SEDUCED BY HER REBEL WARRIOR

Greta Gilbert

MILLS & BOON

First Published in Great Britain 2019
by Mills & Boon, an imprint of HarperCollins*Publishers*
1 London Bridge Street, London, SE1 9GF

© 2019 Greta Gilbert

ISBN: 978-0-263-26902-4

MIX
Paper from
responsible sources

FSC® C007454

This book is produced from independently certified FSC™ paper
to ensure responsible forest management.
For more information visit www.harpercollins.co.uk/green.

Printed and bound in Spain
by CPI, Barcelona

For Mike Noble—
the kindest, wisest, funniest, bravest,
most wonderful stepdad in the universe.

Chapter One

❦

Rome—101 CE

Atia always knew she would die young. Even before she visited the ancient sisters she sensed her days were numbered.

On the morning of her twelfth birthday, Atia's mother shook her awake. 'Dress quickly, my dear,' she said. 'Today all will be revealed.'

Together they hurried down the Via Sacra, their heads hooded, their eyes fixed upon the paving stones.

'Faster, Atia,' her mother urged, for gossip moved like brushfire through the streets of Rome. 'If your father finds out about our errand, we will feel his wrath in lashes.'

Atia hurried after her mother as they made their way into the Subura slum. They entered a towering *insula* and began to climb—one floor, five floors, ten. Finally, they reached the highest floor and stood before a door. Atia's mother knocked and it creaked open.

'May I help you?' called an ancient voice. Atia peered into the shadows and beheld a short, round woman with hair as white as the moon.

'We have an appointment,' said Atia's mother. 'A reading for my daughter.'

'Ah yes—the ladies of Palatine Hill,' said the woman. She gave Atia's mother a second glance, as all people did. 'Please, seat yourselves,' the old woman said, then disappeared down a dark corridor.

Atia and her mother took their seats at a large circular table. Soon the round woman re-emerged, carrying an incense lamp. A chunk of amber-coloured rock smouldered inside the lamp's wide belly, producing a rich, otherworldly scent.

'Frankincense,' her mother remarked admiringly.

'To invite the goddess's favour,' said the woman. She set the lamp on the table, then pulled a large scroll from beneath her belt and ceremoniously unfurled it.

Atia gazed in wonder at the eerie drawing: a perfect circle divided into twelve proportionate wedges. Strange symbols decorated the insides of the wedges and colourful lines crossed between them—some of the lines blue, but most of them red.

The round woman placed the scroll on the table and studied it, then fixed Atia with an onyx stare. 'The girl is good,' she pronounced.

Atia released a breath she did not realise she had been holding.

The woman pointed to a blue line. 'This means her heart is tender. She abhors the suffering of others.'

'It is true,' trumpeted her mother. 'Atia has always been kind. A blessing from Juno.'

'And look at this,' said the woman. 'Mercury conjunct Saturn. A disciplined mind. Like a general or a politician.'

Her mother smiled wistfully and Atia knew what she was thinking: *If only Atia had been a boy.*

'Sensitive to the thoughts and feelings of others!' exclaimed the woman.

Atia took a long whiff of the sacred smoke and began to relax. 'The girl is loving and helpful,' said the woman. 'The girl likes to jest.' Atia was almost enjoying the game now. 'She is a natural peacemaker.'

The woman puzzled over the wheel some more, tugging her silver chin hairs. She pointed to a symbol that looked like the moon. 'Here is the girl's mother. Very well aspected in the house of Venus. So much beauty.'

Since Atia could remember, strangers had remarked on her mother's uncommon beauty, often expressing disbelief that Atia was indeed her mother's daughter.

'You speak only of my daughter's gifts, Grandmother,' said Atia's mother, turning the subject back to Atia. 'What of the ill? What challenges will she face?'

'The ill? I am sorry, *domina*. We do not usually speak of ill in such a reading.'

Atia's mother gave a loud *tsk*, then plunged her fingers into the depths of her coin purse. She held up two gold coins. 'One for the good and one for the ill,' she said.

The old woman shook her head. 'The ill can be difficult for some to bear.'

'You mean that it can be difficult for some *patricians* to bear,' her mother said.

The old woman only bowed her head.

'Grandmother, I was born in this very neighbourhood. I rose to my station by the blessing of this alone.' Atia's mother gestured to her own face. 'I can bear whatever it is you have to say and so can my daughter. We are stronger than we look.'

Atia had never heard her mother speak so

forcefully in all her life. Nor had she heard her lie with such conviction. After all, her mother had been born to a family of Roman patricians from the province of Hispania.

Had she not?

Her mother pressed the coins into the old woman's palm and a kind of knowing passed between the two women.

'Decima!' the round woman called.

Suddenly, another old woman emerged from the corridor. She was tall and thin and wore a pronounced scowl. Her bones made creaking complaints as she walked.

'At your request, I present you with my sister,' said the round woman. 'She has a talent for seeing the ill.'

The thin woman gave a curt nod and seated herself beside Atia. She pointed a bony finger to a symbol inside the seventh wedge. 'Here is Saturn in the girl's house of marriage. It bodes ill. Many obstacles. And look here—it makes a bad angle to Jupiter, the planet of progeny.'

Atia's mother nodded gravely. 'Anything else?'

The thin woman sighed. 'Where to begin?' She pointed to a red line. 'The girl will labour beneath the control of a wicked, powerful man.' She pointed to another red line. 'She will travel to foreign lands where she will face grave danger.' She pointed to yet another red line. 'She will witness terrible things and her heart will break a thousand times.'

Atia did not understand. She looked to her mother for reassurance, but her mother's expression was ghostly. 'What can be done?' her mother asked.

The thin woman shrugged. 'The girl must weather the storm and wait to be reborn.'

What did she mean, *wait to be reborn*? Atia opened her mouth to ask, but no words came.

'Look, Decima!' clipped the round woman. 'You have upset the girl!' She patted Atia's hand reassuringly. 'The girl must not dwell on the bad,' she told Atia.

'Why not?' asked the thin woman. 'If it is the truth?'

'It is not all of the truth!' said the round woman. She pointed to one blue line. 'Look here. She will appreciate the beauty of the world.'

'But she will seek to escape from it!' croaked the thin woman, pointing to a red one.

'She will be bold.'

'She will also be shy.'

'She will have many husbands.'

'Disappointments all.'

'She will be very clever.'

'Yes, but she will never be beautiful.'

Atia heard her mother draw a breath. *She will never be beautiful.* The words were like burning coals dropped into Atia's lap. She closed her eyes and pretended they were not there. She did not like this game any more.

'What do you mean, *she will never be beautiful*?' asked Atia's mother. 'Just look at her. She is well on her way.'

'The girl is indeed lovely,' said the round woman, nodding approvingly at Atia. 'She has nice large eyes and such fine auburn hair. And her lips are shapely and abundant, are they not?'

The thin woman shook her head. 'Yes, but look at that nose. It is not lovely, and nothing can be done to change it.'

'The nose is a small flaw,' said the round woman. 'It means nothing.'

'It is a distasteful shape. And it occupies far too much of her face.'

Atia placed her hand over her nose. The thin woman was right. It was not lovely. Her two older sisters had jested about it all her life. It was overly large and bony, with a terrible, hooking angle that made it resemble nothing so much as an eagle's beak.

'But she has beauty pronounced in her chart!' protested Atia's mother. 'Just look at her fourth house!'

'That house does not describe the daughter's beauty, but the mother's,' said the thin woman. 'The mother's beauty is a part of the daughter's life.'

The thin woman might have said more, but Atia had ceased to listen. All she could hear were those five terrible words: *she will never be beautiful.*

What could a woman become if she were not beautiful? Beauty was necessary for women, for it meant they married great men, and what other ambition was there for a woman but to marry a great man? Beggar, barmaid or brothel dweller—those were the alternatives, at least according to Atia's mother.

'I do not agree with you about my daughter,' her mother was saying, but the thin woman was already pointing to another part of the wheel. 'It is this relationship here that is of most concern. It bodes very ill for the mother.'

Atia's mother shook her head. 'This is my daughter's chart. How could it bode ill *for me*?'

The thin woman glanced at her mother's stomach and Atia saw her mother's lip quiver slightly. 'You cannot know that.'

'The threads of the Fates bind the members of a family as surely as they bind the world,' said the thin woman. 'When one thread comes unravelled it affects all the rest.'

'Will I lose it?' whispered Atia's mother, gently touching her stomach. The thin woman remained silent. 'Tell me!' her mother shouted. 'I command you!'

'I am afraid you will lose more than just the child, *domina*.'

Atia's mother began to weep. Fearful tears sent drops of green malachite down her lovely cheeks.

'Why do you tell me this?' sobbed Atia's mother.

'Because you asked for it, my dear,' said the round woman. 'Do you not remember? The good and the ill. You said that you could endure the knowing.'

Atia rose from her chair. She did not wish to hear any more of what the sisters had to say— good or ill.

'I will wait for you outside, Mother,' she said, though her mother was no longer listening to anything but her own sobs.

Atia was hurrying towards the exit when she heard a third voice. 'Do not go,' it crooned. 'You should not leave in such a state.'

'I am not in a state,' snapped Atia, pausing before the dark corridor.

'Come closer, dear.'

Atia peered into the shadows and saw a tiny, ancient woman surrounded by shelves full of scrolls. 'Do not be shy,' said the woman.

'The thin woman says that I am shy,' Atia said, hovering beneath the corridor's low arch. 'But the round woman says that I am bold.'

'Can you not be both?'

Atia cocked her head.

'Sometimes I am shy,' continued the woman. 'Other times I am bold. Sometimes I am even ruthless.' She flashed Atia a toothless grin.

'Ruthless? What is that?' asked Atia. There was something menacing about this tiny woman, yet Atia could not bring herself to leave.

'You will learn,' said the woman.

'Who are you?' asked Atia.

'Who I am matters little. Step closer.' Atia took one step through the archway, though it felt more as though she was being pulled.

'Now tell me what has upset you.' The woman's eyes were on Atia, but her hands were busy knitting. A fine-threaded white shawl stretched up from a basket on the floor beside her. Inside the basket, Atia caught the glint of a pair of shears.

'The women speak in circles,' said Atia, gesturing towards the others. 'They make me confused.'

'I understand. If I were twelve years old, I would be confused, too.'

'How do you know my age?' asked Atia.

'I know many things.'

'Do you know if I will ever be beautiful?'

'You will and you will not,' said the woman. 'What else do you wish to know?'

Atia shook her head. 'You are just like the other two. You speak in circles.'

'I assure you that I am nothing like my sisters,' creaked the woman.

'Then tell me one true thing about myself,' said Atia. 'No more circles.'

'Ah, one true thing...' The old woman lowered her voice to a whisper. 'For that you must come closer, lest the goddess overhear us.'

Before she even knew that she had moved, Atia found herself bending her ear to the old woman's wrinkled lips.

'I can tell you the time and the day of your own death,' she whispered.

A chill tickled Atia's skin. 'That is impossible. How could you know something like that?'

'It is written in the stars, my dear,' she said. 'It is the one true thing in your life.'

In a single motion, the old woman lifted the shears from the basket and sliced through a strand of yarn. She offered the shawl to Atia. 'Well? Do you wish to know it or not?'

City of Bostra (modern Bosra in southern Syria),
Roman Province of Arabia Petraea—119 CE

The trouble started with dates—sweet, cloy-
ing dates from the plantations of Palmyra. The
camels were wild for them and Rab fed the beasts
handfuls before they raced.

It was the sweetness of dates that had spurred
his white camel to victory that day, or so Rab believed, and what had made her so skittish in the
winners' circle. The agitated giant danced about
the enclosure like a harem girl, her large hooves
calling up clouds of dust.

'Calm her, Zaidu!' Rab urged his nephew, who
was perched high in the saddle.

'I am trying!' the boy shouted. His arms flailed
uselessly as the white beast lurched towards a
group of admirers. Rab seized the camel's bridle
and attempted to tug her backwards, but she re-
sisted, apparently wishing to be admired.

'Shush her to her knees,' Rab told his nephew.
'Now!'

Zaidu nodded, filling his small chest with
air and hissing out a fearsome *down* command
that would have sent a normal camel to the dust.
But not the white. She reared up, then wheeled
around, tugging Rab with her and sending him
stumbling into the person of a woman.

A Roman woman.

'By Jupiter...' The woman cursed in Latin and for a fleeting moment Rab felt the softness of her body against his.

She was clad all in white—just like the camel—and had covered her hair with a shawl so ethereal and white it seemed to be made from the sheen of a cloud.

'Apologies,' Rab said, righting himself, then heard the sound of tearing thread. *No*, he thought, cringing. *Not the shawl.*

The woman gasped. Her flowing headpiece had somehow become attached to the belt of his robe and had torn slightly.

'Untether it quickly,' she commanded, glancing behind her. 'Lest my father see us.'

'By the gods!' Rab muttered, and in his efforts he somehow yanked the shawl from atop the woman's head to reveal a cap of shiny auburn hair gathered into a tight, oiled bun. It was a practical coiffure—not meant to be seen—and Rab could not conceal his blush at having glimpsed it.

'Forgive me,' he said, freeing the damaged shawl from his belt and thrusting it at her. Their eyes locked and desire rollicked through his body. 'I will pay you for it.'

'There is no need to pay for the damage,' she said. 'It is an old shawl.'

As she rearranged the garment on her head,

Rab rearranged his wits, which seemed to have gone the way of the camel.

The camel! Curses, he had forgotten about the camel. He spun around, fully expecting to see its humped silhouette bounding towards the horizon. But the beast stood calmly behind him, his little nephew perched high in the saddle. Both boy and camel wore the same placid grin.

Rab smiled back. 'Well done, Zaidu,' he told his nephew. 'You brought her to heel.'

'It was not my doing,' said Zaidu, glancing at the woman.

The woman frowned and her strange beauty hit Rab like a hot wind. Mystic eyes, hooded and sad, perched above a nose so large and regal it might have belonged to Cleopatra herself. So much stern dignity—and almost totally undone by her lips, whose rosy extravagance brought to mind an abundance of cherries.

'It appears that you have calmed my camel,' he said.

'Do you really think I could have any effect whatsoever on such a beast?'

'Yes, yes, I do,' Rab replied stupidly.

'But how?'

'Perhaps she was drawn to your white clothing? As you can see, she also wears white.' It was the most ridiculous thing he had ever said and he was shocked to discover a smile traverse her lips.

'May I touch her?' she asked.

'You are welcome to do so,' said Rab—with far too much enthusiasm. What in the name of the Great God Dushara was the matter with him? The woman was Roman. Rab did not converse with Romans and he certainly did not allow them to touch his camels.

But there she went, stroking the white beast's nose, and he did nothing at all to stop her. Nor did he say anything when she began to coo softly in Latin. He only closed his eyes, as if she were whispering the sweet words to Rab himself.

An angry voice split his reverie. 'Daughter, why do you engage with these dirty Arabs?'

A man in a purple-trimmed toga stepped forward. He pointed a bejewelled finger at Rab. 'Can you not control your own camel?'

Rab opened his mouth to respond, but no words came.

'I am speaking to you!' shouted the Roman. He gave Rab a mighty shove, sending Rab crashing against the camel's middle. Zaidu shouted something from his perch in the saddle and the agitated camel thrust out her long leg.

Rab could almost hear the Roman man's bones splintering as the camel's heavy foot pounded against his shin. He collapsed to the ground, his toga tumbling into the dust. 'Father!' the woman shrieked. She glanced up at Rab. 'Please get help!'

Rab staggered to his feet only to find two sets of hands seizing him by the shoulders. A fist crashed into his jaw, followed by a foot into his stomach. A throng of Roman guards was pouring into the circle and Rab watched in horror as several other guards wrenched his nephew from atop the white camel. 'Zaidu!' he cried, then felt a heavy blow against his side.

'Take them to the fort!' he heard a man shout. Rab could not find his breath. 'And somebody call a litter! The Governor has been injured!'

At first, there was nothing but pain—sharp, mind-splitting pain and the memory of blows. Then there was the taste of blood inside his mouth and the hardness of stone beneath his head. A silken voice split the silence. 'Awaken.'

Rab opened his eyes to find himself surrounded on three sides by walls. Before him stretched the thick iron bars of a prison cell. Beyond the bars stood a figure bathed in torchlight—a vision of curves and white linen. A woman.

She turned and he knew her instantly. It was *the* woman—the one from the camel races. He would have recognised her anywhere—her soft curves, her auburn hair, her strong, determined nose, so like his late mother's. Her shadowy profile sent a strange pang of nostalgia through him, though when she neared his cell and squatted low that nostalgia quickly transformed into an unexpected lust.

She pushed a water bag through the bars. 'Drink,' she said.

'What is it?'

'Water. You have been asleep for many hours.'

He sensed a lie lurking behind her words, but he was too thirsty to refuse her. As he reached for the bag, her fingers grazed his. He nearly recoiled: they were as frigid as a corpse's.

'You are very cold,' he remarked. Without thinking, he removed his head tie and pulled off his long white head cover. 'Wrap my *ghutrah* around yourself,' he said, pushing the garment through the bars. 'It will warm you.'

He seemed to have forgotten that she was Roman and thus did not deserve his charity. Still, her fingers had been terribly cold and her cheeks were bereft of colour.

She gave the voluminous white headscarf a long, suspicious stare. 'It is just a head cover. It will not bite you,' he said.

As a gesture of goodwill, Rab grasped the water bag she had offered him and took a long quaff. The liquid tasted vaguely of flowers.

He held out his *ghutrah* once again. 'Come now, you are obviously cold.'

'How could I be cold?' she clipped. 'It is the

middle of August in Arabia, by all the vengeful gods.'

The absurdity of the comment struck them both at once and for a second their voices mingled in laughter, bouncing off the prison walls like two parts of a song.

Her lips returned to frowning. 'I am not cold,' she repeated. She sprang to her feet and placed her hands authoritatively on her hips.

'Why do you gape?' she asked.

'I do not gape.'

'You are most certainly gaping.'

'Hmm,' grumbled Rab and looked away. He reminded himself that it was folly to engage with Romans. Their manners were bad, their greed never ending and their moods as changeable as the desert winds. Romans were, in a word, savages, no matter how lovely their frowning lips and curving hips.

He returned the *ghutrah* to his head and fixed it into place with his head tie. He brushed the arms of his long grey robe and folded his legs beneath him. 'Where am I?'

'In a holding cell beneath the Roman fort at Bostra,' she said, and when he did not respond, she added, 'In the Roman Province of Arabia Petraea.'

'Arabia Petraea,' he echoed.

As if he needed reminding. Despite over a

dozen years of Roman occupation, the words still tasted vile on his tongue. Whatever name she wished to call his homeland, to Rab it would always be the Kingdom of Nabataea, with its capital not of Bostra, but of Rekem, that great southern city of stone.

'Why do you keep me here?' he asked.

'Do you not recall? Your camel injured the new Governor of Arabia—a man who happens to be my father.'

'That man was the Governor?'

Curses, he should have guessed it. The bejewelled hand, the purple-trimmed toga, the imperious demeanour. Of all the confounded ill fortune.

'It broke his leg,' she said with indifference, 'though the break has been splinted and we are told it will heal normally.'

'I did not intend—'

'It does not matter what you did or did not intend,' she said. 'What matters is what my father believes.'

'And what does your father believe?'

'That you commanded the kick.'

'That is impossible. Where is my nephew?' Rab started to stand, but his legs seemed to be growing weaker by the moment.

'Why is it impossible?' she asked.

'Where is my nephew, by the gods?' Rab demanded.

'He is in another cell not far from here. Why is it impossible that you commanded the kick?'

'Is he injured? Has he eaten?'

She pursed her lips together. 'He has been treated in the exact same manner as you have. Now please answer my question. I am trying to help you.'

'So you beat my nephew and hold him in a cell and tell me you are trying to help me? He is only eleven years old!'

'I had nothing to do with your nephew's beating or his captivity,' she said. Then, in a whisper: 'And I was able to sneak him a corner of bread.'

Rab paused, feeling a strange gratitude, then reminded himself that there was no room in this conversation for such a sentiment. 'I demand that you release us both,' he said.

She stiffened. 'You are not in a position to make demands.'

'And you are?' Rab craned his neck to observe the empty hallway in which she stood. 'You approach my cell all alone, a beautiful woman without any protection... On whose authority do you question me?'

She appeared confused. She glanced around the prison as if she believed him to be referring to someone else. 'On my father's authority, of course,' she said at last.

He struggled once again to stand, but this time

the effort made him dizzy. 'Do you know who I am?'

'No,' she replied carefully. 'Who are you?'

He bit his tongue. By the gods, what was wrong with him? Had he really almost revealed his identity? 'I am my nephew's only protector.'

'And I am your only friend,' she added.

'Why do I find that difficult to believe?'

'Just answer the question,' she pressed. 'Why is it impossible that you commanded the kick?'

'Because a camel is incapable of learning such a command.'

'My father will investigate the veracity of that claim. If it is a lie, you will lose your life.'

Savages, he thought. *Every last one of them.* He shook his head and studied the floor.

'So it *is* a lie,' she said.

'Why does the Governor care whether the kick was commanded or not?' he asked. Better she discover the second lie than the first.

'It amuses my father to discover the truth,' she replied. 'And I can assure you that he always does.'

'Does he not have more meaningful sources of amusement? Roads to build, riches to plunder, slaves to drive?'

She would not take the bait. 'Your story must match your nephew's.'

'And what does my nephew claim happened?'

She looked away. 'I cannot tell you that.'

'I thought you said you were my friend.'

She sighed. 'Everything you tell me I am obligated to tell my father. Now please, answer the question.'

Rab measured out his words. 'Yes, it is possible for a camel to be trained to kick on command.'

'And have you trained your camel in such a skill?'

Rab paused. 'I have.'

He had not. He knew very little about training camels, in truth. Or racing them, for that matter. The camel races were simply a ruse—something to distract attention from Rab's more important activities. Still, Zaidu loved the races and had been working with the camel for some months now on a variety of commands.

'Did you order the kick?' the woman demanded.

No, he did not, but he feared that Zaidu had. He needed to protect the boy. 'I did.'

'Why did you do it?'

'Because your father pushed me,' Rab explained. 'I was merely defending myself against him. I was unaware of his identity.' At least it was mostly the truth.

The woman nodded thoughtfully and seemed satisfied. 'You may have just secured your nephew's release. And saved your own life.'

'Am I supposed to thank you?' he slurred. His head had begun to spin. She did not answer him, though she was watching him like a shepherd observing a doomed sheep. All at once he understood why. 'It was not just water you gave me, was it?' His vision blurred.

'No, it was not,' she admitted.

'And you are not my friend.'

'No, I am not.'

Chapter Two

Atia stopped to smell the roses. They had been placed in a vase on the shelf outside her father's *tablinium* by some well-meaning slave. She paused with her nose enveloped in petals. *What a strange compulsion*, she thought. She had stopped smelling flowers years ago—back when she had begun to count down the days until her own death.

She breathed deeply now and was rewarded with a sweet, subtle scent. Even more rewarding was the rose's lavish hue—like the ruddy burn of the sun through smoke. It reminded her of the colour of the tie the camel man used to hold his *ghutrah*.

The *ghutrah* he had offered to keep her warm.

She had been so shocked by the gesture that she had not even been able to properly decline it. What prisoner offered to aid his own interrogator? Even more startling had been their reaction to the gesture: they had laughed together like thieves.

Laughter? It was another strangeness. She had hardly recognised her own voice. How many years had it been since she had laughed? Ten? Fifteen? Back before her mother had died and delight had still seemed possible.

Now, at the advanced age of thirty, Atia had learned to view delight as suspect. Obviously the camel man had been trying to endear himself to her—to trick her into trusting him.

Still, something in the way his dark, sun-flecked eyes had smiled down at her had made him seem sincere. Even now, as she thought back upon those eyes, it was as if they were warming her very thoughts.

She knew that warmth could not be trusted. And when he had called her beautiful? That had been a trick as well: a sly attempt at flattery designed to gain her sympathy.

Because beautiful she was not—not with the terrible protrusion occupying the middle of her face. Well dressed, yes. Properly coiffed and painted, certainly. Rich. Powerful. Connected. She was the daughter of a Roman Governor, by the gods—one of Emperor Hadrian's most trusted men. But beautiful? It was a gift that Venus had declined to grant.

Still, there had been something resembling sincerity in the way the man had spoken the compliment. *You approach my cell all alone, a beautiful woman without any protection...* It was as if he were not talking about her, but some fantasy version of herself—a bold, attractive woman who explained herself to no one. It amused her to think of herself in such a way.

Then there had been the strangeness of his expression after he had spoken the compliment. The tight lips and pulsing jaw. The eyes narrowed dangerously in something resembling hunger. It was quite possibly the best imitation of desire she had ever seen.

Of course, what he really desired was to be released from his prison, just as all prisoners did. Still, he had spoken the words—*a beautiful woman*—and, however false, they had had the effect of buoying her spirit, such that she had caught herself smiling all afternoon and, apparently, stopping to smell roses.

'Come forward,' called her father from inside his office. Atia returned the rose to its vase and entered her father's sparsely decorated *tablinium*, pausing before his sprawling ebony desk.

He appeared to be reviewing some official scroll. Beside him, a stony-faced scribe stood sentinel, his eyes flitting across the parchment in time with her father's.

'Sit down, Atia,' he commanded without looking up. As she made her way to one of her father's client chairs, she caught the gaze of her father's first officer, Plotius, standing in a corner just behind the desk. The fleshy, thick-muscled military man took his time assessing Atia's figure and Atia wasted none in volleying him a sneer. He replied with a *just you wait* look.

Seating herself, Atia nodded her gratitude at a boy operating a palm leaf in another corner of the room, though its small wind did little to alleviate the midday heat. It was August, after all—the sweltering month—and even the cool marble and high ceilings of her father's villa were futile against the Arabian sun.

Trying to resist the heat was useless. In that way, it was much like her father himself.

'You are looking well, Daughter,' said her father, finally glancing up from his scroll. 'Unusually so.'

Atia thought of the camel man and felt a small trickle of sweat trace a path down her cheek. 'I should say the same, Father,' she said. She glanced beneath the desk at his bandaged leg. 'Only two days after your injury and you are already at work.'

'The business of Empire waits for no man,' he said. It was Emperor Hadrian's favourite aphorism and her father recited it like a prayer.

'A new prohibition?' asked Atia, glancing at the scroll.

'Execution warrants,' he said, dipping his quill into a tub of ink.

Atia gulped a breath. 'Which prisoners?' There had been so many of them lately. Young men and old. Rich and poor. All Nabataeans—many of whom Atia had interrogated herself. They had been ripped from their homes under charges of collusion with the rebels, though Atia believed most of the men to be innocent.

'We must clear out the holding cells,' pronounced her father. 'We will behead all prisoners who have been in captivity for more than a month.'

Atia's throat felt dry. 'You will not try them?'

'Trials are expensive.' The ink dripping from her father's pen was like blood. 'Besides, we must send a message to the populace.'

Atia pasted a smile on her face and gave a small nod. Later that afternoon, she would tip three drops of poppy tincture into her wine and try to purge the vision of a dozen innocent Nabataean heads on spikes in Bostra's central square.

It was wrong. Nay, it was barbarous. To kill a man without trial? To take a human life just to send a message? The thought made Atia dizzy with despair. Her father's method of government bore a strong resemblance to his method of war, yet Atia could do nothing to stop it.

Forty days, Atia thought suddenly. In only forty days she was supposed to die. She had been counting down the days since the age of twelve, when the exact day of her death had been foretold to her. For a long time she had feared the date, but had gradually come to look forward to it. If the prophecy was true, then in only forty days, she would no longer be complicit in her father's wicked deeds. In the meantime, she only wished for a few drops of poppy tears to help her through.

'I am also banning that silly scarf the men wear over their heads,' her father said.

'The *ghutrah*?'

'It makes them all look the same. How will we find our rebels if we cannot tell one from the other?'

Atia thought of the camel man's face: the round cheeks and liquid gaze; the eyes like big dark suns; the short black beard surrounding thick, sensuous lips; the bottom lip so much larger than the top—like the promise of abundance and its immediate fulfilment. She could have easily picked him out from among a hundred *ghutrah*-wearing men.

'A clever strategy, Father,' she said.

Her father scrawled his signature across the bottom of the scroll. 'We are going to find every last one of these damned rebels and slaughter them where they stand,' he said. 'We will make Quietus's massacre look like a child's tantrum.'

Atia nodded and fought a wave of nausea. The Roman General Quietus had recently defeated an encampment of rebellious Jews in the adjacent province of Judea. According to rumour, he had taken over twenty thousand lives, including those of women and children.

'We must strike fear in the hearts of all Nabataeans,' her father explained. 'They must understand that there is no resisting Rome.'

'Yes, Father.'

Nor was there any resisting her father. To him, disagreement was a form of disloyalty, and disloyalty was meant to be punished. Once, Atia's eldest sister had questioned her father's actions and he had sent her to labour in a temple. When Atia's second eldest sister had disgraced the *familia* through adultery, she had suffered twenty lashes. But those punishments were small in comparison with their mother's. The one time she had questioned their father's will, she had paid for it with her very life.

'Now tell me,' her father said. He was blowing gently on the ink of his signature. 'What news of the Nabataean cameleers?'

Atia took a breath. 'The boy claims that he commanded the kick, not his uncle.'

'And his uncle, what did he say?'

'That he commanded the kick, not the boy.'

'You loosened the man's tongue before discussing the matter?'

'I gave him the poppy tears, yes.'

'So he lied to protect the boy?' asked her father. He lifted the scroll by its sides and passed it to the scribe.

Atia nodded. 'An honourable thing to do.'

'You sound as though you favour him,' her father said, arching a brow.

'I merely observe him,' Atia said. She felt his gaze burrow into her.

'Then you would agree that his physical conditioning does not match his vocation?'

Atia beat back a blush. The man's lithe, muscular form brought to mind the hero Achilles—all taut muscle and long-limbed grace. Atia nodded.

'Do you believe him to be a rebel?' her father asked.

'It is possible,' said Atia, aware that any denial would betray bias, 'though he seemed too concerned with the well-being of his nephew to harbour greater motives.'

'You trust too easily, Atia, but that has always been one of your flaws.'

'Yes, Father.'

'We must be vigilant if we wish to wipe out

these rebels completely. Hadrian is depending on our success.'

Emperor Hadrian and Atia's father had come from the same *gens* of Spanish immigrants, along with former Emperor Trajan. As Hadrian had risen through the political ranks he had elevated Atia's father along with him and the two had become commanders together in Emperor Trajan's Dacian campaigns.

When Emperor Trajan died and Hadrian took the purple, Atia's father had worked tirelessly to make Hadrian's enemies disappear.

As the news of the executions flooded into the dining rooms of Palatine Hill, Atia had been careful to appear surprised. 'Who would do such a thing?' she always replied.

But she knew who would do such a thing, for she had seen the bloodstains on her father's toga and the black look in his eye as he sneaked through the kitchen late at night. And when she passed by his doorway in the darkest hours, he had spoken the names of the doomed in his sleep—four Senators, along with a handful of their closest men, executed without trial. Murdered.

'I have some disappointing news,' her father had told Atia towards the end of the killings. She had been sitting in one of his client chairs much like she was now, his large ebony desk sprawling before him like a black pool. 'I am afraid your husband's ambition became threatening to the Emperor.'

'My husband?'

When her father retrieved her third husband's finger from the drawer of his desk, she had carefully concealed her horror.

'He was a traitor,' her father had explained. He had tugged her late husband's jade ring from its severed digit and held it in the air. Then he had placed the ring on his own finger. 'He was disloyal. Unlike you, Atia.'

Loyalty. Utter, unquestioning loyalty. It was what Hadrian demanded of her father and what her father demanded of her. So when a rebellion erupted in Rome's newest province of Arabia Petraea, Atia had gone along to aid her father however she could. Of course she had. Her father was Emperor Hadrian's man and she was her father's daughter.

Now her father studied her closely. 'I sent for you, but you did not come straight away. Why?'

'Father?'

'You lingered outside this very *tablinium* before entering.'

'Ah, yes. I was smelling the roses.'

Her father cocked his head. 'I have never known you to enjoy the fragrance of flowers.'

'I was simply wondering if Arabian roses smell

differently than Roman ones,' she stated, but he seemed not to hear her.

'Is there anything else I need to know about the interrogation? Anything the man may have said? Think carefully.'

Atia paused. She did not wish to condemn the camel trainer, but if she tried to conceal the strange comment he had made, she would have to hope for the rest of her life that her father did not discover it. He began to tap his fingers gently against his desk. The green glint of her late husband's ring caught Atia's eye. *Loyalty*, she thought.

Utter and unquestioning.

'He asked me if I knew who he was.'

Her father ceased his tapping. 'And?'

'And he quickly changed the subject, so I did not pursue it. Better he think I did not perceive the revelation.'

Her father sat back in his chair. 'Perhaps I have taught you something after all,' he said. He motioned to Commander Plotius and whispered something in the tribune's ear. Atia felt the blood leaving her limbs. She knew that she had just condemned the camel man to some wicked punishment.

The man who had offered her his *ghutrah* and made her laugh.

The man who had called her beautiful.

'Consider it done, Governor,' said Plotius, who cut her a glance before marching from the office with terrifying purpose.

Four drops, she thought. She would put four poppy tears into her cup tonight, not just three.

'Are preparations complete for tonight's banquet?' her father asked.

'Yes, Father.' She glanced briefly at his leg.

'You doubt my fitness to attend?'

'Not at all.'

'The injury is nothing. The doctor says it will heal in a month.'

'So you still plan to journey to Rekem in the autumn?' she asked him, though all she could think of was the camel man. What would Plotius do to him? And what of the camel man's young nephew? He was only eleven years old.

'Of course I shall journey to Rekem in the autumn,' said her father.

Rekem, located far to the south, was the most important city in the province. As the new Governor, her father owed it an official visit. 'The business of Empire waits for no man,' he added. 'My injury changes nothing.'

'And the camel man's nephew?' Atia asked with careful uninterest. 'Shall I question him further?'

'What you really wish to know is if I will release him,' said her father.

Atia gave a shy nod. 'Sometimes I think you know me better than I know myself.'

'You have always had a weakness for children. Understandable—since you were never able to produce your own.'

'Yes, Father.' She braced herself for what always followed.

'If only your husbands had wanted you more.' The rest of the statement he left unsaid, though it haunted the air like a ghost. *If only you had been more desirable to them.*

He closed his eyes and the silence spread out between them. 'I will release the boy,' he said at last.

'You are merciful, Father.'

'Merciful, yes, but not foolish. There is a condition.'

'What condition?'

Her father's face split with a jackal's grin.

Chapter Three

'He wishes for you to apologise,' the woman said. Her voice was as smooth as a dune.

Rab coughed and attempted to sit up. 'Excuse me, but what did you say?' he asked. His head throbbed and his throat felt as if it had been stuffed with wool.

'At the banquet tonight, my father wishes for you to apologise to him before his guests and to pledge your loyalty to Rome. He does you a great mercy.'

She had changed her tunic. In place of her simple white wool, she had now donned an elegant garment of flowing bronze linen. Worse, she had kohled her eyes and reddened her lips with the dregs of wine. She was the embodiment of loveliness, though her expression was grave, as if she were heedless of it.

'You stare at me as if I am Medusa herself,' she snapped. 'Did you not hear what I just said?'

Rab struggled to his feet. 'You drugged me.' It seemed she was drugging him still—with that cursed, silken voice.

'I helped you sleep,' she said.

'A sleep of the dead.'

'I gave you the gift of peace.'

He gripped the bars of his cell. 'A strange way to describe a poppy haze.'

She tilted her head at him in that careless, haughty way of Romans, but he noticed a throbbing pulse in the side of her neck. *Pulse, pulse, pulse.* Was it possible that she felt it, too? This strange pull between them?

'I was ordered to give you the poppy tears,' she said. 'I had no choice.'

Pulse, pulse, pulse. Her neck was pale, as was the rest of her. He imagined she spent most of her life indoors. She probably wasted hours each morning anointing herself with expensive oils and perfumes just like all Roman women of her station.

He imagined her seated at her makeup table gazing into her copper mirror. The vision should have angered him: it was the picture of Roman decadence. But instead he thought of her lovely auburn hair hanging at her shoulders—free of its ties and buns. He wondered how long it took her to comb.

He released his grip on the bars and ran his

hand through his hair. What was wrong with him? He had every reason to doubt this woman and no reason at all to be imagining her at her makeup table.

'The poppy tears dulled your rage,' she explained.

He shook his head—which only increased its pounding—and tried to revive his indignation. 'Drugging a man is no way to dull his rage. When the rage returns it is stronger than before.'

She shook her head, having none of it. 'The drugging of prisoners is a common practice. It softens their tongues.'

'You speak like a damned politician,' he said. Though she did not look like one. She looked like one of those lavish Roman goddesses sculpted from the sandstone.

'I am a politician's daughter.'

'As if that is all there is to you.'

She cocked her head. 'What do you mean by that?'

What *did* he mean by that? 'I mean that you do not seem quite as heartless as a politician.'

She laughed bitterly. 'I assure you that I am very heartless.'

'You sneaked my nephew a corner of bread.'

She frowned, as if unsure of what to make of the comment, and seemed to decide to dismiss it entirely. 'As soon as you agree to apologise to my father, your nephew and the camel will be released.'

Zaidu's freedom in exchange for an apology? It sounded too good to be true. 'How can I trust you?' he asked.

'You have no choice but to trust me,' she said. 'If you can perform your apology with enough conviction, my father may decide to release you as well.'

'What do you mean, *perform*?'

'You must take the knee before him and speak your apology with great humility,' she said.

'So your father wishes to humiliate me before his guests?'

'He wishes to demonstrate his clemency as Governor.'

'He wishes to flatter himself.'

'What does it matter, as long as your nephew is released?'

Rab felt vaguely ill. The last thing he had ever imagined doing was asking forgiveness of a Roman governor. But Zaidu's safety—nay, his very life—was at risk.

'Fine. I will do it,' he said.

'You will?'

Was he mistaken, or was that a smile ghosting her lips?

She motioned to the three guards standing nearby. They took positions behind her as she produced a key from the belt of her tunic. She unlocked the barred door and stepped into Rab's cell.

Her perfume swirled around him—some wicked mixture of honey and myrrh. He breathed it in, despite himself, and stole another glance at her neck. It was pulsing faster than ever. It seemed to be keeping time with his own beating heart.

'Drink this,' she said. She motioned to one of the guards, who held out a water bag.

Rab nearly exploded with laughter. 'Do you think me that much of a fool?'

The woman's expression was all innocence. 'I vow that the water inside this bag is clean and unaltered.'

'And I am the King of Babylon.'

Her eyes flashed and there it was again—that ghost of a smile. Why did it please him so much to see it?

'I understand your hesitation,' she said, recovering her stony façade.

'My *hesitation*?' He gazed at the poison-filled leather serpent dangling before him. 'Have you always had such a gift for understatement?'

'I am not proud that I drugged you,' she said. 'But I promise that I shall not drug you again. I would never compromise the moment this evening when you kiss my father's signet ring.'

'Kiss his ring?' Rab echoed, feeling the room begin to spin. He pressed his arm against the wall.

'Dizziness is a common side effect of poppy tears,' she observed. She gazed wistfully at the floor. 'And, of course, a craving for more poppy tears.'

'I am afraid I feel no such craving,' he shot back.

'That is well, for this water contains no such medicine.' She took the bag from the guard and thrust it beneath his nose. 'Drink,' she demanded and then, more gently, 'and afterwards we shall witness your nephew freed.'

And thus the battle was over almost before it began. Witness Zaidu freed? Rab tipped the bag into his mouth and drank down every last drop.

Moments later, they were standing on the rampart of the fort, watching Zaidu's small figure lead the white camel back to Bostra. Rab felt a weight slowly lifting from his chest.

He knew that in less than an hour, Zaidu would walk through the big cedar doors of their family's home and be greeted by his three sisters, who would shower him with love and care. Zaidu would explain that Rab had been captured and the news would spread to those who needed to know. Rab was certain that a rescue party would come for him. But even if one did not, the work would go on. That was all that mattered.

'Come, let us prepare you for the banquet,' the woman said. She was standing beside him—not an arm's length away—and he stole another glance at her neck. *Pulse, pulse, pulse.*

She walked ahead of Rab and the guards across the fort's central courtyard. Soon they stood before an elegant, columned building gleaming pink in the late afternoon light. As he stepped inside the towering structure, Rab found himself surrounded by brightly painted frescoes and unnatural heat.

'The guards will stay with you while you bathe,' the woman explained. 'I will leave your undertunic and toga in the dressing room and await you here in the entry hall. Go now.'

She was gone before Rab could protest and soon he was sitting naked inside a hot, luxurious, marble bath, sweating layers of dirt and blood from his skin.

All around him were signs of opulence. Fine glass pitchers. Thick, embroidered towels. Water ladles inlaid with precious stones. Rab scraped the fine bronze *strigil* along his oiled limbs and gazed up at the high, stained-glass windows. Their light poured down in pools of colour on to the new marble floor.

He might have been impressed. The Romans were excellent builders and baths like this one were among the most lavish in the world—true palaces of leisure. But Rab could not bring himself to relax, for he knew the source of all this gaudy wealth.

Taxes. Nabataean taxes, to be precise, stolen from every Nabataean trader and merchant from Bostra to Rekem.

Rab gazed at the gilded rail leading into the hot pool and envisioned the camel-loads of frank-incense that had surely purchased it. Twenty per cent. That is what the Roman tax collectors took from every load, thus robbing the Nabataean incense traders of virtually all their profit. In the thirteen years since the Romans had come, the richest Nabataean traders had become paupers. Many were now so desperate that they had gone on to the Roman bread dole.

Twenty per cent. The Romans made it sound trifling—the price of acquisition, they called it. As if it had little impact on Nabataean lives. As if it had not slowly, systematically, fleeced the Nabataeans of their wealth and greatness. He scraped a bronze *strigil* along his bruised limbs a little too roughly. 'Twenty per cent,' he muttered. Reason enough for a fight.

The lamp flickered. It was too damned hot. He needed to get out of this cursed bath. He dropped his *strigil* and pushed past the guards. 'Stop!' called one, though Rab could hardly hear him as he strode down the hall to the dressing room, where he thrust aside a chair and crashed into something soft.

Or someone, rather.

'Titans of Olympus!' she gasped, stumbling backwards. He saw a blush creep up her neck and his stomach leapt with an unwelcome lust. Against his will, he stepped towards her.

'You might have announced yourself,' she protested, stepping backwardss.

'In the men's changing room?' he asked.

She was sweating. Her lovely robe was clinging to her breasts, emphasising their shape. He felt his desire begin to rise.

'I told you I would leave your clothing here,' she said. Her voice was unusually thick. 'You might have remembered that.'

'I apologise for my poor memory,' he said, sounding in no way apologetic. He saw her eyes range across his naked chest and then turn away. She took another step backwards.

'Why did you leave the bath so soon?' she asked.

'The gleam of gold began to sting my eyes,' he said, stepping forward.

'Where are the guards?'

'On their way, I'm sure.'

He was now only a few steps away from her, yet it was not close enough. He could feel the fullness of his desire and puzzled over how quickly he had lost command of himself. Here he was, standing before the enemy—captured, powerless, naked—yet all he wanted was to get closer to her.

'Please, robe yourself!' she commanded, keeping her eyes carefully locked with his. 'Your toga is just there.'

'Where?' he asked and, when she turned to indicate the toga, he saw her eyes slide down the length of him and behold his naked form once again.

The entirety of it.

And for one unexpectedly satisfying moment he saw her heavy lids disappear and her eyes open wide.

Chapter Four

The guards burst into the dressing room and seized the camel man by his arms. 'Robe him!' Atia shouted as she pushed back through the doorway and out into the main hall.

She felt as if she had just escaped a burning building. She fanned herself with her hand and began to pace. Did the man have no shame? But the question was unfair. Once inside the baths, men were not required to remain clothed. Still, he had appeared almost triumphant as he watched her take in the vision of him.

And what a vision it was, in truth. So much glowing bronze flesh. So much taut, sinewy muscle. He had seemed taller without the trappings of cloth and there was a solidity to him that she had not perceived before. His arms bulged, his chest sprawled, his thighs were as thick as logs and between them…

She stopped pacing. Shook her head. It was

not as if she had not seen a man's desire before. After three marriages, she had long since learned to dread the sight, for it meant only one thing: submission to her wifely duties.

And yet now her mind wanted nothing but to consider that large, fascinating blur of flesh that she knew many men would call a blessing. Many women, too, she thought wryly.

By holy Minerva, why was she even thinking of such a thing? She was the Governor's daughter. She was supposed to be a model of modesty and decorum. She gazed up at the hall's high ceiling where an image of the goddess Juno floated in diaphanous robes. The goddess held two pomegranates in her hands, as if weighing them. Her cool expression seemed full of judgement.

'It was not my doing,' Atia explained to the placid goddess. What was not her doing? The toga? The bath? The unreasonable attraction she felt towards a man whom her father suspected to be a rebel? 'It is not my fault,' she muttered weakly to the goddess. 'He trespassed the boundaries of propriety.'

Though to be fair, it was Atia who had trespassed on him.

She returned to pacing. It was not just his nudity that had unnerved her. In addition to his highly improper display of flesh, there had been that look in his eye—the same one he had flashed when they had first met and then again when he had called her beautiful.

Strange things had happened to her body all three times he had looked at her that way. Heat had pulsed through her, followed by a kind of melting feeling and a weakness in her legs. It was as if his very gaze had the power to cook her—to turn her limbs into noodles and her insides into bubbling *polentum*.

They bubbled even now, just remembering that look. And then there was that barely detectable smile that she saw traverse his lips just afterwards. It was as if he knew she admired him.

As if he believed that, in some small way, *he* had conquered *her*.

Ha! He had done no such thing. He was her father's prisoner! How could he have any power over her at all? His life was not even his own. Nay, if she felt anything for him at all, it was pity.

In that instant, she heard the door to the men's changing room swing open. She turned to discover him striding towards her, the flowing white *toga virilis* draped elegantly around his body. Her stomach turned over on itself. If she had believed that the trappings of clothing would erase his appeal, she had been woefully mistaken.

By the gods, he was well made. Even the draping toga could not conceal his finely sculpted strength. The flowing fabric hung from his broad left shoulder and swept beneath his right arm, revealing the contours of his chest through his snug-fitting undertunic. As he walked, the heavy woollen garments seemed to whisper across the floor.

Pity. Deep, abiding pity, she reminded herself as he planted himself before her and nearly slew her with his gaze.

'You wish to make me into a Roman,' he growled.

He did look rather Roman—with all his pursing lips and broad-shouldered arrogance. Closely trimmed beards such as his had become popular among the equestrian class recently and even his long black hair was of the latest Roman fashion. It brushed the tops of his shoulders, giving him a carelessly regal appearance—like a scholar fresh from the baths.

'The toga suits you,' Atia observed. She studied the creases of the garment's folds, careful not to meet his gaze.

'Is that supposed to be a compliment?'

'It is merely an observation.'

'The toga is a mockery,' he said, swatting the air.

'It is not my doing,' she said, though she had no idea why it seemed important to clarify. 'My father wanted you to be presentable at the banquet. He has also asked me to learn your name.'

'Ha!' the man scoffed. 'What else did he ask for? My domicile? My sandal size? The breed and lineage of my finest camel?'

The humour of the statement struck them both at once and they chuckled together.

What was this strange thing between them, this laughter? And when had his dark eyes acquired that glint of gold?

'Rab,' he said at length.

'What?'

'Your father wished for you to learn my name. It is Rab.'

'As in Rabbel? The last Nabataean King?'

'Half the men in Arabia are named Rabbel,' he said absently.

'Are they indeed?' Atia said, though she was barely listening. She had become distracted by Sol, the Roman sun god. His long arms were stretching through the bathhouse doorway, staining Rab's face with golden light.

'Rabbel was a popular king,' Rab added, 'though not any more.'

'And who is your father, Rab?' she asked, for her own father had commanded her to find this out as well. 'And what is your father's profession?'

Say he is a farmer, or a herder. Let him be of no political interest. A nobody.

Rab paused and gazed at the ceiling. 'My father was a man called Junon. Before his death he was…a pomegranate farmer.'

Atia exhaled. A nobody, then. A glorious, unassailable nobody. 'Come then, Rab, son of Junon, farmer of pomegranates,' she said. 'We must prepare you for your performance.'

She glanced over his shoulder at the guards. 'Please await us outside.'

The three men exchanged looks and Atia knew she had just made a grave error. The guards would certainly notify her father of the unusual command. Atia would have to devise some story to explain it. But not now. Now was about preparing Rab to preserve his own life. With Fortuna's favour, he might even earn his freedom.

'If my father senses insincerity in your apology tonight, he will punish you further,' she said. 'You must believe me in this, for I have seen it before. He demands a moving performance.'

'He wants theatre?'

Atia sighed. 'All banquets are political and all politics are theatrical,' she said.

'You speak in knots,' he said.

'Just give me your best apology and let us see if it will suffice.'

Rab cleared his throat. 'Honourable Governor Magnus Atius Severus of Arabia Petraea, I, Rab, son of Junon, do beg your forgiveness for the harm done to your person by my camel and I pledge my loyalty to Rome. Good?'

'Beyond terrible.'

Rab frowned.

'Your words are too terse and your demeanour far too proud. Just look at how you hold yourself. In that toga, I might have mistaken you for Augustus himself.'

A sly smile spread across Rab's face and he puffed out his chest comically.

'It is not a compliment,' Atia warned. 'You must hunch your shoulders and hang your head low. Do not appear comfortable in that garment. Appear as if you feel unworthy of it.'

Rab gave a dismissive grunt.

'I do not think you understand what is at stake,' Atia said. 'My father wishes to humiliate you and receive your submission. If he is not satisfied, he will pursue other means.'

'What means?'

'He will take a finger, Rab. Or a toe. He will have you disrobed, or thrust your arm into the snake charmer's basket. I have seen all these things happen to slaves and prisoners who have come before my father at banquets. He likes to put on an entertaining show.'

The colour left his cheeks. He paced away from her, his silence betraying his fear. *Good*, Atia thought. He should be afraid. Only the gods knew what manner of humiliation her father planned for him.

'And as for the nature of your apology,' she continued, 'you must make it as detailed and elaborate as possible. Sorry is not enough—you must fawn and you must beg.'

She watched him cringe. 'You must bury your true feelings deep. Watch me now and listen closely.'

Atia dropped to her knees and assumed her most miserable expression. 'Honourable Legatus Augusti Pro Praetore Magnus Atius Severus,' she said. 'I come to this banquet in the manner of a lowly dog. I am embarrassed, ashamed, contrite. I sit on your couches, I eat your oysters, I avail myself of your endless generosity, yet I deserve none of this.' Atia sat back on her heels. 'Do you see? Now continue where I left off.'

Rab gave his shoulders an exaggerated hunch. 'Honourable Governor, I stand before you as a beggar, a sand-scratcher, a worm. A fly on the back of the world's ugliest toad. The stinking excrement of the lowliest jackal in the foulest—'

'Perhaps a bit less description,' Atia interrupted, suppressing a grin.

Rab nodded gravely. 'Only two days ago, my camel did the unthinkable. The mindless beast thrust out his wretched leg and crushed your own. It was a crime for which both beast and owner deserve the worst of punishments. And yet you, Honourable Governor, in your magnificent mercy, have allowed us to live.'

'Better,' said Atia. 'Now drop to your knees.'

Rab dropped to his knees before her and she felt a wave of heat pulse through her body. Now they were kneeling before one another with half-an-arm's length between them. The bubbling in her stomach returned with new force.

She gulped a breath and willed herself to focus. 'You must speak your apology with great humility,' she advised. 'Ideally, you must begin to cry, but only if you can produce real tears.'

'It will be difficult enough to hide my disgust.'

'You must not simply hide your disgust, you must swallow it whole,' said Atia, 'and after your apology, you must declare your loyalty to Rome... with thunderous enthusiasm.'

He rolled his eyes. 'You wish for me to raise a cheer, then? Summon the trumpets?'

She frowned. His arrogance was exasperating. He certainly did not comport himself like the son of a pomegranate farmer.

'Senatus Populus Que Romanus,' he was saying now. 'I have come here to pronounce my loyalty to Rome. First I shall perform a Roman salute, followed by a prayer to Magna Mater. Then I shall recite a few lines from the *Aeneid*.'

He arched a brow and it was all she could do not to laugh.

'You will say none of those things—lest my father throw you to the lions!'

'Just the lions?' He was making light of her advice, but his words had grown edges. Beneath all his bluster, she knew he was afraid.

'After your apology, you should straighten your posture and lift your chin thusly.' She tilted her head so that her face gazed up at his. 'Then passionately declare your loyalty to Rome.'

'I am beginning to understand the nature of this drama,' he said.

'And that is?'

'A debased, uncivilised Nabataean man is transformed by his submission to Rome.'

She did not deny it.

'And if I do not wish to be your father's performer?'

'You risk losing more than your dignity,' she said.

Rab exhaled mightily, then rose to his feet. 'I declare my complete and undying loyalty to Rome,' he said, his rich, gravely voice resounding against the marble. 'For Rome's greatest Governor has lifted me from squalor and shown me mercy.'

'Bravo,' she said, feeling unreasonably happy. 'You have learned the dance.'

He flashed a begrudging grin and extended his hand down to her and when she rose to her feet it was as if they were really dancing.

'If Fortuna wills it, you will walk free tomorrow,' she said. If Fortuna willed it, this would be the last time they would ever speak again.

'You do me a kindness,' he said. 'Why?'

'I find it…tedious to watch other people suffer.'

'I am grateful to you,' he said. She noticed that he had not released her hand. She glanced at the floor, unsure of how to respond. 'Truly,' he said, willing her to look at him again. 'I owe you a debt.'

Atia blinked. Obviously he was trying to win her favour again. What prisoner ever expressed gratitude to his captor?

'Yes, that is it,' she said. 'That is the tone of sincerity you must strive to convey.'

He lowered his voice. 'It is not a tone. I am sincere.'

What a strange thing for him to say. *But of course you are not sincere*, she wished to tell him. *You are a prisoner. You will say anything to engineer your escape.*

'When you stand before my father tonight you must work hard to veil your thoughts,' she said. Meanwhile, her own thoughts had begun to run riot.

'You appear to know quite a lot about the veiling of thoughts,' he observed. He squeezed her hand. There was very little distance between them now. She could smell his clean olive scent.

'Yes, I believe I am something of an expert in that particular skill,' she admitted.

She had been veiling her thoughts all her life, in truth—from a father who used her, from husbands who despised her, even from her own awareness. Thoughts were dangerous, because they always led to pain. 'If my thoughts are concealed, they cannot be used against me,' she said.

'And yet perhaps you are not so very adept at concealment as you think,' he whispered. She glanced at his lips, the bottom lip so much larger than the top, like a pillow upon which she might lay her secrets.

'I am extremely adept,' she countered. She had meant the statement as a kind of jest, but the words came out thick and heavy.

'Can you guess my thoughts in this moment?' he asked.

'No, I am afraid I cannot.'

His lips were so close. It was as if he wished to kiss her. 'I am thinking that you are very beautiful.'

His breath washed over her, bathing her skin with sensation. It flooded down her limbs, making her feel relaxed and alert all at once. What had he said? That she was beautiful?

Beautiful?

She froze. She was many things, but beautiful she was not. Something was amiss.

She stepped backwards. He was watching her closely, his eyes smouldering with…with that look. That very well-crafted, remarkably believable approximation of desire. Something was very, very amiss.

He tilted his head back to take in the length of her body and his eyes fixed on the belt of her tunic—the place where she had stored the key to his cell.

And there it was—a glimpse of the truth. His mind was not on her—of course it was not. Had she forgotten how her terrible hooked nose made her completely undesirable? Nay, he was thinking of the key. He did not desire her. He desired escape.

She took another step backwards. And to think that she had tried to tutor him in the art of performance! What a fool she had been. She had almost been taken in by him, had waited for his kiss, had longed for it, even. How could she have forgotten herself in such a way?

'Do you think me that naive?' she asked.

'Apologies, I do not underst—'

'Guards!' she called.

Chapter Five

Atia tipped the vial into her goblet and watched two cloudy drops mix with her wine.

'How many for you, Lydia?' she asked her friend.

'Only one, dear,' said Lydia, glancing at the door. 'And be quick.'

Just beyond the small bedroom, every bored patrician in Bostra had gathered. They milled about the column-lined courtyard of her father's large villa, trading compliments and spoiling for gossip.

'You are making me look bad,' said Atia, tipping a single drop of the poppy tears into Lydia's goblet, then a third into her own. She swirled the liquid inside her glass and thought of the moment that afternoon when she realised Rab had been lying to her. *The tears will wash away the pain*, she told herself.

It was a long-practised refrain—a phrase she

had invented in the days after her first marriage, almost eighteen years ago now. She had been only twelve years old at the time—a full two years younger than the proper age for a Roman marriage.

It had been a trying time. After her mother's death, her father had been eager to rid his *doma* of his three daughters. Her eldest sister had refused to marry, so he had sent her to serve at a temple in distant Crete. He had rewarded a military ally with the hand of Atia's second-eldest sister, who had inherited the beauty of their mother.

He had had more difficulty finding a husband for Atia. 'Your nose is a problem,' he had told her. 'No man wishes to pass such a thing along to his children.' Eventually, however, her father had found a beneficial match in the person of an elderly Senator—a political ally with a taste for young girls.

The tears will wash away the pain, Atia would always tell herself when she heard the heavy treading of the Senator's sandals on the marble floor outside her bedchamber. She would quickly tip the vial to her lips and, when he turned her over and laid his wrinkled stomach across her back, she would close her eyes and find peace.

'Come, Atia,' urged Lydia. 'Before we are missed.' Atia tipped one last teardrop into her goblet and the two women slipped back into the courtyard. They followed a crowded walkway to the dining room, where they stretched out at opposite ends of a lounging couch surrounded by tables full of delicacies.

Lydia raised her goblet. 'To Arabia Petraea.'

'To Arabia Petraea,' Atia repeated, then took another long sip of her wine.

It was a sly joke the two women shared, for neither had wished to come to Rome's easternmost province. Lydia had followed her husband here three years ago. A lesser tribune in Trajan's Second Legion, the womanising commander had survived the change of administration from Trajan to Hadrian thanks in no small part to the wise counsel of his wife.

'What troubles you, Atia?' Lydia asked now, casting a wary eye on her husband. The old lecher had cornered a young Greek woman and was shamelessly caressing her cheek.

'Nothing at all, my darling,' Atia said, because her troubles seemed insignificant in comparison to the humiliation Lydia currently suffered.

'Come now, I can see that something worries you,' Lydia prodded. She reached for a fig. 'Beyond the usual worries, of course.'

Atia sifted through her catalogue of worries to find one suitable to discuss publicly. Her stomach twisted as she envisioned burning *ghutrahs* and starving prisoners and innocent Nabataeans doomed to die. She wondered if her own death would come before all of them.

'You are familiar with the science of astrology?' she asked her friend.

'Of course, my dear,' replied Lydia. 'We recently hosted Dorotheus of Sidon at our villa in Gadara. A wretched man, but his astrological treatise is quite famous.'

'Did I ever tell you that an astrologer once predicted the day of my death?'

'Really? But you must know that such predictions are impossible. Astrology is a general science.'

'Of course,' said Atia. She plucked an olive from a plate and gazed at it.

There was a long silence. 'Now you have made me curious,' asked Lydia, also gazing at the olive. 'What day did he give you?'

'It was a she, not a he—a very old woman in the Subura slum,' said Atia.

'And?'

'I cannot recall the exact date she gave,' Atia lied. *In forty days.* Atia popped the olive into her mouth and swallowed it whole. 'She only said it would take place in my thirtieth year.'

'How perfectly morbid! And how old are you now?'

Atia raised a brow.

Lydia laughed. 'Come now, Atia. You do not really believe it, do you?'

Atia shook her head dismissively. She did not need to tell her friend that not only did Atia believe it, she had been looking forward to the date.

'If the reading took place in the Subura, she was likely a charlatan,' Lydia added. 'Besides, old women will say anything to amuse themselves.'

'We most certainly will,' said Atia, sending Lydia a playful grin. A pair of centurions' wives had taken up residence on the couch near them and a pair of young lovers were seating themselves upon the third of their trio of couches. Even in the furthest reaches of the Empire, it seemed, Atia could not escape the risk of gossip. 'My real worry is the heat,' said Atia, turning the conversation to a safe subject. 'I fear it has begun to vex my nerves.'

'It is a brutal time of year,' replied Lydia. 'Though not without its charms.'

'Charms?'

'I am speaking of the nights.'

'Ah, the nights,' said Atia, as if that explained everything. She shot Lydia a confounded look.

'The nights being the only respite from the heat, of course,' Lydia said with a wink.

'Of course,' said Atia. Her friend might have been speaking Latin, but she sensed another language at play.

'To enjoy the nights more, I have begun to sleep on the roof of our villa.'

'Have you indeed?' said Atia. Her head swirled. She was beginning to feel the effects of the poppy.

'I sleep on the roof of our villa because there is a wonderful view of the night sky.' Lydia continued. Atia frowned. Why was Lydia repeating herself?

'You sing of the night sky like a Grecian choir boy,' Atia teased.

Lydia rolled her eyes and leaned forward, and the two women met in the middle of the couch. 'I have taken a lover,' Lydia whispered. 'Is it not obvious?'

Atia sat back, mildly stunned. No, it wasn't obvious, though now that she considered it, she did notice something of a lightness to her friend's mood. She raised her glass in honour of Lydia. 'Have you found it as satisfying as you had hoped?' Atia asked in her public voice. 'Viewing the night sky, I mean.'

'It is utterly spectacular, my dear,' said Lydia. She shot a glance at her husband, who had now begun to caress the Greek woman's arm. 'I highly recommend viewing it yourself.'

Atia tossed her friend a scolding grin. 'You know my father would never allow me to…ah… sleep on the roof.'

'But you are a grown woman, are you not?'

'A Governor's daughter does not sleep on the roof at all,' Atia said. 'And I fear she has never even seen the night sky.'

It was the unfortunate truth. Atia had never learned to enjoy the pleasures of the flesh, despite having been married two more times. Atia's second marriage had been worse than the first. After the old Senator had died, her father had married her to an ill-humoured tax collector as payment for a debt.

The man had been spiteful and rough with Atia, and had often criticised her looks, calling her less than what he deserved. On the rare occasions that he had visited her bed, he had been intent on harming her. And though the poppy tears had helped her endure the pain, they had not been able to shield her from his anger, or the bruises that had always decorated her skin after those terrible nights. Thank the gods her father had chosen to end the marriage and make Atia available for a better alliance.

Though that better alliance had proven to be folly. A prominent Senator, her third husband had claimed to be her father's ally and had eagerly sought Atia's hand. But on their marriage night, he had explained to Atia that he preferred not to see her face during the coupling act. The very next day he had introduced Atia to his mistress.

As it turned out, the Senator had been a spy.

He had married Atia to learn more about her father's efforts to secure Hadrian's rule. When her father had learned of the Senator's treachery, he had slain him at the baths and taken his finger as a prize.

Atia took another sip of wine. Now Lydia was motioning Atia towards her once again. Atia leaned forward and her friend whispered in her ear. 'Love will always be elusive to women like us. But why not seize a little bit of life before it passes us by? A bit of pleasure? We are not getting any younger.'

Atia lay back on the couch and nodded her assent. Indeed they were not. Lydia was already a grandmother and Atia would have been if... She paused. If she had appealed to her husbands enough to get with child. She smiled and took another drink. The tears of poppy were simply a wonder. They made even the most difficult thoughts somehow easier to think.

'I have been sleeping on the roof for many months now, in truth,' said Lydia, tracing the rim of her glass. 'I enjoy the night sky every night.'

Atia peered at Lydia. Was it the effect of the tears or did her friend seem to glow? 'How would one go about such an endeavour?' she asked casually, then filled her mouth with a wedge of melon.

Lydia grinned. 'One must simply select the rooftop mattress one desires and then pay for it.'

'Pay for it?'

'Of course. Or offer some kind of gift in exchange. I recommend the Nabataean-made mattresses. They are especially comfortable.'

Atia could not conceal her wonder. Her closest friend was having an affair with a Nabataean man, whom she compensated with coin and gifts.

It was all very commercial, though she supposed that, in a sense, every union was so. Marriages were always negotiated and every woman was for sale. Or perhaps rent was a better term. Atia herself had been rented three separate times, in three separate marriages. She had never had any aspirations of love or pleasure. She was simply an object of trade in the economy of her father's shifting alliances. If she survived beyond her prophesied death, she did not doubt that she would become such an object again.

Atia gazed at her friend in admiration. Why should she not strike her own bargain for a change? There was something liberating about the idea and it occurred to her that one would not have to be beautiful or desirable in such an arrangement. One would only need to be rich. And rich Atia was.

A vision of Rab's dazzling grin filled her mind. *Go away*, she told it. He was her father's prisoner, after all—the worst possible candidate for a lover. Besides, he had exploited her good will and sought to flatter her towards his own ends. It terrified her—how close she had come to believing his deception. She was certain that, had she allowed their encounter to go on for even a few more seconds, he would have tried to kiss her.

And she would have kissed him back. That was what scared her the most. It was as if his body had been beckoning hers, pulling her towards him by some invisible force.

Thank the gods she had not fallen into his trap. She was not a desirable woman: her father and all three of her husbands had made that abundantly clear. And for the first time in her life that knowledge had served her well.

The tears were hitting her now—a great rush of them. They cooled her limbs and flooded her mind with bliss. She began to laugh. How little any of it mattered, she thought. In forty days she would likely be dead.

Her laughter bubbled over the couch and flowed out into the dining room, mixing with the chords of a lute and catching the attention of her father, whose raised couch gave him full view of the room. His arm was a blur of movement. It was almost as if he was motioning to Atia.

Atia's heart took a plunge. He *was* motioning to her. She ceased her laughter. Her head swirled. She could hardly stand upright in such a state, let alone face her father. Yet she knew she did not have a choice. She stood and steadied herself, then smoothed her *stola* and crossed the room.

'Good evening, Father,' she said, squatting at the side of his couch. She struggled to gather her wits.

'May I ask what is so funny?'

'I was just speaking with Lydia,' Atia said. 'About sleeping on the roof!' Her father gripped her wrist and pulled her close.

'You are cold.' He searched her eyes. 'You have indulged in tears of the poppy.'

'Just a few drops. To relieve my headache.'

His grip on her wrist grew tighter. 'They cloud your judgement. They make you even weaker.'

'Yes, Father.'

He released her wrist. 'The guards tell me that you asked for time alone with the camel man this afternoon. Why?'

Here it was—the moment she had been dreading. 'To gain his confidence,' Atia stated. 'For further interrogation.'

'And what did you discover in your time alone with him?'

Atia paused. She felt as if she were balancing on some invisible rope. 'He claims his father was a pomegranate farmer.'

'That is all?'

'He was very tight-lipped.'

Her father scowled. 'Did you at least discover his name?'

'Rabbel. He goes by Rab.'

'Rab, son of…?'

'Junon.'

'Junon? What kind of a name is that?' Her father paused. 'Ah, it is as I suspected, then.'

As he suspected? What exactly did he suspect? Atia could not think. A panic was rising inside her. It was mixing with the softness of the drug, making her dizzy and confused. Her mind seized on a vision of Rab cowering in his cell, his bright new toga stained with his own blood. 'What will you do with him?' she asked.

Her father only shook his head. 'You have grown too attached to the tears, Atia. But that will soon be remedied.'

'Father?'

But he motioned her away and Atia could do nothing but plaster a smile on her face and make her way back through the dining room to Lydia, her heart filling with dread.

Remedied? Did he plan to take away her poppy tears? Gods, no, not that.

'Make way for the prisoner,' announced a herald.

The crowd parted and there was Rab's hunched figure standing at the entrance to the dining room. Behind him stood a host of guards.

Atia's father made a show of hoisting his injured leg on to a footrest. 'You may approach, prisoner,' he said.

Rab reached the base of the dais in a few long strides. He bowed his head.

'Tell me, prisoner, what category of audacity compels you to present yourself at this elite gathering?' asked her father.

Rab shook his head and studied the floor. 'Forgive me, Honourable Governor. I am as a dog who prowls at a lion's banquet. I embarrass myself.'

There was a smattering of laughter and her father nodded gamely. 'You are worse than a dog, Camel Man. By allowing your camel to injure me you have placed the well-being of this province at risk. You are a menace.' He stomped his good leg on the floor and Rab wisely jumped.

'That is why I have come to apologise,' Rab continued, 'for guilt consumes me and I fear the judgement of the gods. But mostly I fear your judgement, Good Governor, for despite the atrocity of my actions you have granted me mercy.'

Her father was pressing his fingers together—a good sign. 'Go on.'

'I am but a witless, humble cameleer and I curse the day that, in my ignorance, I ordered my camel to deliver the kick that resulted in your injury. Had I known that I was in the presence of the Governor of this great Roman province, I would have rolled beneath the offending hoof myself.'

He was doing well. He had heeded Atia's advice. The audience was looking on with sympathetic interest and her father was nodding gravely. It seemed quite possible that Rab would emerge with his freedom.

'And that is why I beg your forgiveness,' Rab was concluding. He fell to his knees. 'I do not deserve it, just as I do not deserve this fine toga, which in your generosity you have seen fit to provide. Please, Honourable Governor, forgive me, if only so that I may spend the rest of my days singing your praises.'

Atia's father paused dramatically. 'You fail to mention my greatest mercy, Camel Man.'

Atia saw Rab's eyes search the floor. She held her breath. 'My nephew,' said Rab at last. 'In your mercy you released my young nephew. And for that I thank you, Honourable Governor.'

'It was a pleasure to release the youth,' said Atia's father. 'My guards followed him all the way to your home east of Bostra, just to ensure his safety. It is a fine home for one such as yourself. Two floors, a big garden. Beautiful acacia trees.'

Rab's eyes flew open.

'Oh, I know much about you, Rabbel, son of

Junon,' continued her father. 'What I do not know is where your loyalties lie.'

Rab swayed on his knees, as if he had just received a blow. 'Ah, with you, Honourable Governor,' he said, recovering himself. 'With you and with Rome.'

Atia's stomach twisted into a knot. She had not prepared Rab for threats to his family. 'Then you would not deny your Governor a request?'

'I—' Rab glanced at Atia. 'I would do anything in my power to fulfil it.'

'Tell me, have you heard of the Nabataean tax thieves?'

'I have not.'

Atia's father gave a theatrical harrumph and his guests tittered. 'I find that hard to believe, Camel Man,' he continued, 'but since you claim ignorance, I will enlighten you. Every month for the past year, the caravan that conveys the Roman tax payment from Rekem to Bostra has been robbed along New Trajan's Way. We believe the thieves are using the riches to fund the Nabataean rebels.'

'Fools!' cried someone from the audience.

'Fools indeed, but as a result the rebel army has grown bolder,' said Atia's father. 'Two Roman tax collectors were killed just last week. And we all know about the attack on the Rekem *contubernium*.'

There was a collective sigh. Just two months before, a squad of ten Roman soldiers had been killed on their way from Rekem to Bostra. 'New Trajan's Way is no longer secure,' continued Atia's father. 'I assume you know the alternative routes, Camel Man? The locations of the water holes and such?'

'I do,' Rab said carefully.

'Good. As a demonstration of your goodwill, I would like you to guide my daughter and a host of guards to Rekem. Departing tomorrow.'

Atia caught her breath. A journey to Rekem? In the middle of August?

'I wish for you to convey a precious package to Legate Julianus, the commander of the legion stationed there,' her father continued. 'In addition, my daughter has some business with him.'

Atia felt every eye in the room settle on her. There was only one kind of business that could take place between the commander of a Roman legion and the daughter of a Roman governor: marriage.

There was a spate of hushed talk and Atia felt as if she were sinking into the floor. He had done it, then. Her father had selected her fourth husband and was sending her to him along with her precious dowry.

It would be a *sine manu* marriage—as they all had been—with her father retaining control over Atia and her dowry. Whoever her new husband was, Atia would be expected to submit to his every wish—at least until such time as her father determined the alliance of no further use.

Atia laboured to keep the emotion from her expression. She could tell her father was relishing this moment. He had given the bored patricians exactly what they craved. She could hear the gossip starting already—whispers about the meaning of the match, along with a smattering of comments on Atia's advanced age, unfortunate nose and general plainness. She had never been more grateful for the effects of the tears.

Her father returned his attention to Rab. 'You will guide my daughter and her armed escort and help ensure their safety from rebel attack. It is a dangerous mission, but it is how you may prove your loyalty to Rome.'

'Yes, Governor,' said Rab, his head bowed.

'Good, now kiss my ring.'

Rab betrayed only the slightest hesitation as he bent to do the deed and kept his expression blank as Atia's father pulled him close and whispered something in his ear. When Rab returned to standing, he appeared smaller somehow. Defeated. He had managed to get free of his first prison, but now he was obviously trapped inside a new one.

And this time, Atia was trapped with him—the

man who had offered her his *ghutrah* and called her beautiful and tried to kiss her.

The man who had done all those things not out of desire, but in a desperate, futile effort to get himself free.

Chapter Six

The elephants. They haunted Rab's dreams. Giant, fearsome creatures that stormed his restful hours in thundering armies, giving him no peace. He had never actually seen elephants, though he had heard them described by his father so often that he felt he knew them intimately. And he hated them.

When his father had returned from his first trade mission to India, he would not stop talking about the strange beasts. He said that they were as common as camels in that distant land and that they were larger and smarter and gentler than any other creature that walked the earth.

After Rab's mother had died on the birthing bed, his father had made several more trips to India, though each time he returned he had seemed a little sadder. Speaking of India's elephants was the only thing that seemed to cheer him. He had been so fascinated with the beasts that soon he had stopped saying India altogether and instead begun to say 'the land of the elephants' and finally just 'the elephants.'

On the night his father took his own life, Rab had been dozing on the roof of the palace, gazing at the night sky. He and his new wife Babatha had had another argument and Rab had taken his comfort in a bottle of Nabataean wine and the company of the stars.

The memory gave him a chill. Had the warning trumpets not sounded when they did, he would likely have fallen asleep. He would have never seen the Roman legion marching into Rekem: five thousand men treading softly along its sacred way, their helmets gleaming in the moonlight.

If he had not heard the trumpets, he would have never sent orders to the head of the palace guard to surround the most important tombs and speed his family from the city. He would have never rushed into his father's chamber to discover him sprawled on the floor, an empty bottle in his hand.

'My son!' his father had exclaimed. His eyes had been shot with blood and his limbs quivering.

'Father, what have you done?' Rab had asked, though the bottle's purple paint told him everything he needed to know: His father had drunk atropa—the deadliest of poisons.

'Forgive me, Son,' his father had breathed. 'We cannot beat them.'

'We can draw them into the desert, can we not? Just as our forefathers did? The desert is our home. Our enemies are defenceless in it.'

'It is we who are defenceless now.' His father's eyes had fluttered. 'I have written a letter explaining all. You will find it in my tomb.'

'Father, do not go. I do not understand. Please—'

'The elephants, my son,' his father had murmured. 'The elephants.'

And then he was gone.

Rab never found the letter. By the time he'd been able to sneak into his father's tomb, the Romans had taken everything. He and his sisters had travelled north to Bostra, where they had gone into hiding. Rab had grown out his hair and beard and thrown himself into recruiting the rebel army.

'You must let go of your vengeful thoughts,' his young wife had urged him. 'The Romans are here to stay.'

And so he had divorced her. He no longer had any patience for compromising Nabataeans, nor did he have any room left in his heart for love. There was only the relentless, all-consuming work of getting back what Rome had taken.

The elephants. Rab considered the phrase now as he watched their party's leader—a towering Roman commander by the name of Plotius—

berate a young soldier for the dull condition of his sword.

Could his father's reference to elephants have meant the Romans themselves? They were certainly large and they stampeded all over the world. But that was where the comparison ended, for there was nothing gentle or particularly intelligent about the Romans.

And now Rab would be guiding them across his own homeland, aiding them in their business of colonisation. In other words, he would be helping them build what he had been working for thirteen years to destroy.

He watched another soldier place a large bag of onions atop the back of a donkey and saw the beast stumble. The bag added too much weight to the donkey's load and the wrong kind of weight at that.

Rab caught the donkey's eye and tried to convey his apologies. In response, the miserable beast let out a long, squealing bray.

They were Rab's sentiments exactly. It was already mid-morning and the heat had grown fierce, yet their large party of ten donkeys and thirty soldiers still had not left the fort and even the Governor had abandoned them.

This was beyond madness. A journey from Bostra to Rekem in the middle of August?

Nobody travelled in the heat of August. Not

the herders, who followed mountain pastures, nor
the farmers, whose donkeys ploughed the low-
land fields, nor the traders, who plied the desert routes in their caravans of thousands. Even
the wild ibex knew better than to range during
the month of August. Sensible creatures, they
hovered in the shade near their water holes and
waited for the more reasonable temperatures of
autumn to arrive.

It was not the first part of the route that worried him. It would be hot, of course, but there
would be some grazing for the donkeys through
the rolling hills of the north and they would find
supplies and relief in the towns and small villages
that dotted the route.

Nay, it was not the first twenty days that would
break them, it was the second twenty: the desert.

Rab imagined their large party trying to find
shade. There were simply too many of them to
fit beneath the thin overhangs that the badlands
offered. He pictured their cumbersome group attempting to navigate a slot canyon in their heavy
chain mail shirts, or struggle across a dune with
their swords and shields.

That was when he noticed the donkey carriage.
They could not possibly be thinking to bring it
along. 'We cannot bring a carriage,' Rab told
Plotius.

'We can bring whatever we like,' snapped the commander.

'Why do we not employ camels for our journey?' Rab asked.

'Dirty beasts,' Plotius scoffed. 'Camels are for Arabs.'

Rab bit back his anger. 'The donkeys are not suited to this kind of heat. They will expire of thirst.' *As will we all if we are not careful.*

'It is your job to lead us to Rekem,' said Plotius, his fleshy jaw flexing. 'Not to give advice. Understand?'

No, Rab did not understand—not when their very survival was at stake. 'We should carry dates and nuts, not onions, and we should not travel at this time of day.' Rab pointed to the sky. 'You must respect the sun. Your own great Emperor Trajan was defeated by it.'

Plotius paused and Rab could see that the statement had had its intended effect. It was a scandal among Roman soldiers that the Emperor, whom they considered one of the greatest military leaders of all time, had died by fever resulting from exposure to sun.

'Go to Hades,' Plotius responded. He sent a string of spit on to Rab's sandal, then strode away.

You fool, Rab thought, for even spit was something precious in the heat.

The soldiers were lifting their heavy rucksacks, preparing to depart. Rab peered into the crib of the carriage, expecting to see more ill-considered provisions. Instead he beheld the Governor's daughter, gazing listlessly through a rift in the shade cloth. Her face was already a dangerous shade of red.

'You must shield yourself from the sun,' Rab told her. He moved to adjust the shade cloth and lowered his voice. 'If you wish to survive this journey, you must listen to the story that the desert has to tell you. It will be your life...or your death.'

'Please do not try to endear yourself by pretending you care about me,' she replied, waving him away. 'There is nothing I can do for you now.'

They were the first words she had uttered since she had called the guards on him the previous day and he was alarmed at how much they stung. But he should not have been so surprised. They merely underscored what he should have accepted from the beginning: that she was not his friend.

Of course she was not. He was Nabataean and she was Roman, or so she had so helpfully reminded him yesterday inside his cell. Not that he should have required any reminding. He hated Romans. They were unlike the Greek conquerors who had swept through Nabataean lands before them. Romans did not attempt to understand the peoples they conquered. They invaded kingdoms and bled them of their riches, then gifted their broken peoples with the title 'citizen' and expected their undying love.

Rab could see it happening already. There were now over two thousand Nabataeans in the Third Cyrenaica Legion based in Bostra and there was news the that the Twenty-Second Deiotariana based in Rekem had an equal number in its ranks. Many of Rab's poorer friends now donned Roman armour and his landed friends wore Roman togas. They mixed with Roman settlers and married their daughters, abandoning their Nabataean gods and embracing Jupiter and Juno and the rest.

It was a disgrace. They were dishonourable men, at least in Rab's mind—traitors to their people. A true Nabataean would never consider any kind of an alliance with a Roman. A true Nabataean would stay as far away from the Romans as he could possibly get.

In other words, he was not her friend, either.

Which was why he was finding it difficult to get the previous day's events out of his mind, for she had helped him in a way that had seemed utterly selfless. Had she not guided him in the manner of his apology, he would have surely landed himself back in the cell. Or worse.

And there was the problem of her nearness. When he had pulled her up to face him in the bathhouse reception hall, it had felt as if he were standing before a woman he had known all his life. Against everything he knew and believed, he had found himself wanting to kiss her.

Though that was perhaps not the best way to describe the elemental yearning that had him sweating and trembling and swilling her scent.

And she had wanted to kiss him—he was almost certain of it. She had closed her eyes and parted her lips—those lush, welcoming lips—and then—

'You, Camel Man, on the point,' commanded Plotius. The soldiers were moving into position around the woman's carriage, pushing Rab to the side.

Good. He did not wish to be near her. Nearness was dangerous. It scrambled his wits and made his body want things it should not. Besides, he suspected she was now betrothed. What other business could she possibly have with the Roman Legate at Rekem?

'Take your places,' Plotius called to the men. The armoured soldiers were donning their helmets and preparing to depart. Rab scanned the group in search of an augur or holy man, but failed to discover a one. 'Will we not request the favour of the gods before we begin?' he asked. 'Will we offer them nothing?'

There was a long silence. The Roman woman

sat up in her cart and sighed with annoyance. 'Plotius?' she barked. 'Prepare a sacrifice for Janus.'

Rab watched Plotius remove his helmet and scan the fort in search of something to kill. But not even the pigeons would oblige him in this kind of heat. He stalked towards a donkey and rifled through its saddlebag, finally seizing on a large glass jar.

Plotius flashed the party a thick-lipped grin as he uncorked the container and pulled out three dead dormice dripping with vinegar. 'Still fresh,' he said to no one in particular. 'They will have to suffice.'

Rab cringed as Plotius held the tiny corpses up to the heavens. What mockery of a sacrifice was this? Were Romans so blinded by their own dominion that they had ceased even to fear the gods? Plotius mumbled some incomprehensible thing, then placed the mice beside the road.

'Leave the jar as well,' said the woman. She reached into her pocket and produced several silver *denarii*. 'And place these coins with it,' she continued, 'lest Janus think us stingy.'

With a roll of his eyes, Plotius placed the jar on the ground next to the corpses and tossed the coins upon the crude display. He gave the sky a defiant stare, then addressed his troops. 'Let the infernal march begin,' he said. 'To Rekem!'

Suddenly the men were moving. They fell into

position without effort, flowing around Rab as if he were a rock in the stream. They would march, it seemed, even without their guide to lead them.

Rab sent a quick prayer to Shay' al-Qaum, the Nabataean god of caravans, and stepped silently past the mice, imagining their tiny corpses roasting in the sun all day. By evening they would draw the dogs, who would feast on their cooked flesh, then smash the fragile jar and consume their pickled companions as well.

Rab gazed out at the heavily armoured soldiers and realised that he was the only one who saw it—the suffering ahead of them. The first part of the route they would survive. The hills of the north had reliable water and there was never a town more than two days' journey away. But as they journeyed further south the desert would begin to claim them: first their energy, then their water, then, finally, their minds.

The Romans did not understand. They would never understand. The desert in summer was a dog. And they were the dormice.

Chapter Seven

 Atia never went looking for trouble, but trouble always seemed to find her. It had found her the day she was born, for she was supposed to have been a boy. It had found her the day of her first marriage, then the day of her second, then the day of her third. It had found her the day her father had ordered her newborn sister taken away to the dump and the day after that, when her mother had taken her own life and Atia had sought comfort for the first time in the tears of poppy.

And then it had found her again just three days ago, when her father had taken away the tears from her for good.

Gods, the heat.

Quiet and suffocating, it had cooked her where she lay inside the cart each day, crushing her will, turning her thoughts into *polentum*.

The donkeys. Did no one else worry for their well-being? The poor beasts had been grossly overburdened and so Atia had spent all of the second evening going through their saddlebags trying to balance their loads. Her efforts had helped a little, but not enough, and so this third evening she had dedicated herself to placing the heavier items in her own cart.

'What are you doing, *domina*?' Plotius asked her. He had removed his officer's armour and his sweat-soaked undertunic clung to his outsized muscles. Atia noticed that he looked down at those muscles regularly, as if congratulating himself on them.

'I cannot rest, Plotius,' she said. 'I am worried about the donkeys.'

Plotius gazed at the carriage full of supplies. 'But where will you sit tomorrow during the march?'

'I will not sit. I will march like the rest of you.' She had grown restless over the past two days and a walk sounded most welcome. She had never gone this long without a few drops of tears to calm her nerves.

'You are trembling, *domina*,' said Plotius.

'I am nervous for the donkeys,' she said, though in truth she had never experienced such a trembling before. 'I fear for them.'

'And I fear for you. You seem to be ailing.'

'I have a headache. That is all.' But it was more

than that. She felt as if she was crawling out of her skin.

'How can I help you?' asked Plotius.

Atia glanced around the camp. The men were sprawling on their bed mats, exhausted and unable to move. The sun had set, but the heat lingered, tormenting them all. Many paces away, two of the soldiers laboured over a small fire upon which they had arranged several pots of *polentum*. Sweat poured from their brows, landing in the soup.

The only man who did not appear to be suffering was Rab. He had found a seat on a large boulder at the perimeter of the camp. He had caught the current of a breeze, for his *ghutrah* fluttered behind him in a way Atia could only describe as graceful. He was staring out at the stark rolling hills, sipping from his water bag, calm as a camel. He seemed to know something she did not and it irritated her.

'There is a way you can help me, Plotius,' Atia said, lowering her voice. 'Do you have any tears of poppy potion? I fear it is the only thing that will quiet my headache.'

'I do,' Plotius said carefully, 'but I am afraid your father has forbidden me from giving it to you.'

'I only need a few drops. Please, Plotius.' She must have spoken a bit too loudly, because she saw Rab turn slightly as if to listen. Atia lowered her voice. 'The tears will cure what ails me, you understand? I need them badly.'

Plotius flashed a crooked grin. 'Not a soul can know of this.'

'Of course. Just tell me what to do.'

'Meet me on the other side of that hill around the second watch,' he whispered, glancing at a low rise about a half-mile beyond the camp. 'You will have your poppy tears.'

You will have your poppy tears. The words were like a balm. They echoed in her mind for the rest of the evening, crowding her thoughts. She scratched her skin and swatted at flies, trying to be patient. The soldiers were eating now. One of them was approaching her with a bowl of *polentum*.

'No, thank you,' she said, waving him away. Just the thought of food made her sick with nausea.

She turned to find Rab still sitting on his rock, regarding her disapprovingly. What right did he have to watch her that way, his eyes so full of judgement?

She stomped towards him, utterly annoyed. 'Why do you stare at me?' she demanded.

'You are foolish not to eat,' he said.

'Pah,' she spat out. How arrogant he was—

presuming he knew what was best for her. First the shade, then the gods and now this.

'The journey requires that you preserve your strength,' he added. He held out a handful of dates. 'Take these.'

She shook her head, looked away. She reminded herself that he had been charged by her father to see her safely to Rekem—that was all. He was only pretending to care for her.

Still, there was something almost tender about the way he held out the small fruits. They appeared to be all he had to eat, yet he was offering them to her.

She reached out to accept them and noticed that her hand was trembling. Overcome with shame, she pulled it back to her side.

'It is your choice not to eat,' he said, 'but it will be your fault when you are too tired to scale the steep slopes ahead of us.' He brushed away a fly and tilted his face to the breeze, and her irritation returned.

'You act as if you own the desert,' she barked.

'No one can own the desert,' he returned.

'Well, you have certainly made yourself the mayor of this wretched patch of earth,' she said.

He blinked, then erupted in laughter.

'What is so funny?' she clipped.

'You are.'

'Me?'

'Funny and foolish.'

She shook her head, realising only after many moments that such vigorous denial *was* both funny and foolish. 'I am the Governor's daughter and the highest-ranking person here,' she reminded him. 'I am the embodiment of our party's *dignitas*.' A fly buzzed around her face and she swatted at it uselessly.

He was laughing again.

'I am glad I am able to entertain you so much,' she said and could not suppress her own small grin. Curse him. Even in her agitated state she was a victim to his charms.

She drew a breath and held her arms tightly at her sides. She tried not to scratch the itches that seemed to be breaking out all over her body. If only she could stand before him in a state of indifference—not wavering with this terrible restlessness.

'It is not just yourself you harm by not eating,' he said at last. 'It is everyone else in the party.'

And there it was: how he truly felt. It was the party's well-being he cared for, not hers. The offer of dates was his way of telling her to pull her own weight, nothing more.

She stalked back into camp, consoling herself that in only a few hours, she would have her tears and a measure of calm. But moments made up hours and the moments were passing far too slowly.

You have grown too attached to the tears, her father had told her.

The morning of their party's departure, he had summoned her to his office. He had been sitting at his desk, holding a candle carefully over the lip of an envelope. Plotius had stood behind him and both men had watched with interest as the crimson wax dripped on to the delicate white page.

'This letter is for Julianus, the commander of the legion in Rekem,' her father announced. He had pressed the face of his signet ring into the circle of wax and held it there. 'You must deliver this to him without fail,' he said, blowing softly on the wax. 'It contains important instructions, and will explain the contents of the box that Plotius carries.'

Atia had glanced at the sandal-sized iron box in Plotius's arms. Why had her father not just said that the letter was a marriage contract and the box contained her dowry? Perhaps he had not thought it necessary. It was an obvious match, after all—the Governor of Arabia, stationed in the north, allied by blood with the Legate in charge of its most powerful legion in the south. The north and south of Arabia, bonded through family. Of course he was sending her to be married.

But he had said not a word. It was as if he

wished to keep her in suspense. Or perhaps punish her with it.

'Remember to deliver this letter to the Legate personally,' he said, and handed it to her. 'And the seal must remain unbroken, do you understand?'

'Yes, Father.'

'Consider it a test of loyalty.' Atia had bowed, then turned to take her leave. 'And, Atia?'

'Yes, Father?' He was thrumming his fingers upon the desk.

'No more poppy tears.'

It was all he had said. There had been no sharp words or bitter admonitions. Just those four words accompanied by the quiet thrum of his fingers on the desk.

She could still hear their steady thumping inside her mind. The sound was at war with her nerves, which cried out for relief. What difference would a few drops make? She was already far from home and Plotius would not dare tell her father he had given her the tears, lest he implicate himself in the deed.

Besides, if the foretelling of her death was true, she would likely never even make it to Rekem, for in exactly thirty-seven days, Atia was meant to die.

She paced about the camp until she was certain that all the men had gone to sleep. The thought of her own demise had always brought with it a sense of relief, but that night it felt almost thrilling.

In only thirty-seven days, she would quite possibly be free of this itching, trembling, restlessness. She would no longer ache for her mother and sisters, or be complicit in her father's wicked deeds, or cringe as she recalled the uselessness of her life. She would no longer have to depend on the tears to numb the pain inside her heart. She would be permanently numb, for she would be gone from this terrible world for ever.

Until then, she would do what was necessary to return herself to comfort. She made her way over the hill and waited upon a rock for Plotius.

Soon she heard the soft snapping of twigs and saw the flash of a candle drawing near.

'You are early,' said Plotius in a honeyed voice. The candle lit the flesh of his face in an eerie glow.

'My headache grows worse,' Atia said. 'Do you have the tears?'

'I do,' he said, lifting a small bottle from beneath the belt of his dagger. Atia moved to take the bottle, but he pulled it out of her reach.

'Do you realise the risk I am taking by giving this to you?' he said. 'If your father were to find out, I would be stripped of my command.'

'He will not find out,' said Atia.

'How can you assure me?'

'I can assure you because he would do worse to me. Much worse,' she said. She held out her palm.

'I am afraid I need one more small assurance.' He wedged the candle between two rocks and placed the bottle between his teeth. Then he pulled off his tunic.

Atia froze in horror. He was standing before her in only his loincloth, which he was hurriedly unwrapping. The length of cloth tumbled to the ground.

She stepped backwards, catching sight of the growing column of his flesh. 'I am sorry,' Atia said, trying to keep her voice even. 'I think we have misunderstood each other.' She took another step backwards. It was so dark. She wondered how fast she might be able to run back to camp.

'Do you want the poppy tears or not?' he demanded. He took himself in hand.

Terror shot through her. 'I have changed my mind,' she managed to say. 'I must go.' She turned to run, but he caught her by the wrist.

'You are not going anywhere, my dear,' he breathed. His long nails dug into her flesh.

'Release me!' she shouted, as if anyone could hear her so far from camp. She twisted her arm, but could not seem to break free of him. He grasped her other wrist and pulled her towards him. Terror split her mind.

Suddenly, the candle blew out. There was

scuffling in the dirt, followed by a soft, choking sound. Plotius gasped, then released his grip on both her wrists. Atia stumbled forward.

'Go!' cried a voice, and Atia did not stop to think. She just ran.

She had shivered beneath her blanket that night, despite the heat, and had not slept a minute. When their march began the next morning, she found a place as far away from Plotius as she could get. She did not wish to see his fleshy face or remember the feel of his hands on her wrists, though the pain of the bruises was making it difficult to purge the memory entirely.

He had almost defiled her. Right there in the lonely wilds of the Arabian north, with no witnesses but the stars. The thought was quietly terrifying. No amount of poppy tears was worth such a risk. And yet in her desire to obtain the treasured potion, she had walked blindly into his trap.

Trouble. She had always thought that it searched for her, but this time, it seemed, she had searched for it. And she had found it. If her anonymous saviour had not miraculously emerged from the shadows to stop Plotius, she knew she would be suffering from more than just bruises.

The sun rose higher in the sky and she watched the soldiers closely, trying to discover some clue to the identity of her hero. But the soldiers' laboured movements and blank faces told no tales. He could have been anyone.

She marched on. The sun was hotter today than it was yesterday, or so it seemed. The naked, boulder-strewn hills sprawled before them, their spring flowers gone, their wild grasses long dead. She knew that they were to avoid New Trajan's Way to the east, but there was a perfectly good river valley a distance below them to the west. A river by the name of Jordan flowed lazily through it, wandering past a mosaic of dry farmlands with its meandering swath of green.

'Why do we not follow the River Jordan?' she asked weakly, but nobody seemed to hear.

How lovely it would be to take a plunge in that river, Atia thought. She was growing more nauseated by the minute and these endless hills were devouring her strength.

'Halt,' Plotius commanded towards the end of the day. A small flock of goats had appeared and was pouring down a steep slope into the dry *wadi* in which their party had been marching all afternoon.

'I see our dinner, men,' Plotius said. He motioned to a soldier, who seized one of the goats and held it to the ground. 'Snap its neck,' Plotius commanded.

Atia moved to protest. It was a crime to take another man's goat anywhere in the Roman provinces and Plotius knew it. Besides, Roman soldiers were not allowed to consume meat while on duty. Plotius knew that, too.

But Plotius shot her a glance that froze her in place. The soldier dutifully snapped the goat's neck, then hoisted the dead beast over his shoulders while the other soldiers cheered.

In the same instant, an old shepherd rounded a bend in the *wadi* and gasped.

'What are you looking at, old man?' said Plotius. He placed his hand on the hilt of his sword and strode forward. 'Get yourself gone before we take another.' Stunned, the man did not move. Plotius unsheathed his sword as if to strike.

Stop! Atia's mind shouted. She saw a small trickle of urine run down the man's leg.

'Leave us, shepherd!' shouted Plotius, lunging forward, and the man threw off his staff and stumbled back around the bend, narrowly escaping the sting of Plotius's blade.

Atia stole a glance at Rab. His granite expression betrayed no emotion, but the colour had left his cheeks. 'We must leave the cart,' Rab said suddenly.

'What?' said Plotius. 'We will do no such thing.'

Rab pointed down the *wadi*. 'Nabataean shepherds are dangerous enemies and you have just made a small army of them. They will wait for us further down the *wadi*, where they will ambush us and attempt to stone us to death. So we cannot follow the *wadi* any longer.' He pointed to the steep, cliffy mountain rising to their left. 'That is our route now. We must transfer our supplies to the donkeys' saddlebags and leave the cart behind. Now.'

Rab did not wait for Plotius's reply. He simply started up the steep slope.

Atia looked around in desperation. Did Rab really expect them to scale such a cliff?

The soldiers were watching Plotius, awaiting instruction, when a terrifying shriek resonated from down the *wadi*. The cry was followed by another and then half-a-dozen more.

Plotius motioned to Rab. 'You heard him. Now move quickly.' The men transferred the contents of the cart into saddlebags, then started up the slope. There was so much loose rock. For each step the soldiers took, they seemed to fall backwards an equivalent distance.

Atia stood and stared, unable to move. It seemed that she was just swimming in trouble now. Drowning in it.

Atia began to climb—though climbing was a poor way to describe the stumbling, slipping, lunging efforts she made.

Once again, the only one who seemed at all

comfortable was Rab. He was cutting a path vertically up the mountain, not attempting to ease the route. It was as if he meant to punish them.

'Why do you not ease the way?' she shouted. No reply. 'I command you to answer me!' She stopped to await a response, but that only made her fall behind.

The ground was not behaving. It was beginning to undulate beneath her feet, making her stumble. How did the goats do it? she wondered. How did they scale such mind-bending heights every day? She could see their small round droppings. They were so very sweet—like small, plump olives fallen from imaginary trees.

And then suddenly there they were—goats! A hundred of them. A thousand. A million. They were travelling across the hillside like a flowing stream.

She sat down and they began to flow towards her. She opened her arms.

She did not recall what came next. There was the sound of voices near and she was scooped up by a pair of arms. Now she was no longer walking, but floating up the hillside. And that was well, because her head felt light and full of air.

The heat. Gods, the heat.

She felt sick. Her stomach heaved and, for the final time that day, trouble found her.

Chapter Eight

Until this moment, Rab had never in his life watched another person sleep. The realisation hit him as he sat in the cave beside the woman, watching her writhe and shout and mutter.

He was certain she would wake soon—the pale light of dawn was already painting the cave walls pink. He had been wise to settle her in this small cave well away from the rest of their party, for she had been suffering wailing terrors throughout the night. Her voice had been loud and commanding. It was as if she were a centurion leading troops on the field of battle.

He smiled at the thought. It was an apt description, as there had been a markedly militant quality to her demeanour of late. The way she had shouted at him on his way up the hillside that afternoon reminded him of certain Nabataean commanders he knew. And it definitely appeared as though a battle had taken place where she slept.

She lay amid a tangled confusion of shawl and *stola* and bedsheet, all twisted and coiled around her like the bonds of Prometheus.

'Release me,' she mumbled, lost in a dream. Her arm flailed to the side and he caught sight of a cluster of bruises on her wrist. Anger gripped his chest. Roman or not, no woman deserved to be harmed in such a way. Rab fought the urge to gut Plotius and leave him for the crows.

Though he could do nothing of the sort, for Plotius was the Governor's most trusted commander and Rab was the Governor's dog.

Rab could still hear the Governor's thick voice inside his ear the night of the banquet, whispering his terrifying promise.

'No, Father,' the woman muttered, as if somewhere in the tumult of her dreams she had heard the promise, too. She thrust out her leg, nearly kicking Rab in the chest. 'You are as bad as the white camel,' he whispered.

Her expression went soft and she seemed to enter some quiet, peaceful space. She was lovely at rest. Her nose was no longer stern, only chiselled and strong, and her big brown eyes could accuse him of nothing. Her cheeks were soft and full, her chin round and sweet, and her lips made the shapeliest of blooms. Peace became her.

Yet he knew her heart was full of torment. What did Plotius have that she needed so badly?

What powerful demon compelled her to meet with such a crude, violent man in the middle of the night?

The very thought of her in the clutches of such a man made Rab ill with disgust. If only Rab could understand why she had gone to meet Plotius in the first place, he might be better able to protect her.

Though right now all he wanted was to feel the reassurance of her breath. He held his hand over her mouth.

A soft white hand reached up and gripped his wrist. 'What are you doing here?' she demanded, her eyes flashing open. He jumped backwards. There was nothing heavy about her lids now. Her gaze was quietly ferocious.

'I am here to aid you,' he said. 'You have had an ordeal.'

'I do not need your aid,' she said.

He held out his water bag. 'Drink,' he said.

'What is it?' she muttered, sitting up.

'Water. You have been asleep for many hours.'

She gave the bag a puzzled look. 'Have we had this conversation before?'

'You must drink.'

She untied the mouth and peered into the bag. 'There would not happen to be any poppy tears mixed with this water, would there?'

'No,' said Rab. 'Unlike you, I do not drug people without their consent.'

'Good,' she said, but her eyes lacked conviction. She took a long swallow of water, then gazed around the small cave. 'I feel as if I am remembering a dream.'

'Yesterday you were harmed by the sun and too much exertion.'

Her lips twisted into a scowl. 'I seem to remember that we were *all* harmed by too much exertion. You led us up a cliff face!'

'There was no choice, *domina*,' he said.

'Call me Atia.'

'Atia...' he said, testing the name on his lips. It was noble and retreating all at once, he thought. Doubtful but kind. It suited her.

'I see you are trying to become a Roman after all, Rab, son of Junon.' She glanced at his short red tunic.

'A temporary evil. There was an...accident that required me to wash my robe.'

He gave her a significant look and watched as she retrieved the memory. 'I lost my stomach upon you, did I not?' she asked. She covered her nascent smile with her hands. 'I am so sorry.'

He quirked a frown. 'You do not appear very sorry.'

'I am very, terribly, extremely sorry.' She was trying so hard not to laugh that it was all he could do not to smile himself. She moved to rise, but was prevented by the confusion of cloth surrounding her. She fell back to the ground with a thump.

Then he did laugh. 'You are a tangled mess,' he said. 'Arachne herself could not unravel you.'

'I am quite capable of unravelling myself,' she said. 'But how do you know of Arachne?'

'Do you think me a barbarian? Of course I know of the Greek gods. As for Arachne, I believe I see a certain minion of hers just there in the mess of your hair.'

He pointed teasingly to her hair and she shrieked. She shook her hair, then fell backwards, hindered once again by her tangled wraps. He doubled over in laughter.

'You wicked beast!' she shouted. 'I thought there was a spider!' She punched him in the arm.

He gazed at the sight of the blow and gave a loud *tsk*. 'I am afraid that was the most ridiculous, womanish punch I have ever received.'

'That is well, for I am a woman!'

'That you are,' he said, meaning to sound pragmatic, but the words had leapt from his tongue in a tone of admiration.

She scowled playfully. 'Do you wish for another blow, then?'

'I certainly do,' he said, 'for I pity you and wish to assist you in retrieving your honour.'

She raised her arm as if to strike him again, but he caught her elbow in the air. 'You are very slow. I fear your honour remains in a shambles.'

Her lips balanced at the edge of a grin. Gods, he wanted to taste that grin. He pulled her arm closer and her body leaned towards his. Suddenly they were back where they had been that day at the baths. Her lips were so close. He could feel her warm breath on his cheeks.

Suddenly her expression became confused. She pulled her arm back to her side and leaned away. 'I am afraid such gestures will no longer deliver any advantage,' she said.

'Apologies, I do not understand.'

'I no longer carry any keys beneath my belt.' She raised a brow, as if awaiting his response to the puzzling statement. When he gave none, she moved to stand, then swayed with dizziness.

'You are weak,' he said.

'I am not weak.'

'You have not eaten for two days.' He pointed to a small bowl of dates he had set beside her bed mat. 'Those are blessed dates from the plantations of Palmyra. They will help you break your fast.'

She frowned at the bowl. 'That is very kind of you, but I am not hungry,' she said.

'You must eat now,' he ordered.

'Whether or not I eat is my own concern.'

'I am afraid it is also my concern, for you are

a member of the party I am guiding and I have promised your father to deliver you safely to Rekem.'

'Yes, of course,' she bit back. 'Gods forbid the ship of goods not arrive to port.'

'I have no choice in this mission,' he said.

'Nor do I.' She was wrestling with the cloth now. She seemed to be tangling herself in it further.

'Will you at least allow me to help you up?' he asked.

'I do not wish for your help now—or ever,' she said. She wrangled herself free, jumped to her feet and exited the cave.

Rab felt as if he had just been kicked by a camel. What on earth had he done wrong? He had only been trying to help her. Though that was not the whole truth. He had only been trying to help her at first. After they had touched, he had only been trying to help her lips connect with his. He could not seem to overcome it—that maddening, irresistible pull.

A pull towards a woman who was a Roman and also likely betrothed.

Thank the gods she had spoken when she did. Had they got any closer he might have kissed her and kissing a betrothed woman was nothing less than adultery. A Roman woman, no less! He would have dishonoured his family name, not to mention himself.

I no longer have any keys beneath my belt. What on earth did she mean? But there was no time to think, for she had already returned to the cave and was hovering over him like a battle-ready Athena. 'You did not answer my question,' she said.

'What question?'

'Why on earth would a Nabataean camel racer have occasion to learn Greek religion?' She was doing it again—trying to steer the conversation away from what had just taken place. 'Well?' she prodded.

Had she no idea how distracting were her curves from this angle?

'Is my question so very difficult to answer?' she asked.

And what question was that? He could no longer recall. *Could you please repeat it?* The morning sun was not helping matters. It shone through the skirt of her tunic to reveal the profiles of two very shapely legs. 'I am simply asking how you came to learn about the Greek gods,' she said.

'And goddesses,' he said.

He considered rising to his feet. That would certainly remove several of the distractions she was currently presenting. But he was taller than she and to stand over her now would strip her of the fragile dignity he knew she was attempting to recover.

He folded his legs beneath him and sat up straight. 'Nabataean school children are required to learn the Persian, Roman and Greek pantheons,' he replied. 'We are also required to read a good deal of literature in Greek and Aramaic.'

She cast him a doubting look, so he cleared his throat and switched to Greek. *'Of all creatures that breathe and move upon the earth, none is bred that is weaker than man.'*

'Homer?' she asked. He shot her a wink. 'But I thought the Arabs did not value learning.'

'Who told you that?'

'My father.'

'Your father is mistaken. Learning is all the Arab tribes have ever done. We are traders and trade necessitates learning. I assume you know of my tribe's particular trade?'

She shifted her weight and assumed a scholarly pose. 'The Nabataeans are the shepherds of the Frankincense Road,' she stated. 'Across the Arabian wasteland.'

'The Arabian desert is not a wasteland.'

She paused. 'It is how they refer to it in Rome.'

'There is life everywhere in the desert. One must simply know where to look for it.'

'But how do you exist in such a place?'

'We control the water.'

'What water?'

He lowered his voice. 'The secret water.'

Her expression softened. 'Secret water?'

'Very secret water,' he said, relishing her interest. 'The Nabataeans have cultivated it for hundreds of years and kept its locations—nay, its very existence—from outsiders.'

Atia narrowed her eyes in doubt. 'You cannot cultivate water.'

'Tell that to the men who dig the wells and lay the pipes to channel the rain. Tell that to the builders of the cisterns and the forgers of the dams. The city of Rekem itself would not exist without the elaborate control and storage of water.'

'I have heard the praises of Rekem sung even in Rome,' she said wistfully.

'People say that the great stone tombs are the glory of Rekem. I say it is the great networks of water.'

'I should very much like to see this secret desert water,' she said.

'If I showed you, you would be bound to me for ever,' he said. He flashed a playful grin and was rewarded with her frown.

'But do you not agree that it is foolish to travel in such heat?' she asked.

'With the whole of my heart,' he said.

'Then why can we not simply stay in one of the old Greek Decapolis cities here in the north?

Pella, for example. We can stay there until the heat of August lifts.'

'I promised your father that I would get us to Rekem by the end of September.'

'Then why can we not simply follow the River Jordan to the west? We would have water always near and we could stop in Jericho—'

'I would love nothing more than to follow the River Jordan,' admitted Rab. 'But it is part of Judea now and Jews and Nabataeans have a long, bloody history. I would not be welcome.'

'Surely we could disguise your identity.' She gave another glance at his Roman tunic and he felt her eyes graze across his exposed thighs.

'I am afraid that Romans are not welcome in Judea either—not right now. Your Commander Quietus did a very bad thing in Lydda recently,' said Rab, 'and there are rumours of another Jewish uprising in response. I promise you there would be trouble.'

Her gaze was owlish. 'I know of Quietus's butchery and have also heard the rumours of an uprising. But how would a simple camel trainer know of them?'

'I sometimes work in trade,' he lied. 'I hear things.'

'A trader?' She glanced at his arms and shook her head.

'You doubt me?'

'I observe you.'

'And what do you observe?'

'That you do not have the physique of a trader.'

'And you are an expert in the physiques of Arabian traders?'

'They are tall and thin, like the camels they command. You have the body of a soldier, not a trader.'

He wanted to be angry, but he could not help feeling a strange pleasure at the thought that she had considered him in such a way. Still, he needed to be careful with this woman. She was far too observant for her own good.

'Shh! Scoot!' she shouted and he turned to discover a squirrel stealing one of the dates from the bowl he had placed on the ground. The creature took one brazen look at Rab, then bounded away with his treasure.

'Thief!' shouted Rab and he watched with pleasure as Atia's face split with a grin.

'Will you not have one small date?' he asked. The thought of her starving until lunchtime made him bristle with worry. He retrieved just one date from the bowl and held it up to her. 'Please,' he begged. 'Do it for me.'

Her expression softened and she accepted the date without a sound. Her hand grazed his.

'Your fingers,' he said.

'What about my fingers?'

'They are not cold.'

Nearby, a sword rattled loudly against a shield, splitting the silence. 'Pack your things,' shouted Plotius. 'We march in half an hour!'

Rab watched a cloud pass over Atia's expression.

'Stealing another man's goat is a capital offence,' Rab mused, 'yet not one of the soldiers questioned him about the act.'

'Roman soldiers are trained never to question their superiors,' Atia explained. 'It is cause for a flogging.'

'In that case, the next time it happens, *I* will challenge him.'

'Do not think of it!'

'Something must be done,' Rab replied. He offered his water bag to Atia, who took a final, long draught. Perhaps she would accept another date? He reached for the bowl, only to discover two squirrels now breaking their fasts at the bowl's edge.

'Leave, you cursed vermin!' he spat, swatting the air. Atia began to laugh and her laughter seemed to flow into his body, filling him with energy. He leapt to his feet and gazed down at the two furry creatures. They flicked their tails and twitched their ears, as if they were laughing, too. 'Did you not hear me, you little thieves?' Rab shouted, lunging towards them. 'Go!'

The squirrels bounded away and Atia's eyes flew open.

Chapter Nine

'Go!' he shouted, and it was the same 'Go!' that she had heard two nights before when she had stumbled out of Plotius's grip. There was simply no mistaking the voice. It was the voice of her saviour and that saviour, it seemed, was Rab.

She masked her surprise by feigning anger at the squirrels, causing Rab to laugh. He muttered something about checking the donkeys' loads and departed, leaving Atia to consider the bowl of dates along with this strange new truth.

Rab had saved her from Plotius.

But how? She had never even considered the possibility. An unarmed camel trainer could never subdue a hulking Roman commander, or so she had wrongly concluded. Nor had she considered that he would rescue her from exhaustion, or that he would fill her water bags and bring her dates, or that he would sit beside her as she slept.

No one had ever sat beside her as she slept.

But why had he not just admitted to saving her? They had spoken together for a long time—longer than she had spoken to anyone in many moons. If he truly felt that he owed her a debt, then why had he not simply admitted to the good deed and declared that debt paid?

She suspected that his good deed was not the only thing he was hiding. The man knew far too much about Roman politics to be the simple trainer-turned-trader that he claimed to be. General Quietus's massacre in Lydda was well known, but the rumours of another Judean revolt were quite new. Indeed, her father had deliberately kept those rumours quiet, lest the Nabataean rebels be further encouraged.

Yet Rab had somehow heard them.

It was possible the rumours had been passed to him from one of the soldiers, though it was doubtful that Roman infantry soldiers would be aware of such rumours. She supposed that her father himself might have warned Rab away from a route through Judea—especially given the box of gold coins Plotius likely carried. Gods forbid any harm come to that.

It still did not explain Rab's education. His Greek had been flawless—better than her own. If Nabataea was anything like Rome, then only landed, noble families could afford to educate their children in such a way.

Families of camel trainers surely could not afford to teach their children to recite lines from Homer.

Then there was the question of his appearance. The man was simply too strong for his vocation. A camel trainer would have no occasion to do the lifting, carrying and pulling required to develop such a muscular chest.

And it was not just his chest. The short Roman tunic he donned had afforded her a glimpse of his thighs—two bulging pillars of muscle that had borne Atia herself all the way up the steep slope the previous afternoon.

Not that she had to be reminded of his thighs—or anything else. The image of him naked inside the dressing room—his arousal growing as they spoke—was etched into her mind for ever.

Rab was not a camel trainer, nor was he a trader. Who was he, then?

She watched him closely throughout the march that day. He led their small caravan with easy confidence, picking the best routes up and down the rocky canyons. When the sun became too fierce, he directed their group to a shady overhang that he seemed to conjure from the desert itself.

He was a natural guide and shepherd—that seemed quite clear. As they took their places beneath the shade at noon, she observed him subtly taking stock of the soldiers and donkeys, ensuring that each animal was properly shaded and that any ailing soldiers were helped free of their armour and made comfortable.

He was an experienced leader, or so it seemed, though Atia ceased to ponder the matter when she became aware that he was also taking stock of her.

Except that it was more than a simple assessment. When she lifted her head to meet his gaze, there it was again: desire. Fierce and piercing. Hotter than the midday sun. There was no mistaking it now—she had seen it too many times. Nor did she doubt its veracity, for there was no longer any more reason for him to feign his lust.

Time seemed to stand still and she willed herself not to look away. He desired her—despite her many attempts to put distance between them. Yearning seemed to pour out of his eyes—a great cascade of it—and she realised that she wanted to bathe in it for as long as she could.

'Rab!' called a soldier and the spell was broken.

Atia lay her head back on her mat and remembered to breathe. She told herself not to make too much of that moment or any other. She was the only woman within a dozen miles, after all— the only woman that any of the men would see for the next six weeks. It did not matter how she looked. She was a woman and he was a man and, in the absence of other women, he had settled for her. Proximity bred desire. It was as simple as that.

Still, it pleased her to think that he desired her—for whatever reason. At her advanced age, and with her repulsive nose, it was just nice to be desired. Nay, it was better than nice. It was wonderful.

So wonderful that she could think of little else all that day, or the day after that. The memory of his smouldering eyes was like a candle glowing bright within her mind—bright enough to nearly erase her other, more shadowy thoughts.

The ones she had become determined to vanquish.

The ones that managed to creep in at the oddest moments. Like when she lay down at night and considered that she would soon be married. Or when she thought of the look on her father's face when he had vowed to slaughter the Nabataean rebels. Or when she thought of her sisters' unfortunate fates, or her mother's terrible death…

But mostly she did not think of those things. She tried instead to focus on her legs. She told them how much they loved to walk. They seemed to believe her. They piloted her up and down the endless hills with growing vitality, and when the group camped outside the city of Pella that seventh afternoon, she noticed that her headache was gone and her trembling had ceased.

'Good evening, *domina*,' said one of the soldiers, cutting a bow. 'A group of us are going to Pella to purchase supplies. Is there anything you might wish for us to bring you?'

Atia glanced around camp, finding neither Plotius nor Rab in sight. Her heart beat faster. Pella was a large Greek colonial city with strong trading ties throughout Arabia. There would be alchemists and doctors and tears aplenty available for purchase there. 'Will Plotius accompany you?' she asked casually.

'No, *domina*. The commander wishes to rest here in camp.'

Atia's mind swirled. She could simply tell this soldier to fetch a bottle of tears for her, flip him a gold coin and no one would be the wiser.

Only she did not drink the tears any more. She had given them up.

Though it would be nice to have them for an emergency. *Just one small bottle*, she thought.

'Would you wait one moment?' Atia asked the soldier. She crossed to her bed mat and bent to fetch her coin purse. Perhaps she would have him buy her two bottles instead of one. Then she would have one bottle for emergencies and another for occasional use. In that case, she could have just a few drops with her dinner that night and her sleep would be free of terrors.

As she strode towards the soldier, she caught sight of Rab rising from his bed mat not ten paces away. He flashed her a grin so wickedly handsome that it made her lose her footing. She stumbled, righted herself, then smiled back.

'Atia, come join me for some *polentum*,' he called.

This time it was her heart, not her feet, that seemed to stumble. Something in the way he beckoned her made her feel terribly, inappropriately happy.

'Ah…one moment,' she told Rab and, as her feet continued towards the soldier, Atia remembered the first time Rab had offered her food. It had been that second day of the march when she had been so terribly restless. He had offered her dates, but her hands had been trembling so hard that she had been unable to accept them. She knew that it was the lack of tears that had caused the trembling, as well as the shame. She never wanted to feel that way again.

'What is your order, *domina*?' asked the soldier.

'Apologies,' Atia replied. 'I have changed my mind. I do not need anything after all.'

'As you wish, *domina*,' said the soldier with a retreating bow.

Atia felt quietly triumphant. She had never in her life refused the opportunity for tears. She had not known she was capable of such a refusal.

Her reward came only a little while later when Rab brought her a bowlful of *polentum*. The notoriously bland stew had never tasted more delicious on her tongue. Afterwards, she found a seat on a rock just above the camp and Rab joined her there.

'The sky will be beautiful tonight,' he observed, gazing out at the crimson horizon. 'The moon will rise late.'

He had seated himself very close. His robed arm brushed against her own and, though it was just the touch of cloth on cloth, the contact quickened her heartbeat.

'You know much about the night sky,' she said. She smiled to herself, thinking of the special meaning that Lydia had given to the starry expanse.

'The desert is my mistress,' Rab said. 'The night sky is her robe.' He turned to look at Atia and her stomach plunged in a strange delight. She had a powerful inclination to conceal her nose from his view.

'Do you have a favourite constellation?' she

asked instead, hoping he would return his attention to the sky.

He thought for a moment. 'There is a Nabataean constellation called The Balance. Three stars in the shape of a pyramid: one to hold the balance itself and two to hold the scales. It is beautiful, but mostly I love what it symbolises.'

'And what is that?' asked Atia.

'Justice.'

'In Rome it is the same. Libra—the scales.'

'There are so many things we have in common with you Romans, but you hold yourselves above us and treat us unfairly. You fleece us of our greatness, our wealth, our—' He stopped himself.

'Why do you cease?' she asked.

He shook his head. 'I do not need to bother you with my ranting.'

'Do you think I am so naive as to believe in Roman righteousness?' she asked.

He looked at her as if she had just sprouted wings.

'I remember the day Emperor Trajan marched ten thousand Dacian soldiers on to the Campus of Mars and had them crucified one by one,' she continued. 'It was the greatest tragedy I have ever witnessed, though I have read about many others. I have studied history, Rab. I know how Rome bullies and batters its way around the world. The business of empire is the business of suffering and death. I only wish I did not have to take part in it.'

'You do not have to.'

She laughed softly. 'As if I have any power at all over my fate.'

'You have power. You just do not know how to use it. Your father...'

There was a long silence. 'My father what?'

'He is a powerful demon,' Rab said at length.

She did not answer, but she did not contradict him either.

There was movement in the camp below them. The soldiers who had gone to Pella had returned and fresh bread and rations of wine were being passed around. Soon the men would be deep in their cups. Atia and Rab could remain undisturbed.

'Ah, look, just there,' said Atia, pointing to two stars that had risen near the eastern horizon. 'I think that is the beginning of Libra.'

'We must wait and see,' said Rab, though it seemed he was speaking of something other than the sky.

Atia searched her mind for something to say, but all she could think about was how good it felt to sit beside him like this, with all the universe spreading itself out before them, as if they were not prisoners carrying out their terrible sentences, but simple travelers in a great big world.

Rab spoke at last. 'May I ask you a question, Atia?'

'Of course,' she said.

'Are you betrothed?'

She paused. It was a perfectly natural question, and yet she felt as if someone had just stuffed a scarf down her throat. 'I—I do not know.'

'You do not know?'

It was the last thing on earth she wished to talk about with him. 'My father said nothing to me about any betrothal. He gave me a letter and told me to deliver it to the Legate in Rekem. I do not know what it contains.'

'Can you not open it to find out?'

'He forbade it. I do not know if the letter contains the marriage contract or something else. I know that—' She stopped herself. There was no reason to bring up the dowry.

'You know what?' he demanded.

'I *believe* that there are golden *aureiis* in the box Plotius carries. It is perhaps a loan of some kind—maybe for a public works project. Or perhaps payment for the legion at Rekem.'

'Or perhaps a dowry,' he said.

'Let us hope that is not the case.'

'What quarrel do you have with marriage?'

'I believe it is…dangerous,' Atia said.

'What do you mean?'

'My sister was betrothed once—to a wicked

man. When it was discovered that she had fallen in love with another, my father punished her with twenty lashes.'

Rab gasped. 'Twenty lashes…for a woman?'

'It was a mercy,' said Atia. 'Her lover received fifty.' She bit her tongue. She had said too much.

'Fifty lashes? Who could survive that?'

Atia said nothing, for the man had not survived.

Even in the darkness, she could sense Rab's expression change. He scooted away from her—just enough to make room for the wall that seemed to materialise between them.

She should not have been surprised. She had just described how her father had murdered her sister's lover. If Rab had harboured any intentions of getting closer to her, she had just delivered them a violent end.

'If your father does not send you to be married, then why does he send you to Rekem at all?' He peered over his shoulder, as if fearful of being seen with her.

'Perhaps as a punishment,' she said.

'Punishment? What terrible misdeed would warrant sending you across the desert in the middle of August?'

'I believe it was—'

She stopped herself. Hounds of Hades, was she really about to tell him the truth? *I believe it was my overindulgence in tears of the poppy.* She could never tell him *that.* Even if she could not have his desire, she at least wanted his respect.

'I have no idea,' she lied. 'My father enjoys keeping me in suspense.'

Rab removed his *ghutrah* and ran his hand through his long hair. 'I fear you are not alone in that.'

'What do you mean?'

'Your father said that if I did not deliver you to Rekem by the end of September he will kill my nephew.'

Atia's stomach heaved. Another innocent under threat of her father's blade. 'I am so sorry,' she said. 'I will do everything in my power to—'

'I do not tell you this to elicit your sympathy,' he interrupted. 'I only wish for us to be honest with each other.'

'As do I,' she said.

'Do you?'

Atia thought of the most honest thing she could say. 'I know that it was you who saved me from Plotius.'

He turned to look at her directly, but it had become too blessedly dark for him to see her. 'How do you know that?' he asked.

'I am very observant,' she said.

'That you are.'

'You saved me, Rab,' she said. 'Why did you

not simply tell me? Did you not think that I would wish to thank you?'

'I do not require your thanks,' he said. 'I only wish to know why you agreed to such a meeting at all. Why did you do it?'

It was an impossible question. To answer it honestly, she would have to admit to her weakness for the poppy. How much would he desire her after learning that she was willing to risk her own safety for a single drop of the tears?

But there was another, more basic reason. To voice her weakness for the poppy would give it more power somehow. Power that she did not wish it to have. Power that it did not deserve.

'I cannot say why,' she said.

'You cannot say or you do not wish to say?'

Atia paused. 'Both reasons.' She sensed him stiffen. 'It is not important.'

'It is important to me,' he returned.

They sat together in silence for what seemed like hours. Atia was sure that Rab suspected an affair. It was the obvious explanation for why she had agreed to meet Plotius in the middle of the night so far from camp.

Why should she not tell him the real reason she had put herself in that position? Rab had saved her from a terrible ravaging, after all. He deserved to know the truth.

But she could not bring herself to admit it to

him. The truth was even uglier than her nose, for it was caused by a flaw deep within herself. It was something so very ugly that not even darkness could conceal it.

'It has been so long since I observed the night sky,' she remarked, feebly changing the subject. 'When I was young I would often watch the stars on the roof of our *doma* in Rome.'

'Indeed?' he said absently. With each passing moment he seemed to draw further away from her.

'Especially in the summers,' she chattered on in in growing desperation. 'My sisters and I would play in the atrium pool all day and spent our nights upon the roof, gazing at the stars.'

'How wonderful,' Rab said, but there was little wonder in his voice.

'Our mother would teach us the constellations. She had studied astrology as a young woman, you see. She was so full of enthusiasm back then and so very beautiful. That was before she…'

Atia bit her lip. She squeezed her eyes together to fight the shock of tears. She had not spoken of her mother in years.

'Are you all right?' Rab asked. Thank the gods for the darkness, for it concealed the tears she felt streaming down her face. 'Will you not even answer that question?'

'I am fine,' she said with too much cheer. 'Everything is fine.' She buried her face in her hands.

'It really does not seem that way,' he said. 'What is wrong?'

'Please, just go away,' she said.

Rab exhaled and rose to his feet. 'As you wish. Goodnight, Atia,' he said.

'Goodnight,' she said and listened closely to the soft crunch of his feet against the earth as he walked away.

But then the crunching stopped and she heard his voice cut across the darkness. 'It is a powerful demon you face,' he said.

Chapter Ten

The trail grew rougher. The rolling hills of the north transformed into steep, cliffy canyons that plunged into narrow *wadis* flowing only with sand.

Atia kept her head down as she marched and took one step at a time. *It is a powerful demon you face*, he had told her, as if he already knew of the battle she waged.

It was impossible. She had told him nothing of her fondness for the poppy tears.

Surely he had been speaking of some other demon: her father, Plotius, the Legate of Rekem. Or perhaps he had been referring to the demon of grief, who had shown himself unexpectedly when she had spoken of her mother.

What was abundantly clear was that Rab no longer wished to speak with her, for he left her to eat alone each night, and did not join her again to watch the stars come out. Whatever desire he had once had for her had waned predictably. Nor had she helped matters by describing the gruesome death of her sister's lover.

As if that were not enough, she had refused to answer his question about why she had gone to meet Plotius and when he had asked gently about her mother she had ordered him to go away.

It is a powerful demon you face, he had said and was clearly letting her face it alone.

And that was well. She wanted to be alone. There were only thirty days left until her foretold death, after all. Or was it twenty-nine?

She searched her mind, but it yielded only confusion. How on earth had she managed to lose track of the days? She paused on the goat path. They had arrived outside Pella on day thirty-five, had they not? Or maybe it was thirty-four. And how many days had it been since then? Four? Five?

It was what she had been wondering when a bulging hulk of a man crashed into her. 'Apologies!' he exclaimed, reaching out to steady her.

The man was breathing so hard beneath his chain mail shirt that Atia had the strong urge to lift it off him. 'You saved me from a fall, soldier,' she said. 'I am grateful.'

'But it was I who caused the stumble in the first place.'

'Then we shall call ourselves even,' she said.

'Not in the least!' exclaimed the man. 'I vowed to deliver you safely to the Legate in Rekem. Until that blessed moment I shall never say that we are even.' His expression was so earnest that she could do nothing but bow her thanks.

His name was Livius. He was the most talkative and also the stoutest of the soldiers, though he seemed better suited to kneading bread than tromping up hills. Each morning he would seek her out and attempt to engage her with small talk.

'I do not wish to talk, Livius,' she would say, though it made no difference.

He would always open their one-sided conversation with a remark about the sun, then remove his helmet and scratch his bald head ponderously, as if its light and heat were one of life's great mysteries.

He would go on to describe some detail of his homeland—Gaul—his sisters—unmarried, fine weavers—his family's vineyard—burned by Caesar, since replanted—or his physical state—chafing between his thighs, a toothache.

Then he would urge Atia to ride a donkey for a while and take a bit of rest. 'You must be tired, *domina*. Why not relieve your weary bones?'

'I prefer to walk, thank you,' she always replied. She knew that Livius was secretly speaking of himself and that, if he were given the chance, he would mount the sturdiest of the donkeys and ride it all the way to Rekem.

'If you wish to suffer, I cannot stop you,' Livius always said.

Atia did wish to suffer. She wanted to walk and walk, to feel the burn of muscle and the ache of bone—anything to keep her from thinking of the poppy tears.

It is a powerful demon you face, she told herself over and over again. *And you are defeating it.*

She occupied her mind with games of distraction. How many steps to the next hill? Which was the tallest soldier? How many seconds for a hawk to make a single spiral in the air? She gathered up pretty stones and then threw them away one by one. One evening, she carved a message into a slab of soft sandstone: *Atia was here.*

She was getting better with each passing day, but it was still hard to distinguish herself from the yearning, which had transformed from a physical illness to an illness of the mind. She decided that she much preferred the physical malaise to the mental. One could escape the physical through sheer exhaustion, but there was no escaping the mind.

Atia was not *here*, she carved the next evening. It seemed much closer to the truth.

* * *

Rab kept a blistering pace. The soldiers' limbs grew redder by the day, their search for shade more desperate. Rab began their march earlier and earlier each morning. In the evenings, he roused them for several more hours in the wake of the sun god's retreat.

It was as if he were trying to sneak around the heat, as if he believed that if they marched quietly and stealthily enough, it might not notice them at all.

Inspired, Atia tried to sneak around the yearning. She steered her thoughts to other things she wished for: shade, a good meal, a plunge into a deep pool.

The wish to be desired by a pair of eyes flecked with gold.

It was not an unreasonable wish, for no one had ever desired her before. 'It is your nose more than anything, dear,' her third husband had told her once. They had been strolling together at a banquet, admiring a lovely garden. 'Everything else about you is quite adequate.' He had said it as if he were paying her a compliment, then had motioned to a woman standing nearby to join them.

'Atia, I would like to introduce you to my mistress.'

'Hello,' the woman had said with a shy grin.

Her nose had seemed so small as to be almost invisible.

Atia had nodded at the beautiful woman, but had been unable to say a word.

'Come now, Atia,' her husband had said. 'I thought you would be pleased. You no longer have to perform those duties that I know are so odious to you.'

Though Atia had no love for her wifely duties, she knew in that moment that her third husband had been speaking of his own odium—of Atia.

Though the manner of the rejection varied with each husband, the reason was always the same. And thus her path was laid. With each step she was drawing closer to a fate as familiar as it was dreadful. Another husband. Another series of disappointments. More long years of smiling with feigned contentment through what amounted to a prolonged rejection inside a marble prison.

It was no wonder she craved the tears.

I am tired of being used. The thought came to her on the twenty-sixth day of the march. Or was it the twenty-fifth? She was sitting in the shade of a boulder, noticing the contours of new muscle in her legs. She realised that she was tired of sitting in a haze while her life slowly passed her by.

She was tired, she realised, of doing nothing. They marched and marched and Atia's legs grew stronger still. She was not alone. About half of the soldiers appeared to be growing stronger as well. They seemed to view the heat like Rab did, as a puzzle to be solved.

The others, however, were not faring so well. They spent much of their energy in active rebellion against the heat, not realising that half of the battle lay inside their own minds. Plotius might have been the worst of them. He spent his days kicking rocks from his path and scowling at the sun.

Meanwhile, the New Trajan Way stretched to the east, its wide, smooth surface mocking them as they threaded their way along steep, rocky goat paths.

Another temptation lay to the west: a giant lake into which the River Jordan flowed. The Romans called it the Bitumen Lake after the tarry black substance that floated up from its depths. The Nabataeans had many names for the expanse, including the Sea of Zo'ar, the Sea of Forgetting, and even the Dead Sea, for its waters were salty and void of life. At a distance, however, the water seemed fresh and fecund, like the pool of some divine oasis.

Atia had to remind herself of what Rab had warned—that both routes were traps: to follow either would be to invite attack.

Supplies ran low. The donkeys' loads diminished, only to be replaced by the soldiers' helmets and chainmail, which most men could no longer bear to wear. The more enterprising among them had ripped their bed sheets into strips and wrapped the small pieces of cloth around their roasting limbs.

'You look like an overstuffed mummy, Livius,' Atia said one morning as they broke camp. The portly soldier paused in exaggerated surprise.

'You made a jest! Good for you, Atia,' said Livius. 'I had begun to worry that you resided in the Land of the Dead yourself.'

'Nay, Livius,' Atia said, feeling an actual smile creeping across her lips, 'just the land of dusty spirits.'

'Another jest!' Livius burst out. 'We will need that good humour over the next few days.' He pointed down at the canyon plunging before them—the largest they had yet traversed.

Moments later, Rab stood before the entourage to describe that day's journey. 'They call this the land of the three *wadis*,' he announced. 'The canyon you see to the south is the first—Wadi Ma'in. There will be two others after this one, Wadi Hidan and Wadi Mujib, each larger than the last.'

Atia lent her voice to the chorus of groans.

'You favour him,' whispered Livius. 'I can hear it in your voice.'

Ignoring Livius, Atia focused her attention on Rab, who was pointing at the large peak in the distance. 'Our goal is to reach the third *wadi* by nightfall, for at its bottom we will encounter a perennial stream. It will be our reward.' His eyes found Atia's.

She quickly looked away.

'And he favours you,' whispered Livius. 'That is abundantly clear.'

'You are wrong, Livius.'

'I am always right about such matters. My sisters used to say I have a nose for love.'

'And I have nose for scaring love away,' jested Atia, motioning to her terrible nose.

Livius only shook his head. 'I would not be so sure about that, *domina*.'

Atia wanted to ask Livius what he meant, but Plotius pushed past them. 'Why do we not travel along the Bitumen Lake?' he barked. 'There are many large settlements on its shores and many opportunities to obtain supplies. It is but a day's journey away. All downhill.'

'As I have said, Nabataean rebels patrol the eastern shores. It is not safe,' stated Rab. 'Come, we must keep moving.'

But Plotius held his ground. 'How could you possibly know that?' he demanded. They had gone nowhere, yet Plotius's corpulent face was already covered in a curtain of cloudy sweat.

'I know it from the bitumen traders,' blurted Rab. 'They come to Bostra on the ides of each month to trade their black tar. They talk.'

'I find that hard to believe,' said Plotius.

'I am as concerned as you are about securing supplies,' explained Rab. 'We will pass an encampment of herders just before the Wadi Mujib stream. They will sell us enough wheat to see us through to the next encampment.'

Plotius scowled, but he commanded his men to move out. It was not long before he was groaning once again beneath the sun.

It was their most difficult day yet. Marching out of the second *wadi*, several of the men collapsed and had to be placed atop donkeys. The heat only increased as they descended in the great chasm of Wadi Mujib, but just as Rab had promised, they soon stumbled into an encampment of herders. Atia and the soldiers stood beside a corral of braying sheep while Rab and Plotius bartered with a young shepherd for several sacks of wheat.

'Ask him how much for a sheep,' Plotius said, his eyes shot with blood.

'The sheep are not for sale,' explained Rab. 'They are meant to see this man's family through the summer.'

'Everything is for sale,' Plotius said. 'Ask him how much.'

Atia could hear the apology in Rab's voice as he switched to Nabataean and asked the man if he would be willing to sell one of his sheep. The man shook his head apologetically. 'He is very sorry,' said Rab. 'His family is large. He cannot part with a single one.'

Rab and the shepherd agreed on a price for the wheat and Plotius paid the shepherd from a store of coins. Their food secured, the soldiers fell into line behind Rab as they followed a single narrow path that led over a hill and out of the encampment.

The only one who did not follow was Plotius. Atia noticed him lingering beside the corral, so she stepped behind the tent and lingered, too. The soldiers were almost halfway up the hill when Atia watched Plotius lift the large ewe from her stall.

'Put the sheep down, Plotius,' Atia cried, stepping out from behind the tent. She hardly recognised her own voice. 'Now!'

She planted herself at the start of the narrow path. He could go nowhere without pushing past her.

'Get out of my way, Atia!' he shouted. 'We need her more than they do.'

Atia's heart was pounding. *It is a powerful*

demon you face, she told herself. *And you are defeating it.*

'Leave the sheep,' she said, then added, 'You are acting against provincial law.'

He released a laugh—a long, cold, terrifying laugh that was meant to defeat her. But she held her ground as he attempted to push past her and when he stepped off the path she adjusted her own position so as to remain standing before him, not allowing him to pass.

'Are you mad, woman? Move out of the way, or I will make you regret it!' He was lifting his leg to kick her when Atia saw a large wooden pole rise up behind his head. The shepherd gave a terrifying howl and the staff came crashing down on to Plotius's skull. Goliath went tumbling to the ground.

Chapter Eleven

It had taken time to secure Plotius's stunned body atop a donkey and to apologise to the shepherd, who had made his opinions about Rome and Roman soldiers known to Rab for the better part of an hour. It must have been close to midnight by the time they reached camp.

All of this meant there had been no time for Rab to thank Atia for what she had done.

The next morning, the soldiers tried to wake Plotius, but could not. A half-empty bottle of poppy tears was discovered beside his slumbering figure and it was decided that they would stay by the stream for a day while the commander recovered.

Rab found Atia around midday. She was basking in a secluded part of the stream about a half-mile upstream from the soldiers. He heard her gasp as he approached and watched her dive behind a large boulder.

'You know I can see you,' said Rab.

She swam out from behind the boulder and scowled. 'I thought you were one of the soldiers,' she said, keeping the entirety of her body submerged. 'Why do you laugh?'

'You were trying to hide behind a boulder the size of a rabbit.'

'I was blending into my surroundings,' she countered, which only made him laugh harder. Soon she was laughing, too, though he could see she did not wish to.

'I apologise for disturbing you,' he said, returning to formality. He reminded himself of the last time they had spoken. She had set a clear boundary between them that night. She would not tell him why her father wished to punish her, or why she had gone to meet Plotius, or anything at all, it seemed. *I am fine. Everything is fine*, she had said. *Please, just go away.*

And so that was what he had done. Now he squatted to the level of the stream and quickly announced his intentions. 'I came to tell you that what you did yesterday—when you confronted Plotius about the sheep—it was…very brave.'

He had expected her to ignore him, as she usually did when he paid her a compliment. Instead she smiled, and her cheeks flushed with warmth. 'It is kind of you to say.'

It was more than kind of him to say. It was perhaps the nicest thing anyone had ever said to her.

'And you claim that you are powerless,' he said. 'You are the strongest woman I know.'

'Flatterer,' she said, though the sentiment buoyed her spirit. In a fit of boldness, she sent him a splash. To her amazement, he splashed her back.

And in her cock-eyed glee she splashed him again with so much energy and joy that it was as if she had poured the whole of the river over his linen robe.

He stood and stared down at his drenched figure. 'Siren!' he shouted. She splashed him again and it was as if the wall that had built up between them over the past dozen days had not been made of stone, but of sand.

'So you want to play dirty, is that it?' he asked.

'On the contrary,' she said, pretending to wash herself in the stream, 'I want to play clean.'

She was laughing so hard now that she did not consider that her breast wrap and loincloth were soaked through.

She simply stood, unaware of her near-naked state until his shouting abruptly ceased and he tilted away from the bank as if to get a better look at her.

She hugged her arms to her chest and turned, lunging awkwardly towards the opposite bank where her tunic lay.

But it was far too late for such a dramatic display of modesty. He had seen the whole of her.

Now her blush was no longer limited to her cheeks. It travelled down her neck at great speed. When she finally got her tunic wrapped around her most private parts, it had colonised her chest.

When she finally dared to look at him, he was still gazing at the place where she had emerged from the water. She wondered if she had somehow offended him. 'Is something the matter, Rab?'

'No, ah, I mean, yes.'

'What is it?'

'Apologies. You are just so…beautiful.'

He had spoken it like a confession, like something he did not wish to tell, but simply had to, lest he invoke the wrath of the gods.

And it was the most wonderful thing she had ever heard in all her life.

Their gazes locked, and she felt a rush of heat. There it was—the look. His eyes were so focused, so hungry and alert. They made her stomach feel weak. She never dreamed he would be looking at her this way again.

Blood thundered in her ears. He had no reason to feign his lust. And yet there it was, burning in his eyes, which were now looking her up and down, as if he were tracing all the parts of her he wished to touch. She studied him in return, though she had long ago imagined how she would touch him.

She would first trace her fingers softly along the contours of his arms. Then she would remove his robe and place a chorus of kisses all along his chest. Then she would run her fingers through his long, scraggly hair and touch his sensuous lips. Finally, she would lift her own lips to kiss them.

And that was just the beginning. She had imagined a great deal more and now that she was staring into his eyes it all seemed unnervingly possible.

Still, her wild fantasies meant nothing if he found her unsatisfactory. And she was certain that no matter what fuelled his desire for her—loneliness, isolation, a dearth of other female candidates—he would quickly lose interest in her if she did not give him a reason to keep it. *I will pay him*, Atia thought.

She remembered Lydia's exact words. 'You must simply purchase the right mattress for you,' her friend had advised. Suddenly Atia knew that Rab was her mattress.

She would pay him in gold coins and make it

impossible for him to reject her. She would apologise for not answering his question about Plotius and assure him that she was not betrothed.

What harm could there possibly be in stealing a few moments of joy? Lydia was right, Atia had too little joy in her life and even less pleasure.

It is a powerful demon you face, she thought suddenly. *And you are defeating it.*

She took a deep breath, then stood and unwrapped her tunic, letting it tumble back on to the bank.

He feared it had arrived: the moment when the heat had finally begun to twist his mind. He had long dreaded this moment, though he had never imagined that it would occur on the banks of a river, or that his hallucination would involve the woman he wanted, but could not have, or that the experience of sun madness would be so very... pleasurable.

And yet there she was, standing before him in all her naked glory: beautiful, sensual, irresistible proof of his total insanity.

It was alarming how quickly the sun had worked its evil. Just seconds before, he had watched Atia rise from the stream in a state of distraction, oblivious to her exposed flesh. As soon as she had become aware of herself, she had yelped in surprise and lunged for her tunic on the opposite bank.

Rab had been equally surprised and the vision of all that dripping, curvy abundance had rendered him quite incapable of looking away. She had fumbled with her tunic for a long while, giving him plenty of time to consider what he was seeing.

Surely that was when the sun had gone to work. A thousand forbidden yearnings had swirled inside his head as he stared at the place where she had emerged. But the primary yearning had been this: he wanted to see her again.

Now it seemed he had got his wish, for she had abandoned her tunic and stepped back into the river, her dripping wet undergarments practically inviting him to take a closer look.

And that he most certainly did, for there was no more thinking now. There was only her tight, wet breast wrap that did nothing to conceal her shapely breasts. There were only the shadows of her nipples, which shone through the fabric of the garment like ripe berries. There was only her loincloth, which clung to her delicious curves, wrapping around her legs and then plunging between them to where the dark shadow of her womanhood lay.

He swallowed hard.

This is not really happening, he told himself,

though his desire seemed to disagree. He could feel it rising beneath his loincloth at an alarming rate.

There were other sensations, too: the water she had splashed on him still dripping down his face, the fabric of his drenched robe clinging to his chest, the hot breeze tickling his skin.

Would he be feeling such things if he had truly lost his wits? Perhaps it was not he who had gone mad, but she.

He watched her eyes, searching for signs of sun madness. In truth, they had seemed clearer and more lucid for many days now. Her heavy lids had disappeared, replaced by a curious, wide-eyed watchfulness that Rab had found wildly seductive.

Now that gaze was slowly setting his insides aflame. Perhaps this was not Atia at all. Perhaps this was some splendid goddess who had simply taken Atia's earthly form and was paying him a visit.

She certainly looked like a goddess. So many lovely dips and curves, so much soft, beckoning flesh. To see her march was to believe her made of iron, yet beneath her loose robes was this… garden of loveliness.

Her fingers tickled the surface of the water in slow, seductive circles. Her vivid dark eyes watched him closely, but without the doubt that usually veiled them. It seemed impossible that this was the same bristling, brooding, scolding woman who had eschewed his advances not once, but twice.

'Stop gaping,' she chided.

Well, maybe not totally impossible.

'I'm not gaping,' he replied.

I am throbbing and sweating and lusting, but definitely not gaping.

She took several more steps. She was halfway across the stream now—close enough for him to see the rise and fall of her stomach with her breaths.

It might have been pure wickedness that inspired her to do what she did next. She reached behind her with her long, delicate arms and undid the knot of her breast wrap. Pulling the length of cloth carefully over her head, she unwrapped herself for Rab.

He felt as if he might fall to his knees right there on the riverbank. Two gorgeous breasts appeared before him like precious prizes that he had somehow won. He had not seen a woman's breasts in many, many years and he had forgotten how deliciously arousing was the sight of them.

He wanted to consume them whole.

'You are definitely gaping,' she said, but her voice was as soft as feathers and she was smiling shyly, as if it pleased her that he stared.

'Yes, I suppose I am,' he admitted.

Who was this new Atia? This bolder, stronger, happier woman whose eyes glowed with such a strange new light?

'Rab, I am not betrothed,' she said. 'If I were, I would have been told. Plotius is injured and can do us no harm and the other soldiers are far from this place. There is no danger.'

Rab nodded, feeling that he would have gladly faced any number of dangers if it meant he could continue gazing at her while the sun painted her luscious belly with its honey light.

'Do you want me, Rab?' she asked.

The answer to such a question seemed to demand formality. 'In the name of Dushara, God of the Sun, and Uzza, Goddess of Water, and all the gods that ever were or ever will be, yes, Atia. I want you.'

She flashed a playful grin. 'Then why not come join me?'

He smiled back. Why ever not? It was a brilliant idea. Genius, really. She was always coming up with such clever, good ideas. Yes, just there in the middle of the stream. What better place to do what he had been wanting to do since the day his body had first tumbled against hers?

He pulled off his *ghutrah*, then his robe, and cast both aside. He did not need to look at himself to know the picture of raw lust he presented. He could see it reflected in her eyes, which slid down his stomach and then grew wide with alarm. He needed to close the distance between them lest he scare her away.

He bounded through the stream, lunging and splashing awkwardly.

When he arrived before her she had disintegrated into laughter. 'You have the grace of Egypt's finest river cow.'

'Yet on land I am like a gazelle,' he said with a smirk.

'That you are—or perhaps more accurately a goat,' she chided. She laughed—the most delicious, sensuous laugh he had ever heard. He splashed her again, getting water all over her face. It lodged in her eyelashes and dripped down on to her flushed cheeks. It gathered in beads on her chin and in that sensuous divot just above her lip.

And in that moment she was no longer Roman. She was like Aphrodite's own nymph standing there, anxiously awaiting her pleasure.

And, by the gods, he was going to give it to her.

He slid his hand beneath her hair and gripped the back of her neck. Slowly, he bent and sucked the water from her cheeks, her chin, even her lashes. Finally, he bent to her lips and kissed her.

Time seemed to collapse and a tiny explosion took place inside her heart. She had been yearning for this for so long, wondering if kissing him would be everything she had hoped. It was not everything she had hoped. It was more. Stars and planets. Sweetness and light. A revelation sent by the gods.

His lips.

His beautiful, magical, mystical lips.

So soft, so maddeningly gentle. She was learning their texture, their shape, their secrets. They seemed to have so much to say. Tender, hungry messages accompanied by hot, sweet breath and the scent of musk.

His mouth. So wide and strong. It kissed with slow reverence, as if it were enacting a kind of prayer.

She kissed him back as best she could, hoping her eagerness would make up for what she lacked in skill. None of her husbands had ever kissed her this way and she hardly knew what to do.

She might have been ashamed. Here she was, a fumbling Roman matron offering herself to a man in the middle of a stream. A woman so lonely and desperate that she had decided to compensate him for this pleasure.

Strangely, however, she could not feel any shame. In place of the judgement of Juno, she felt only felt the warmth of the sun. In place of self-doubt, she knew only the soft trickle of the river over the pebbles along the shore. And it was as if her heart was dancing to that music.

'I will make this worth it for you,' she whispered into his mouth. In exchange for his attention, she would pay him a small fortune. For though she was not attractive, she was rich and she would make it so that he never regretted giving her pleasure. 'I will do right by you,' she added. Her words seemed only to fuel him for his lips pressed harder against hers and she knew that he had accepted her offer.

His grip on her neck grew firmer. He paused, breathed her in, then swept his tongue softly through her mouth, barely touching it. He seemed to be holding himself back. It was as if his desire for her was made of clay and he was trying to fashion it into a shape she could understand.

Oh, she could understand.

A strange heat had invaded the deepest part of her. A curious, pleasurable heat that made her feel at once blissful and hungry for more of him.

'What is this thing you do with your tongue?' she asked.

He paused, a delicious smile traversing his face. 'You mean this?' He coaxed her mouth open once again, then moved his tongue across it with such maddening gentleness that she nearly lost her footing.

She sighed into his mouth. 'Yes, that.'

She wanted more of that. And a bit more of his naked chest. And perhaps a sprinkling of neck kisses, as she had heard from Lydia they were quite delightful. She wanted other things, too, though she did not know exactly what those other things were. She only knew that they existed and that perhaps they could be hers.

He nuzzled her ear, then planted a hot, breathy kiss on it. Her hairs stood up like an army of soldiers. Oh, yes, she would pay whatever it cost.

'Atia, you are so very sweet.' He placed his hand upon her back and pulled her closer. The flowing water rushed around their legs.

'Rab, you are so very—' Her breasts crushed against his chest and she felt the whole of his desire press against her stomach. 'So...very...'

Blessed Minerva. He was so very...very.

If she had any remaining doubts about the authenticity of his desire, they were utterly vanquished by the pillar of flesh that now stretched between them.

'Atia, you feel so good,' he said. 'You taste—' he pulled her lip into his mouth and sucked it '—so good.'

His words seemed genuine and she had to remind herself that he would surely be saying the same such words to any other woman in her position. She was the only available woman within a hundred miles, after all. There was nothing special about her—except that she happened to be here.

And that she was willing to pay.

It was a strangely liberating notion. It allowed her the boldness to rock her hips against him and feel her desire begin to flow. It gave her the audacity to wrap her arms around his chest and wonder at the solidity of him.

But it was more than just wonder. As she pressed her body against his, it was as if some darkness within her disappeared, and peace spread through her limbs.

She yearned to lay her head upon his chest, but she sensed that if she did, that same blessed peace would radiate into her heart and she would never wish to leave him.

So she resolved never to rest her head on his chest.

She tipped her head backwards, exposing her neck. He pounced on the invitation. Neck kisses! The smouldering embers deep in her belly flickered to life. Lydia had been wrong in her assessment of them, for they were better than delightful. They were utterly sublime.

And they seemed to be rearranging her wits, for suddenly she wished nothing but to surrender herself to him.

The sentiment gave her a shock. It seemed impossible that she should wish such a thing. She had been surrendering dutifully to her husbands for many years. The only thing she had ever wished was for the odious task to end.

She did not want this to end—not ever. Nor did the surrender she wished for now have anything to do with duty. A kind of knot had tied itself up inside her and she sensed that only he could unravel it.

His kisses became slower. His tongue made soft circles behind her ear. Hot needles of lust tore down her body, so sweet they hurt. This was virgin territory, and she felt rather lost. She had no map for how she was feeling, no guiding principles and, holy Mars incarnate, what was he doing to her neck now?

By the gods, he was sucking it.

And causing the embers in her belly to burst into flame. Her head arched backwards and he caught it in his hand, cradling it. He arched over her and gave her the longest, deepest, most passionate kiss she had ever known.

'I want you so badly,' he breathed into her mouth. The words filled her up, made her dizzy. This was new territory indeed, for no one had ever claimed to want her in such a way. And it seemed he did want her, for he was moving himself over the bump of her loincloth and its folds were slowly giving way.

Good, let them give way, she thought. She

stood on her toes and salted his neck with kisses, then found a place just below his ear and tried her skill at sucking. She must have done something right, for his grip on her waist tightened and she felt his body quake with lust.

Now it was his turn to groan—a groan that was deeper, more consequential and much more dangerous than her own had been.

'Atia...' he breathed. He pushed his fingers through her hair and thrust himself against her. She could feel the fullness of his desire, like a question pulsing between them, demanding an answer.

'Yes.' The answer was yes. 'I want you, Rab. In every way. Just—please be careful,' she said. 'I must not get with child.'

'I will take care. But, Atia, are you sure?'

'I have never been more sure of anything in all my life.'

To prove her certainty, she threw off her loin-cloth, turned around and dropped to her hands and knees in the middle of the stream. 'Go ahead, Rab,' she said, crouching on all fours. 'Do it.'

At first he thought she had tripped and fallen. He moved to help her up, but she made no effort to rise. Instead she dug her limbs more deeply in the stream bed and repeated the command, 'Do it.'

He stepped backwards in alarm. Was she expecting him to mount her? Great Goddess, no. Why was she doing this? She was offering herself to him in the basest, most impersonal way, and before he had even had the opportunity to pleasure her properly.

He felt confused, insulted. Was she so repulsed by him that she did not wish to see his face as they joined? Or was she already so tired of his lovemaking that she wanted to just turn around and have done with it?

None of those things made sense. She had desired him as ardently as he desired her. Moments ago she had told him so.

Though she need not have said a word. He had sensed it in her trembling movements and soft sighs, had felt it in the way she kissed him—as if a bottle full of yearning had suddenly come uncorked within her.

No, this was not an insult. This was something else.

'Atia, please, get up.' He bent and offered her his arm.

'Why should I get up? Did you not say you desired me?'

'Yes, but not like this. Please, Atia.'

He helped her to her feet. The colour was leaving her cheeks. 'Why do you do this?' she asked. 'Why do you truncate our passion?' He might have asked her the same. 'Am I not appealing to you?' she continued. She pulled her arm from his grasp, wrapped it around herself. 'It is my nose, is it not? You find it repulsive? But I turned away from you. Is that not enough? Is not the back of me appealing, at least?' There were tears gathering in her eyes.

'All of you is appealing, Atia.' He could see that she did not believe him. She took a step backwards. The bold, confident woman was in retreat. Her body itself seemed to be shrinking.

'It is all right, you know. I understand your aversion.' She was turning to walk away.

'Stop, Atia!' he burst out. He caught her by the waist. 'Please, do not go.' He took a breath. He needed to take care with his words, lest she misunderstand his confusion for derision. 'I simply do not understand why you would drop to your knees in such a way.'

She turned to face him. 'What do you mean, *in such a way*? Is it not the preferred way for a man?'

He closed his eyes and let the implications of her statement hit him. It was as he suspected, then. The woman had never known any other position. 'Have you ever been married Atia?'

'Of course I have—three times.'

Three times? She had had three husbands and

not one of them had had the desire or even the decency to show her the possibilities of pleasure?

'Oh, Atia...'

'If you do not desire me, then just say so,' she said. 'I do far too much pretending in my life to pretend in this.'

She had misunderstood him anyway, it seemed. Her lips had tightened into a bloodless frown, and her eyes were acquiring their veil of scorn. She was retreating from him with every second. He was losing her. *No, no, no.*

He stepped towards her. 'I desire you, Atia. More than you know. There is nothing I wish for more on this earth than to give you pleasure.'

'You have already given me pleasure. You have kissed me and embraced me and done all the things I had hoped you would do. I simply do not understand why you do not wish to take the man's right.'

The man's right? He almost cringed. What collection of selfish, lowborn, ignorant fools had been allowed to share this woman's bed?

'May I ask you who your husbands were?'

'Who they *were*?'

'Their vocations, I mean.'

'They were Senators, of course. And one tax collector. Allies of my father.'

Rab almost choked. His opinion of Roman patricians had just sunk to a new low—though he knew that to voice his disgust would only trigger her defences. 'The man's right is the woman's right, too,' he said carefully.

'Apologies, I do not take your meaning.'

'You do understand how a woman can take her pleasure?'

Her eyes flew open. 'Of course I understand! Am I not a woman myself?'

'That you are,' he averred. 'So tell me.'

It was an impertinent question, but he had challenged her pride enough to know that she would at least attempt to answer it.

'There is pleasure for the woman in the act of coupling itself,' she stated academically. He could see from her expression that she had not once experienced that particular sort of pleasure.

'Is there any other way for a woman to take her pleasure?' he asked.

'Not that I am aware of,' she said, looking away.

'Why do you lie to me, Atia?' he challenged. He stepped closer. 'As you said, you are a woman yourself. Surely you know.'

'I have heard that a man may kiss a woman in the…forbidden place,' she whispered.

'And did you not ever wish for a man to do that to you?' he asked. He reached out his hand and touched her fingers.

'My husbands said that the act was filthy and repugnant.'

'Gods, those are big words.' He linked his fingers with hers. 'Your husbands must have been extremely educated men.'

'They were quite educated, yes.' She favoured his sarcasm with a sly grin.

'But you did not answer my question.' He bent close to her ear and whispered. 'Have you not ever thought of feeling a man's lips...down there?'

He heard her catch her breath. She was shaking her head. No, no, she had not ever thought of it. That is what he knew she wanted to say. But she could not...because she was thinking of it right now. He could see it in her eyes.

She opened her mouth as if to tell him no, but not a single sound emerged and she made no protest as he began to lead her gently towards the wide, flat boulder that had earlier served as her hiding place.

'May I have the loincloth?' he asked and he spread the large garment out over the rocks and motioned for her to sit.

She took her seat and looked up at him. She had never looked more beautiful or more vulnerable.

'I want to give you pleasure, Atia. Will you let me?'

* * *

She nodded slightly and he bent to her lips and gave her a long, melting kiss.

'I have been waiting for this for so long,' he said. He sat beside her on the rock and eased her to her back.

It seemed that her journey into unknown territory had taken yet another unexpected turn. She had been certain that he had rejected her. He had pulled her from her knees and all but told her he did not wish to perform the act. It was not the first time she had been rejected in such a way.

But then it seemed that he had not rejected her at all. He had merely wished to prolong her pleasure, for apparently that is what paid lovers did. He had climbed on to the flat rock and lain down beside her and now he was showering kisses on her naked breasts. And she did not want him to stop. Ever. What a strange, wonderful world it was.

He covered her nipple with his mouth and gently began to suck. Suddenly, she was compelled to revise her view. No, the world was not simply wonderful. It was spectacular. Sweet hot threads of lust stretched taut within her and she was compelled to grip his head and hold on tight.

He transferred his attention to her other nipple and repeated his work. And what unnervingly fine work it was. So fine that she did not even notice when he deftly slid his finger into her womanly folds.

She tensed, sucked the air, took his hair into her fists.

'Relax, my darling,' he whispered. But she could not relax, for she was so very exposed lying upon this naked rock, trusting herself to a man she had known for less than a month.

A thousand questions crowded her mind, the loudest of which was what? What was he doing? And the second loudest—where? Where was he planning to take this? And finally—how? How did one respond to such a touch?

She had wanted this so very badly for so very long, but now that she was getting it, she was terrified. 'Rab, I…' she said.

He paused. 'What is it, my sweet?'

'I think that I am just a little nervous,' she said.

'I will not do anything that you do not wish,' he assured her, and when she did not respond, he revised his promise. 'I will not do anything you do not command.'

He gazed up at her in all earnestness and she felt a rush of gratitude for this gentle, considerate man who seemed genuinely to wish to please her. 'What is your first command?' he asked.

'Kiss me,' she said. Obediently, he pressed his lips to hers, though she noticed that his finger remained just inside her folds, motionless. 'Kiss me slowly,' she clarified. And he gave a half-grin as he took her lower lip in his and began to suck.

She closed her eyes and tried to focus on the feeling. As they kissed, his finger began drawing slow, sensuous circles around her folds. The sun felt so good on her chest and the water's soft trickle was like a sweet song inside her mind.

'Now on my neck,' she ordered. He nuzzled his lips against her neck and began to kiss softly.

'A little harder,' she said and his kiss transformed into the gentlest of sucks. 'Yes,' she gasped. It was a sensation as sweet as it was painful.

'I can feel how you like that,' he whispered back, sliding his finger around her womanly entrance, which seemed to have grown wet with her arousal.

'Soon you will be commanding me to push my finger deeper,' he observed. And with that he resumed his work upon her neck.

More shivers. More delicious yearning. *Yes, yes, yes*, she thought as his sucking became more intense and the core of her filled with heat.

'Go deeper,' she commanded, making his prediction come true. She felt as if she had little control over what she wanted now. Free will was an illusion of the philosophers. Her body wanted what it wanted. Him.

'Kiss me again,' she ordered, not because it

was the only thing she knew to ask, but because it felt like the most delicious, self-indulgent thing she could possibly demand. As he kissed her, he moved his finger gently in and out of her and her hips began to move in the same rhythm. 'Deeper.'

He pushed his finger deeper, continuing to kiss her until the threads of lust that had been strewn so tautly inside her seemed to twist tighter still and she was overcome with yearning. 'Yes,' she breathed.

She focused on the feeling of his finger's soft plunging. It was like the relentless movement of a carriage over a bumpy road. There was somewhere it was taking her, some strange destination that seemed so important to reach.

New territory.

'Oh,' she gasped. He held his finger still and suddenly the road ceased to exist and she was jumping off the edge of the canyon. Her body convulsed as waves of pleasure gripped her. 'Yes!' she cried as she careened through the air, moaning and sighing and feeling each of the taut threads of herself snap loose one by one.

Her body quaked with pleasure, then gradually went still. Her eyes were closed, but she could feel him watching her. She wondered at this quiet sweetness between them. This strange, unexpected grace.

'Gratitude,' she said at last.

He rolled beside her and put his arms around her shoulders, squeezing her head against the side of his chest. Such a small gesture, yet it threatened to undo her. 'Do you not wish to take your own pleasure?' she asked, pulling her head away. It was just too dangerous to lay her head there. She feared she would never be able to lift it again.

'It was enough to watch you, Atia,' he said.

It was a strange thing for him to say. What man did not wish to take his pleasure with a woman, if given the opportunity? Unless, of course, he did not really desire her.

She smiled at the revelation. It was as she had always suspected, then: he did not truly desire her. He was just like all her former husbands, only nobler, gentler, smarter, kinder, stronger, handsomer and far more affectionate.

In the past she might have been devastated by such a realisation, but now she could only feel a strange sense of relief. It did not matter that he did not want her, for they had a deal.

Now she needed only to complete the transaction. She lifted herself up from the boulder and walked to the river bank. She donned her tunic and retrieved her bag, seizing upon two golden *aurei* within it. She smiled, pleasure still echoing through her body. She would have given him a hundred gold *aurei* if she could have.

She returned to the rock where he sat worrying his beard, his expression puzzled. 'You have shown me what it is to feel pleasure and have placed me in your debt once again,' she said. 'Now I wish to pay it.' She dropped the *aurei* into his palm.

He stared at the coins in confusion. 'If the payment is satisfactory to you,' she added, 'perhaps you would consider some kind of long-term arrangement.' She thought of how happy her friend Lydia would be for her right now. 'I wish for you to be my guide, you see,' she told Rab, 'in the territory of pleasure.'

She took a breath, then congratulated herself on her businesslike comportment. She had even chosen a clever turn of phrase. He was the finest of guides in the territory of the desert, after all. Why not also the territory of pleasure?

But he was staring at the *aurei* as if he did not know what to do with them. Perhaps she was not being clear. 'I realise I am not attractive, but I believe we can come to some understanding.'

He did not seem to hear her. 'You wish to make me your *luper*, your male harlot?'

'Not at all. I only wish for us to be lovers and I wish to ensure your comfort and enjoyment of the process.'

He was shaking his head in disgust. 'You wish to pay me for what happened between us just now?'

'I thought you would be pleased,' she said. Clearly he was not pleased. She could see it in how his body tensed, though she could not understand why. She was offering to compensate him for an act he had seemed to enjoy. Perhaps he had not desired her enough to take his own pleasure with her, but he had willingly shown her how to take her own.

'You wish to take the love we shared today and turn it into trade?' he asked.

'Love?'

'Do you think that just because I am a poor Nabataean camel trainer that I can be purchased? You insult me.'

She felt as if she were sinking into the stream's fine sand. 'Everything is trade, is it not?' she said meekly. 'Give and take? I merely wish to compensate you for the pleasure you have given me.'

He returned the coins to her hand and stood beside her. 'You are not beautiful, you are ugly, and you wish to make me ugly, too.'

'Rab—' she began saying, but she could not finish. His words had been like the arrows of a bitter foe. They had sliced right through her.

He stormed across the river and retrieved his tunic. 'I thought you were a different kind of Roman. I realise now that I was wrong.'

Chapter Twelve

He had been a fool. An utter, inexcusable fool. To think that he had believed her a different kind of Roman—a Roman with a soul. But she was no different than all the rest. They stormed into Arabia with their gold coins and insatiable appetites and expected to do business. *'Curse the Nabataeans!'* they declared in their damnable Latin. *Curse anything of value or meaning.* To the Romans, nothing mattered and everything was for sale.

Including, it seemed, Rab himself.

He could not sleep. He could not even rest. How had he misjudged her? When? Memories crowded his mind, visions of her: Atia fumbling with her scarf; Atia kneeling in her bronze gown; Atia collapsing on the hillside and falling into his arms.

Atia placing two coins into his hand.

It did not make sense.

They had shared more than just lust, after all. They had shared laughter and quiet joy. They had endured each other's anger and come to each other's aid in desperate times. There was more between them than just the maddening attraction of their bodies. Or did their connection mean nothing to her?

No, not nothing. It had meant exactly the worth of two gold coins.

He stared at the stars without seeing them. Debased. That was how he felt. Drained of his humanity and stripped of his soul. It was as if she had taken their bond and smashed it upon the rocks. How could she do this to him?

But he knew how. She was her father's daughter. Had she not told him as much? She was obligated not to feel. She peered out from beneath her heavy lids and pushed away everything she saw. She had pushed him away many times, he had just chosen not to see it. She carried frost in her heart and ice in her veins. Indeed, it was why her hands were always so cold.

But they were not always cold, he reminded himself. And her eyes were not always lidded and she was not always trying to keep her distance. In moments when she was not doubting, scolding, or pushing him away, she was the most wonderful woman he had ever met.

The stars seemed to swirl above him now—a

blur of cloudy light. He had known plenty of women in his time. Before the Romans came— back when his father had lived and life had still made sense—Rab had pursued many women and had been the subject of pursuit himself. Like all young men he had been fascinated by women— their soft, curvy bodies, their sweet, musical voices, their quiet, unassuming strength.

But what he really wished for was what his father had had with his mother before she died on the birthing bed. He wanted that sweet, intangible thing that seemed to bind his parents together and soften them both.

Finally, at age twenty-five, after many years of chasing and flirting and testing the waters of love, Rab had taken the plunge.

Her name was Babatha. They had known one another since their school days, when they had spent hours in the *odeon* together listening to philosophers drone. He remembered her long black braid and how her graceful fingers pressed so diligently into her stylus. She was wildly intelligent and had an ability to explain things better than her tutors ever could.

They had married in a ceremony outside his grandfather's tomb and she had become his Princess. They had moved into her mother's house, as was the custom, and begun construction of their own small palace. Its foundation had already been poured when the Romans had arrived and his father had taken his own life.

After that, time had slowed, along with Rab's own mind. Nothing made sense. Throughout their kingdom's four-hundred-year history, the Nabataeans had fought off the Judeans and the Seleucids, and had for a long time kept even the Romans at bay. Yet when Roman General Palma had led his troops through Rekem's sacred slot canyon to the steps of the Great Temple, there had not even been a fight.

Babatha had tried to assuage him. *Look at Rome's military might*, she had said. *Look at the opportunities that being part of the Empire will bring: new roads, new temples, the expansion of trade.* But they were not good reasons for how quickly and completely the Nabataeans had given up their glory. 'Why?' he had asked Babatha, over and over again.

Why did the Nabataeans do nothing as Palma's legion set up a permanent camp at the heart of the city? Why did they say nothing when Palma began handing out the taxation contracts to Nabataeans, thus turning Nabataeans against themselves?

Rab had looked around at the kingdom he had once held dear and felt nothing but anger. He listened closely to Babatha's sensible explanations, but all he could hear were his father's senseless last words: *the elephants.*

'I divorce you,' Babatha had told him one morning and Rab had made no protest. How could he love when his mind was so confused? How could he feel any joy when his heart was full of pain?

The pain had not gone away. It had only got worse as the years passed. Why had his father given his kingdom to the Romans? No one could give Rab a satisfactory answer.

And so he had thrown himself into his work—the only work that mattered. Resistance. He had grown out his hair and his beard and gone into hiding, maintaining his cover as a camel trainer and moving between the rebel enclaves like a ghost.

If he needed sex, he paid for it, though he rarely needed it. All he needed was something useful to do and the only thing useful was to fight.

Now the stars were perfectly clear—tiny points of light in a sea of endless black. They seemed to confirm his deepest certainty: that the world was an empty place.

And now that Atia had shown her true light, it was emptier still.

The next morning, Plotius was howling. 'I am not going.'

Rab secured the saddle of their strongest donkey and pointed to it. 'We must ascend Wadi Mujib,' said Rab. 'There is no other way out.'

'Of course there is another way out—the *wadi* stream,' said Plotius. 'Why can we not just follow it downhill?'

'The stream drains to the Bitumen Lake. As I told you before, rebels patrol its shores.'

'I do not care,' said Plotius. 'I command this party and I say we follow the sea route from now on.' Plotius gripped the hilt of his *gladius*. 'No more of this canyon hopping.'

Rab shrugged. He had not slept a single minute the night before. His heart was heavy and his head throbbed. He was too exhausted to argue.

It was late afternoon the next day when the entourage finally stumbled on to the shore of the great salty lake. The sweaty, tired men dropped their weapons and rucksacks and plunged into the water like a troupe of boys.

Rab noticed that Atia was not among them. He searched the shoreline and caught her ambling northwards towards a lone date palm.

Her stride had changed. Only days before, she had been bounding up and down the hills in long, energetic steps. Now she was barely picking up her feet. At last she arrived at the base of the palm and took her seat in its meagre shade.

Why was she so crestfallen? Had his rejection of her offer really hurt her that much? It did not seem like the behaviour of a woman without a soul.

'We rest here tomorrow,' Plotius announced to a storm of cheers.

Fools, Rab thought, saying nothing. He turned from the shore and made his way up a craggy cliff overlooking the sea. Arriving at the flat of a natural lookout, he saw the black coal dust of a campfire. Just beyond it, an area had been cleared to make room for several bed mats. There was the small figure of an acacia tree carved into one of the boulders.

Rab was seized with a terrible foreboding. The sign of the acacia was what the rebels used to mark their territory. Clearly a group of rebels had been here recently and likely patrolled the site. If they spotted the Romans, they would not hesitate to attack.

Rab gazed out at the Bitumen Lake, trying to calm his nerves. It was such an unremarkable name for such an unusual lake. Whereas other salty seas held the bounty of life, this sea's only bounty was black and tarry—like the bile of the earth itself.

And that bile was precious.

Bitumen, it was called, and it floated up several times a year to be harvested by the bitumen traders, who would sell the sticky black substance for use in waterproofing everything from boats to mummies. Rab could see the bitumen pontoons still afloat even at this late hour—their figures obscured by a horizontal layer of liquid air.

He peered north. If the rebels were here, they would likely approach from that direction, for the steep, craggy shoreline offered many places to hide. Now, however, the only sign of life along the sun-baked shore was Atia. She was still there, still seated beneath the lone date palm. But she was no longer staring out at the lifeless sea. She was gazing up at a man standing over her, his hands gripping his formidable hips. Plotius.

'I am worried about you, Atia,' said Plotius. A thin line of salt had dried in a circle around the edge of his fleshy face, making it appear as if he wore a mask.

'I do not wish to speak with you, Plotius,' said Atia. She turned away from him, but he only hobbled back into her view.

'You have not been yourself, Atia. Your enthusiasm is lost. You do not even wish to bathe in the lake.'

'It should not matter to you whether or not I wish to bathe in the lake.'

'Oh, but it does,' he said and the fissure of a smile opened across his face. He squatted low and she felt her stomach tighten.

'If you dare touch me, I will let out a scream to shake the heavens,' she said. She peered down the shore, instinctively looking for Rab. He was nowhere to be seen. 'And I will run. Faster than you.'

'Calm down, woman,' Plotius said. He was laughing casually as if they were two old friends teasing each other. 'I have only come to deliver a gift,' he said. He held out a small bottle.

'What is that?' Atia asked.

'What do you think it is?'

Atia shook her head. 'No, thank you, Plotius.'

'I have plenty for myself,' said Plotius. 'Think of it as an olive branch.'

Atia smiled politely. What kind of olive branch came in the form of debilitating poison? 'Gratitude, Plotius, but I no longer use the tears.'

'Yes, instead of using them, you have decided to shed them.'

Was it that obvious? She had been weeping all day, though she thought she had been careful to conceal her emotion beneath her scarf.

Now she wrapped that scarf around her face several times.

'I will leave the bottle here at the base of the trunk,' said Plotius.

'I told you, no!' shouted Atia, but her voice was muffled by her scarf, and by the time she had unwrapped herself, he was already halfway back to camp.

And there was the bottle.

'I do not want it!' she cried out.

Just a few days ago, the statement would have been true. But now it was a lie. She wanted it badly. She knew it was the only thing that would stop the chest-splitting pain she had felt since the moment Rab had rejected her.

The tears will wash away the pain, she told herself. They always had in the past and they were the only thing that could now. She lifted the small but heavy bottle. In its weight she felt the promise of lightness. In the memory of it, the promise of forgetting.

She ran her fingers over the cork and gently tried to pull it free. It would not come loose, thank the gods. It was wedged too firmly inside the bottle. It would take a good deal of effort to get it free.

But once she did get it free, she would have her bliss—perhaps for days. It was a good amount of tears and she would drag out the oblivion for as long as she could. Her energy would flag, of course, and she would be unable to keep up the march. She would have to ride atop one of the donkeys. But it would be worth it, for she would no longer feel this terrible sadness.

And when the tears ran out, what then? The sickness would return, along with the headaches and restlessness and shameful trembling. She would be plunged once again into the realm of Tartarus and have to fight her way back out.

And that was not even the worst of it. If Plotius tried to steal a goat or harm someone or seek to undermine Atia, she would not have the will to stand up to him. She gazed into the bottle and understood for the first time the real danger of the tears: they robbed her of her ability to do the right thing.

She stood and hurled the small bottle into the sea.

When she turned, she peered up at the distant cliffs and caught sight of Rab. He was gazing down at her, his long *ghutrah* fluttering behind him in the breeze. She lifted her arm in greeting and waited for him to do the same. But he quickly turned away from her and disappeared among the rocks.

A tiny part of her soul seemed to break in half. Of course he had turned away. He no longer wanted anything to do with her. And rightfully so, for she had insulted him in the most profound way that one person could insult another. She deserved his disdain.

She walked slowly back to camp and waited for him to return, but he never did.

* * *

That night she could not sleep. She lay on her back and stared at the stars. They seemed dimmer here than they had been in the mountains—smaller and further away.

It was not just the stars, it was as if everything was receding. She had lost her appetite and could find no satisfaction in the trail. Even the ethereal blue of the Bitumen Lake had seemed greyer when she had finally arrived on its shores and she had had no desire to feel its healing waters.

It was as if the world had become a kind of mirage and the only reality was the pain inside her heart.

And every time she closed her eyes, the pain acquired a new facet. Because as she sorted through her memories of him, she could only find joy. Rare, luminous joy, along with a kind of all-encompassing sense of safety in his presence.

And that damnable pull of her body towards his.

She searched her mind, trying to remember the bad, digging for evidence in the case against him. She could find none. The only crime had been the one she had committed. The one that could not be taken back.

The full moon was rising now, its light obliterating the stars. She watched it cast its milky path across the sea. She wished she could follow that path to the end of the world, then simply jump off the edge. Would she become a star? Or would she simply fall off into the darkness, his words echoing inside her ears: *You are not beautiful. You are ugly and you wish to make me ugly, too.*

He had made his thoughts as clear as glass and they hurt her as much as a thousand shards. There was no escaping the pain of what he had said to her. Eyes closed. Eyes open. It made no difference. It only hurt.

Ugly. Not because of her big nose. Ugly because, in trying to compensate him for the valuable thing he had given her, she had unknowingly cheapened it and also cheapened him.

She gazed at the moon, who seemed to wear Rab's face.

Why did you do such a thing, Atia? he asked.

Because I wanted you to feel that it was worth it.

Why would it not be worth it? Do you doubt my desire for you? My love?

Love?

I thought you were a different kind of Roman, Atia. I realise now that I was wrong.

I am different! she wished to tell him. But how different was she really? She was the rich, spoiled daughter of a Roman governor. What more was there to say? Soon she would likely be married. If she survived beyond her foretold death, she would become the complicit, biddable wife of one of the most Roman men in the province.

Suddenly, she wanted that death to come. She wished for it more than she ever had before, though she had somehow lost track of the days until its arrival. Was it coming in twenty days now, or was it nineteen? Eighteen, perhaps? It did not matter. Death was coming and she welcomed it.

She sat up. Her chest felt tight; her breaths were short. She stared out at the vast black lake, instinctively searching for the splash of a fish. But she knew that nothing could live in its salty waters or anywhere along its sun-baked shores.

It was truly a dead sea.

Atia stood and began to walk. The moon was getting higher in the sky. It was flooding the silent landscape with its ghostly light. Across the water, the craggy hills of Judea looked shadowy and forlorn and Atia tried to imagine a time when they had been green and the sea below them full of life.

Perhaps this was the fate of all places on earth. Perhaps all seas eventually salted up and all forests turned to dust. Perhaps there was just a small window of time when life could take hold. A small, precious window. Perhaps it was the same for love and she had somehow missed it.

When Atia arrived back at the base of her lone

palm, she observed the arc of its melancholy arms as moon shadows on the ground. She stepped beneath their strange shade and gazed out at the sea.

That was when she saw the bottle. It had somehow washed up on shore. It was sitting at the water's edge as if beckoning her.

But how was that possible? She had thrown it away, had watched it plunge into the depths of the salty lake. Had the gods somehow retrieved it for her? But Atia was not important enough to be of notice to the gods. And yet there it was, the tiny bottle, like a divine gift.

She retrieved the bottle from the water and studied it for many moments. A memory surfaced—a vision of the first time she had ever tried the tears. She saw herself standing inside her mother's bedchamber, staring at her mother's cold, white body. Even in death she had been beautiful, despite the terrible wound traversing her face.

The wound that, in a fit of rage, her father had made.

Even now, she could hear the sound of her mother's wails inside her mind. She could see the look on her mother's face when her father had announced that they would not be keeping her mother's newborn. 'I married you so that you would give me a son,' her father had said. 'Not another daughter.'

Atia had listened outside her mother's bed-chamber to the sounds of an argument, then violence.

The next morning, Atia had entered her mother's chamber and had at first believed her mother to be asleep. She had nearly tripped on the empty bottles littering the floor and it was many moments before she realised why her mother would not wake. She had gathered them up one by one and smashed them against the wall.

She had sat beside her mother and wept for many hours. When her own tears ran out, she had caught sight of one last bottle inside her mother's cold grip. It was still full.

In a burst of anguish, Atia had wrenched the bottle from her mother's hand and taken a long gulp. The pain inside her heart had disappeared instantly and a kind of bliss had coursed through her young limbs.

Now she craved that bliss once again. She wanted comfort, for she would never again feel the warmth of Rab's smile or hear the spark of his laugh or feel a thrill as his eyes burrowed into her.

You are not beautiful, Rab was repeating in her mind. *You are ugly and you wish to make me ugly, too.*

Pain. Sharp, heart-splitting pain. And right here in the palm of her hand was the antidote. She gazed up at the sky. Rab was still there, staring down at her, shaking his head in disappointment.

Atia uncorked the bottle and raised it up to him, as if in a toast. Then she held it to her lips and took a small sip. She felt a rush of happiness. It tasted so good—like coming home. Her body tingled with joy. She waded out into the water until her feet no longer touched the ground, then she lay back. She was floating! Her body was suspended, cradled by the thick, salty water.

What a wonder was this dead sea! What an absolute joy! Why had she not bathed in it earlier? She could hardly remember the reason. It was something to do with a man who had wanted her once, but did not want her any more. She opened the bottle and took another sip, and then another. She gazed out at the otherworldly landscape. Nothing lasted for ever, she thought suddenly. And if nothing lasted for ever, then nothing mattered at all.

Atia was still floating when Sol's pale light began to paint the sky pink. Her mind was fuzzy with her lingering bliss. She spotted movement along the southern shore. In the distance she could make out the shapes of strange creatures. They had elegant long legs, sloping necks and backs like small brown hills.

Camels. She watched in fascination as they

neared, for their movements were so fluid and they seemed so at ease in this barren place. Equally at ease were their riders, whose long sandy robes and matching *ghutrahs* seemed to fuse with the colours of the camels so perfectly that they appeared as single two-headed beings— like centaurs of the desert.

Camels. She loved them irrationally, for they seemed to represent everything she had come to appreciate about this quiet, desolate land. She laughed aloud as they came more fully into view. So quiet and deliberate in their movements. So graceful and humble beneath the sun.

She wondered if the riders were traders coming to offer their wares. Or perhaps they were bitumen hunters coming to see if there had been any sightings of the large rafts of black tar that they pursued. The camels appeared to increase their pace, then broke into a run.

But why were they running? What rush could there possibly be to arrive anywhere in the barren desert? They were getting closer and Atia saw the outlines of longswords hilted at the men's waists. They were drawing the blades from their sheaths.

'Raiders!' Atia shouted, but it was too late. She stared in horror as the first two riders thundered into camp and began slaying the sleeping soldiers.

'To arms!' a Roman shouted. The Roman soldiers began to wake—though not quickly enough.

The raiders flew down from their saddles with blades fully drawn. There must have been at least twenty raiders and as they fought they shouted expletives in the Nabataean tongue.

Or were they shouting other things as well? Atia listened closely. She perceived the Nabataean word for justice and then the word for freedom. These were not simple raiders, Atia realised slowly. These were Nabataean rebels.

Atia watched as a rebel thrust his sword through a Roman soldier's belly, slaying him instantly. Another rebel gave an ear-splitting screech and charged at a Roman from behind, slicing his head cleanly from his body. Blood spouted from the Roman's convulsing corpse as it tumbled to the ground.

Atia sank deeper into the water. Her thoughts were sluggish, her limbs lifeless and heavy. Her heart beat out a slow, even rhythm.

She should have been feeling horror. She should have been feeling anything at all. But she had drunk a great number of tears and they had smothered her mind and numbed her heart. She watched another Roman take a blade in the throat, then saw a rebel who looked like a boy slain in the chest. She could only stare, waiting for the pain to come. It never did. She was cold and lifeless. Crocodilian. On the shore, the sand pooled with the blood of the fallen.

'Form a phalanx!' shouted Plotius and the remaining Romans scrambled to form a tight group. There was the clang of swords and a chaos of shouting as the Romans attempted to fend off their foes. Only a few of the Romans wore their chain mail armour. Fewer still had use of their shields.

Atia spied two shields between the Roman phalanx and the shore. Perhaps she could retrieve them for the Romans. She swam closer to the phalanx, but when she was near enough to reach the shields, she simply could not summon the energy to get them.

Move, Atia! she told her body, but it would not listen. The Romans were now fewer in number than the rebels, who were swarming the Romans' small, defensive group like bees. Meanwhile, several of the rebels were plundering the corpses of the fallen Romans, taking everything they could.

There was a loud noise from somewhere near and Rab's robed figure came into view. He was bounding down from the craggy hills, his sword swinging, his terrifying bellow filling the air.

Catching sight of him, the rebels ceased their efforts. They stared at the stampeding man in the silence of shock. And in that small window of time, the Romans were able to regroup and become the aggressors.

Atia watched Plotius take down two men and

saw Livius stab another. There was so much blood. It was pooling around the men's feet and filling the air with its stench. So much death and for what?

One of the rebels was making off with the Romans' train of donkeys. Another had gathered what looked to be about a dozen swords. But they were no longer fighting—the Nabataeans were in retreat. They mounted their camels and bounded away into the terrible morning.

The silence was punctuated by groans, the air polluted by the smell of fresh blood. Needles of horror were finally beginning to poke at Atia's heart. The tears were wearing off, but not quickly enough.

The flies. Where had they all come from? They were buzzing around the living and the dead. Of the living, there were only ten left. They threw down their swords and collapsed in the bloody sand.

Nobody seemed to notice as Atia emerged from the water. She sat beside two men who were weeping into their hands. Atia envied them, for she wanted to cry. She wanted to feel anything besides this terrible numbness.

The remaining men spent the next several hours gathering fuel for a pyre, then watched the dreadful black smoke carrying the fallen soldiers' souls to the sky.

* * *

The sun was low in the sky when at last Atia wept. She sat beside the smouldering embers and mourned the lives of men who had not deserved to die. And not just the Romans. She mourned for the dead Nabataeans, for she knew their suffering had turned them desperate.

She wept and wept, and had never been more grateful for her own tears. They anchored her to what was true, reassuring her that there was right and wrong—and what she had just seen was very, very wrong.

Images of the fighting haunted her mind. The senseless violence. The terrible chaos of it all. Over thirty men—Roman and Nabataean—had lost their lives in a matter of minutes. Thirty men who would never again laugh, or love, or gaze up at the night sky in wonder.

Atia's head throbbed. The sun burned down on the bronze landscape, but there was a new darkness everywhere she looked. Shadows and despair. Pain and waste. The world itself seemed to have changed.

If only she had been in her right mind, she might have helped the Romans defend themselves. If only she could have delivered the shields, she might have prevented one of those men from meeting his death. But she had been too numb to do the right thing. She had been paralysed by the effect of the tears.

She gazed down at the tiny half-empty bottle, which she somehow still held in her hand. 'I hate you,' she said. She squeezed with all her strength and the bottle burst open. The small shards sliced into her hand and the precious liquid spilled on to the ground.

Pain. Perfect exquisite pain. It shot through her with terrifying efficiency. Opening her hand, she discovered a mess of blood and glass. She closed it again, just so she could make it worse. Pain. It seemed to invade her whole body. A deep aching awareness of what was true. Pain was not bad. It was necessary. And in that moment Atia knew that she would never allow herself to become numb again.

'We must leave now,' Rab announced. His face was ashen. He placed a final branch into the fire and cringed, and Atia wondered if he had been injured. 'Gather your things,' he told the remaining soldiers. 'We must return to the hills.'

Beside him, Plotius was stirring the ashes with his sword. 'We will do no such thing.'

'The rebels will return soon to collect their dead,' Rab said to Plotius. 'If we are still here when they arrive, they will finish us.'

Plotius gazed into the flames. 'Where were

you, Camel Man?' he asked. 'When the rebels arrived?'

'I was scouting in the hills behind camp,' Rab said, turning to face Plotius.

'A convenient time to go scouting,' commented Plotius, glancing around at the other men.

'What are you suggesting?' asked Rab. He stepped closer to Plotius. *No*, thought Atia. *Do not provoke him.*

'How many rebels did you kill?' asked Plotius. 'Just curious.'

'None,' Rab said. He stood frozen before Plotius. His tall, muscular frame looked almost thin against Plotius's thick, bulky mass.

'Not a one? Why does that not surprise me?' Plotius said. He pulled his sword from the flames and rested it on the ground.

'I arrived rather late to the fight,' said Rab through clenching teeth.

'Exactly,' said Plotius.

'If you would like to accuse me of something, then do it,' said Rab, retrieving his dagger from the sheath against his leg.

'Stop this madness,' Atia said. She lunged between the two men. 'There will be no more fighting today, lest you would like to kill me as well.'

Plotius hissed, but he sheathed his sword. 'We are not returning to the cursed hills,' he growled.

'We will follow the shores of the Bitumen Lake and come what may.'

'Certain death,' said Rab. 'The rebels will find you and they will kill you all.'

'What makes you so certain?' Plotius asked. He lifted aside a boulder to produce the small metal box that Atia's father had given him. He held it aloft. 'This box contains all the coin we need to make our way to Rekem. And in our current circumstances, I do not think the Governor will mind if we use it.'

'Coin cannot keep you safe from rebels,' Rab remarked.

'Of course it can. We can buy whatever we need, including mercenaries.' Plotius turned to address his men. 'What say you, soldiers? Will you follow this slithering Arab back into the hills, or will you follow me along the shore and help me seek our revenge?'

'Revenge!' the soldiers shouted.

There was only one man who did not shout. He sheathed his sword and stood by Rab's side. Livius.

'You betray me, Gaul,' said Plotius.

'My orders are to deliver the woman safely to Rekem,' said Livius. 'That is what I plan to do.'

'Idiot!' Plotius shouted. 'The woman will come with me!'

'Will she?' asked Livius.

Atia felt all the men's eyes on her, but she could only keep staring into the flames.

'Well, Atia?' said Plotius. 'Whom will you follow to Rekem? The man with weapons and coins and…medicine for what ails you, or the man with nothing?'

Chapter Thirteen

At last he had seen the shape of her demon. It was small and round and full of liquid and the day before the slaughter she had thrown it into the sea.

He had seen the shape of the demon's servant as well—a large, fleshy man who called himself a commander, though all he commanded was the gates of oblivion.

Suddenly everything had made sense—her cold skin, her heavy lids and listless expression at the banquet. The difficulty she had had those first days on the trail. It was the tears of poppy.

They were why she had gone to see Plotius all alone that night and were likely involved in the death of her mother. It was why she did not wish to speak of either subject with him.

She used the medicine regularly, or so it seemed, though from what Rab knew about the tears, it was more correct to say that the tears used her.

Though after the night he had saved her from Plotius, he remembered that she had ceased her trembling. Her eyes had grown brighter, her skin warmer, her steps strong and energetic. She had fought her craving for the medicine, it seemed—had slain the demon—and had transformed before Rab's eyes.

She had vanquished the tears and become a warrior.

Now she was crouched over the spring, filling her water bag. When Rab approached, she hurriedly finished the task. She had been avoiding him like this ever since they had parted ways with Plotius and the others—a full three days now.

The evening they set out, neither Atia, Livius nor Rab had been able to speak. They channelled all their energy into their march and fought to keep their despair at bay. Darkness had been heavy and they had not got far. They made camp in silence. It was as if they were still trying to escape the battle.

Tears had clouded Rab's vision throughout the next day. He had recognised several of the fallen Nabataeans and could not get their faces out of his mind.

They had died with honour—that was what

Rab kept telling himself. They had died fighting for what was right.

Still, nothing seemed right about what had happened that day and the thought of all those lifeless bodies lying on the ground filled Rab with a despair so powerful he had found it hard to concentrate.

He had not been alone. Atia and Livius had been fighting their own grief. Livius had limped along on an injured knee, lost in thought, and Atia had wandered off during their noon rest—though not so far that Rab had not been able to hear her sobs.

Rab fought to keep his attention on finding their route. The hills were no longer hills—they were canyons. They did not roll—they plunged. He searched his memory for the locations of the secret springs and the places of shade.

But visions of the battle kept clouding his mind and the wound on his arm had begun to ache painfully. Sometimes he would arrive at the edge of a cliff or the bottom of a canyon and have no idea where he was.

They had run out of provisions and become very, very hungry. 'We shall come across a settlement soon,' Rab reassured them that second day.

In truth he was confused. They should have come upon the settlement already—at least according to his faltering memory. His arm had begun to ache and a worrisome fever heated his head.

He was not alone. Livius's injured knee seemed to be worsening as well. He limped along behind them, cringing in pain. It was Livius who finally broke the silence. 'I believe the sun god is an indiscriminate tormentor,' he said, 'for he punishes the good souls and the bad with equal fury.'

'Aye,' Rab had said, grateful for the sound of Livius's voice. 'I wonder which type of soul is my own.'

'I have been wondering about my own soul as well, Brother,' he echoed.

Rab had hoped that Atia would voice her response, but she only continued to watch her own feet. Surely it was her exhaustion that kept her silent. Grief coupled with hunger could steal a person's strength.

But deep in his soul he knew that it was none of that. On that third afternoon, as he gathered the spring water in his water bag and gently removed his robe, he admitted to himself that she did not speak because he had silenced her.

He had called her ugly—a word he had regretted even as it had rolled off his tongue. She was not ugly, of course. She was one of the most beautiful women he had ever seen. He loved her strong nose, whose unusual hump gave her a regal quality and played off her other elegant features:

her mysterious dark eyes, her big, sensuous lips, her proud, high cheeks. She was utterly gorgeous to him—the furthest from ugly that a woman could get.

What she had done to him had been ugly— that was all.

Though perhaps ugly was not the correct term for it. It might have been more correct to say that what she had done had been destructive. She had taken what they had shared and tried to make it into nothing.

Why did it matter to him at all? If anything, he should have been pleased at her attempt to put distance between them. He had violated his own code of honour by kissing her as he had done and he could hardly forgive himself for what had happened next.

It was a travesty, really, how badly he had wanted her, a total breach of ethics how he had envisioned taking her right there, right in the middle of the stream.

He had stopped himself, thank Dushara, knowing that he could never take his pleasure with a woman who did not know her own. Helping her discover that particular knowledge had been one of the most gratifying things he had ever done.

But there was also no excuse for it. She was Roman—as Roman as they came, as it turned out. And yet he could still hear her quiet moans inside his mind, could feel the way her body had relaxed around him, trusting him, wanting him, how her desire had slowly transformed into her obvious pleasure. Even now, he could see the sheen of her skin in the rosy sunlight, feel her soft, urgent breaths, smell her scent. It was almost too much to bear.

Kissing her alone had been a kind of revelation. Those lips. Those sweet, sultry lips. They were at once soft and demanding, naive and knowing, and so very warm and wet. They represented everything he stood against, yet he could have kissed those lips for a thousand years.

But it was not just the kissing or the touching that had him feeling totally reprehensible. It was the bliss. The complete, terrifying bliss he had felt with their closeness.

He had held her body against his and for the first time since the Romans had landed in his fair kingdom he had remembered what it was like to be happy.

It was unacceptable, that happiness. Completely inappropriate for a man of his background and birth. The Romans had not ceased their conquest of Nabataea, after all. They continued to extract their booty and the Nabataeans continued to suffer.

And she was Roman. Hence, Rab should have been relieved when she had splashed away to retrieve his coins. He should have let the insult serve as a reminder of who she was—and who she most definitely could never be.

But instead, an arrow of pain had sliced through his gut. How could she do that to him? To them? How could she cheapen the precious thing that they had shared?

You are ugly, he had said. He had likely said more, though he could not remember. All he could recall was how that arrow had caught fire inside him and how it had burned so viciously that the only thing he could do to alleviate the pain was to turn it around and aim it back at her.

And that was what he had done. With the skill of a *sagittarius*, he had aimed that arrow right back at her heart.

You are ugly. He had known immediately that the words had hit their target, for the colour had drained from her cheeks and the breath had gone out of her. She had actually stumbled backwards, as if having been hit by a real arrow, though instead of reaching out to steady herself, she had done something strange. She had lifted her hand to cover her nose.

He had had days to consider that moment. Hours and hours to ponder why she had reacted that way. When he had called her ugly, he had been referring to her behaviour, yet she had immediately moved to conceal her nose. Her strong, unique, and, to Rab's mind, rather sexy nose.

Could it be that she considered that part of herself distasteful? When he had called her beautiful that day at the baths, he vaguely remembered she had concealed her nose then, too. Now that he thought of it, there had been numerous times she had covered her nose in his presence.

Her behaviour was beginning to make a heartbreaking kind of sense. *'I realise I am not attractive, but I believe we can come to some understanding.'* Those were the exact words she had used when offering Rab her coins. She had assumed that he found her distasteful—so much so that making love to her would be a kind of chore. No wonder she had presumed that he would not wish to see her face during the act of love.

By the gods, what had he done? In calling her ugly, he had unknowingly said the most harmful thing he possibly could have. She had hurt him, that was true, but his retaliation had gone far beyond hurt. Ugly she was not and what they had shared that day in the stream had been the opposite of ugly.

It had been…holy.

He was tired of denying it. Lying there beside her in the sun, pressing himself against her so hard that their skin seemed to fuse, a strange new feeling had invaded him—a kind of rightness. Suddenly there was nothing more important in the world than pleasing the woman beside him and there would be nothing more terrible in the world than losing her.

What had begun as a powerful attraction had become something different in those few glorious moments. Their lips had met and the sun had burned down and a kind of alchemical change had taken place within him. He did not just want her. He wanted to love her. If he denied it any more he might as well have been denying his own life.

He needed to speak to her—to apologise for what he had said, to tell her what was in his heart. But three whole days had gone by without a word and he was beginning to wonder if she would ever speak to him again.

He was pouring water on his wound when at long last she did. 'Ack!' she shouted. He nearly jumped out of his skin.

'What is that?' she asked, pointing at the oozing yellow fissure in the middle of his arm. She moved towards him, sniffing the air. 'Rab, it does not smell good.' She squatted at his side and studied the gash. 'It festers.' She searched his face. 'You have lost your flush.'

'It is just a small wound,' said Rab.

She pressed her hand against his forehead. 'You feel very hot.'

'I imagine we are all feeling a bit hot,' he jested.

Livius limped over to join them. Upon seeing Rab's arm, he wretched. 'Fires of Vesuvius, why did you not say anything?'

'What good would it do to speak of it? We must reach Rekem above all else. And we must do so in nine days or my own family will be harmed.'

Atia shot Livius a look. Their silence spoke what the two could not say aloud: *There will be no reaching Rekem at all if you are dead.*

'How much further to the settlement you spoke of?' Atia asked.

There was no more reason to lie. 'We should be there already. I fear it no longer exists.'

'It must exist,' said Atia. She slung her water bag across her back. 'And I shall find it. Where will I encounter the next spring?'

She was gazing out at the canyon with a fearsome determination.

Rab tried to stand, but could not seem to gather the energy. 'You cannot just go traipsing off into the desert alone.'

'I most certainly can, for neither of you is in any shape to go on.' She arranged her shawl atop her head like a turban. 'If I have not returned in two days' time, you must return to Bostra.'

'Atia, this is madness,' said Rab, though he had

never seen a more magnificent woman. 'Please do not do this.'

Livius was on his feet, cringing at the effort. 'Do not go, Atia. It is beyond foolish.'

'Apologies, gentlemen, but I simply do not have a choice. I will never again sit idly by while good men die.'

Chapter Fourteen

The men were right, of course. It was beyond foolish to set out alone into the mountainous desert. It had only been a handful of hours and already Atia was lost. She had tried to draw a mental picture of the canyon lands she traversed, but once she had descended into them, she found herself inside a maze.

A maze that was also an oven.

An oven that could very well be her tomb.

She gazed up at the angry white sun. Sol. The Greek Helios, the bright, handsome servant of Zeus. How could he be the same god who now threatened to melt Atia's bones?

She seemed to recall that Heracles had once shot an arrow at Helios while crossing a desert of similar menace. His arrow pierced the sun god right in the heart. Incredibly, instead of punishing Heracles, Helios rewarded him for his boldness. Why would the sun god not reward Atia right now? She was in a similar fix, was she not? In a fit of frustration, Atia lifted a rock and hurled it at Helios. 'Where is my reward?' she shouted, but received no reply.

It was impossibly hot. Heat like the heaviest of burdens or the strongest of winds. It beat her down, made her stumble and grope for balance. It made her care not whether she walked in this direction or that. It made her see things that were not there.

Like sheep, for example.

Sheep?

A single sheep actually, or was it more of a lamb? It was standing at the end of the ravine just ahead—its puffy white coat unmistakable against the dusty cliffs.

She felt the whisper of hope tickle her skin. She descended the side of the small gorge slowly, half-expecting the lamb to evaporate before her eyes. Soon she was standing inside the ravine facing the cutest, cuddliest creature she had ever seen.

'What news, little lamb?' she asked. It gave a small bleat. It was staring up at a steep, rocky slope. 'Is that where your flock went? Would you like some help to find them?' Another bleat.

Atia took it as a yes. She undid her belt and tied it around the sheep's neck, then led the creature up the slope. As they crested the hill, the lamb tugged free of its leash and bounded across the flats of a small plateau.

Atia followed after it, though she felt rather more like a turtle than a lamb. When she finally arrived at the plateau she was no longer looking for her escaped captive, but instead searching desperately for shade. It was many moments before she noticed movement in the boulder-strewn valley below her.

It was a great flock of sheep. They covered the valley bottom like a great white cloak.

Atia's heart thumped. Where there were sheep, there were shepherds. She unwrapped her scarf and waved it wildly in the air. 'Hello!' she shouted and there amid the tumble of rocks she saw a *ghutrah* waving back.

Atia nearly tumbled down the slope. Arriving in the ravine, she stood before the tall, robed figure of an old man and bowed. 'I am Atia,' she said. Why had she never bothered to learn more Nabataean? She began to gesture towards the hills. She flailed her body about, trying to mimic Livius's damaged knee.

The old man stared at her curiously. She placed her hand atop her forehead and pretended to swoon, trying to depict Rab's fever. Still he stared. She needed to convey their hunger, so she pointed to her stomach, then collapsed before him upon the ground.

'You appear to be hungry and lost, lady,' he said in slow, careful Greek. 'I am Adelze. May I help you?'

The shepherd led Atia up the canyon towards a sprawling camel-hide tent tucked among the cliffs. A small column of smoke was snaking its way out of an opening at the apex of the structure. She could almost smell the *polentum* cooking on the fire inside. He gestured to it. 'My daughters are there,' he said. 'They will help you.'

'I am in your debt,' she said to the man, but when she turned to bow he was already gone.

Two children were playing outside the large enclosure and, when Atia stepped towards them, they scattered like leaves. Atia pulled back the door flap.

At the far end of the room, a young woman adorned with clanking bracelets was busy milking a goat. Several paces away, a handsome woman with long, raven-coloured hair sat picking through a pot of beans. Closest to the door sat a stout woman with kohl-painted eyes. She shot a look at Atia that froze her in place.

'Identify yourself,' she demanded in Greek.

'I am Atia, daughter of Atius, citizen of Bostra. I come to your doorstep in need. Can you please help me?'

The three women exchanged a series of looks that seemed to substitute for conversation.

'How did you find us?' asked the kohl-eyed woman.

'An old shepherd pointed me here. He said you were his daughters.'

The raven-haired woman gasped. 'That is impossible. Our father has been gone for nearly twenty years now, may the Goddess Mannat watch over him.'

Atia was confused. 'He told me his name was Adelze,' she said.

The three women exchanged another series of looks—this time tinged with alarm—then appeared to come to some decision.

The raven-haired woman rose to her feet. 'I am Shudat,' she said. 'You are welcome here.'

'Gratitude,' said Atia, feeling a tear work its way down her cheek.

'Breath of the Goddess, you are thin,' said Shudat. 'When did you eat last?'

'Ahh…'

'And how long have you been walking in the sun?' asked the kohl-eyed woman.

Before Atia could answer, the young woman who had been milking the goat was offering Atia a cup of milk. 'I am Gamilath,' she said, her bracelets clanging. Atia stared at the creamy liquid she offered, wondering if it was real. 'Go on, drink.'

Atia tipped the cup to her lips, and suddenly the only thing that existed in the world was the warm, life-giving liquid that poured into her like the gods' own nectar. She drained the cup, then realised that she was weeping.

'Hasten slowly, my dear,' said the kohl-eyed woman. 'I am Hageru. Welcome to our home.'

Atia gave a deep bow. When she returned to standing, Gamilath was placing another cup of goat's milk into her hand.

Atia raised her cup to the three women in a salute of gratitude. She drained it once more, and Gamilath quickly fetched her another. So went their interchange until it became clear that Atia would not refuse a drop. Gamilath gently ushered Atia to the milking bench. 'Let us put you in touch with the source,' she jested and all four women laughed. Atia had the unusual sensation of being home.

By the time they reached Rab and Livius the next morning, the sun was already high in the sky. The men lay motionless in the shade, their eyes closed, and did not even respond when one of the donkeys announced the women's arrival with a bray.

The men's conditions had worsened. Livius's

knee had swollen and a swarm of flies buzzed over Rab's wound.

Atia crouched beside Rab and shooed the flies away. He opened his eyes and reached for her wrist. 'You again?' he said.

'I am afraid that you are not rid of me yet,' Atia said. She could feel the heat of fever radiating from his skin.

'I am afraid that I missed you,' he said.

'Then the fever has clearly attacked your wits.'

'You found the settlement?'

'Of course.'

'But how?'

'I listened to the story that the desert wished to tell me,' said Atia. She pressed her hand to his brow. He was so hot that he might have been the sun god himself.

'You are frowning. You think it might be too late for me,' he said, reading her thoughts.

'Do not fear. I do not let good men die.'

'And what if I am not a good man?'

'You are a good man.'

'Then perhaps the fever has attacked both our wits,' he jested, but she could see the sheen of tears veiling his eyes.

They arrived at the tent in time for the evening meal, though Rab was in no condition to eat. He collapsed on to a bed mat at the corner of the tent.

'Stay with me, Atia,' he breathed, then plunged into a fevered oblivion.

He remained senseless as Atia cleaned his wound and packed it with salt, then pulled his hair into a loose bun and patted his face and neck with water. Hours later, he continued to sleep as she dressed the wound with honey and wrapped it in cloth.

'Fight it, Rab,' she whispered as darkness began to fall. Atia knew he was in grave danger. They all knew. They brought her water for washing and supplies for changing the wound. A girl who looked like Hageru laid a flower at Rab's feet.

Atia gazed at Rab's face and tried to imagine the world without him. No, it simply could not be. He could not die. She would not let him.

She lay beside him all night, listening to the rhythm of his breaths.

'S-savages,' he slurred, thrashing and kicking his legs. He was breathing as if he had just run a hundred miles.

'Keep fighting, Rab,' she said. She soaked a piece of cloth in water and dribbled it into his mouth. His breaths slowed.

'Atia,' he muttered. 'Forgive me.' He turned away.

Early next morning, she woke to discover his arm wrapped around her waist. She was facing towards him, and could see the slow dance of his eyes beneath his lids.

'It is a powerful demon you face,' she whispered to him, 'and you are defeating it.' She wiggled closer and, ignoring the cries of the roosters, she closed her eyes and returned to slumber.

When she awoke once again, Rab had turned away from her and for a long while she watched the rise and fall of his breaths. The sun god's long arms lingered on his broad shoulders, as if consoling him, and she watched the light travel slowly down his back.

That was strange. The light should not have been travelling down his back at all, but up it. And what had happened to the cries of the roosters? Unless... She heard the clanking of plates. She sat up to discover the family seated on a carpet around a low table strewn with food.

'Greetings, Atia,' exclaimed Livius. 'You are just in time for dinner.'

Chapter Fifteen

Dinner. It was perhaps the most beautiful word Rab had ever heard. No matter that it had been uttered in Latin and by a Roman soldier no less. He could only smile hearing Livius's voice and knowing that he, too, had survived.

Somehow, Atia had saved them both.

'How do you fare?' Atia was asking Livius now. Rab's back was turned to them and he breathed deeply as if he were still asleep, but was listening to everything they said.

'Better than I have in years,' Livius replied. Rab heard the clanking of plates, smelled the rich aroma of roasted mutton. 'But if you are asking about my knee, it is improving. It seems to be healing in direct proportion to the number of honey cakes I am fed.'

There was a woman's soft giggle, and Rab heard another woman's voice speak in Nabataean. 'I think Livius favours you, Gamilath.'

'Don't be silly, Shudat.'

It was nice to hear his mother tongue—like donning an old pair of sandals.

'Hageru, pass the bread.'

Bread. Rab's stomach rumbled—a terrible, growling noise that sounded as though it had come from the depths of the earth.

And yet he made no move to get up. He kept his eyes closed, grateful to be alive. He wished to savour this moment.

'The stew is delicious,' remarked Atia.

Her voice was like a soft ribbon. Gods, how he loved the sound of it. It had wrapped around him in the depths of his fever, consoling him, cajoling him, keeping him anchored to the world.

'Have you always lived in this place?' Atia asked.

'We grew up here,' said the woman who had been called Shudat. 'But before the Romans came, two of us—my brother and I—lived in the open desert. We were frankincense traders.'

There was a long silence. 'I envy you that freedom. A Roman woman would not be allowed to engage in such trade.'

'You must become a Nabataean woman then,' said the woman who had been called Gamilath. 'We have always enjoyed more freedom than our Roman sisters.'

'So I have heard,' said Atia.

'You can marry our brother!' exclaimed Gamilath.

Rab's eyes flew open.

Atia was laughing gamely. 'If your brother is anything like his sisters, then I would be a fool not to consider it.'

Rab tried to keep his breaths even. The thought of Atia marrying any Nabataean other than himself gave him a strong desire to throw fists.

'What does your brother do now if he is no longer plying the routes?' asked Atia.

'Oh, he is still plying the routes—just not the desert routes,' said Shudat. 'After the Romans came, there was no more profit to be had in the desert routes, so our brother went to work at sea.'

'I am sorry,' replied Atia.

'What is there to be sorry for?' said Gamilath. 'He works on a large sailing vessel that runs between India and Egypt. He makes more coin than he ever did before. He brings us beautiful things.'

Rab heard the clanking of what he guessed to be bracelets and then the sounds of children squealing. 'Why do I frighten them so?' asked Atia.

'They think you are a Greek goddess,' Hageru explained.

Rab smiled to himself. She was a goddess— a strong, fearless, beautiful goddess whose divine determination had brought him back from the dead. How could he let her know that? How could he make what was wrong between them right again?

'Why on earth would they think me a goddess?' Atia asked. Rab could almost picture Atia putting her hand over her nose.

'I believe it has something to do with your unusual dress.'

'Ah, yes, the *stola*,' said Atia.

'That and the fact that you speak perfect Greek,' said Hageru.

'That is very kind of you to say,' said Atia.

Suddenly, Rab saw his chance.

'But that is not the only reason,' he said, rolling over to face the group. 'You are also beautiful.' He smiled and propped himself on his arms.

'Rab!' Atia exclaimed. She moved to stand, but he motioned her to stay seated. 'Please, if I cannot manage to make my own way to a tableful of food, then I am truly lost.'

Though what he had truly lost was the moment, for in her excitement to see him awake, she had not heard what he had said.

Slowly, he stood. He stared down at himself. His long robe seemed to hang from his wasted bones and his knees shook with weakness. But all he could think about as he made his way across the tent was how good it was to see her.

He took his seat across from her and noticed

the sheen of tears in her eyes. She covered her face with her hands and feigned a sneeze.

'An omen!' shouted the woman whom he assumed to be Gamilath. Her bracelets chimed as she clapped her hands together and grinned. 'The gods intend to favour us.'

'They favour us already,' said Livius, sliding Gamilath a wink.

Rab had the distinct feeling of joining a party that had begun long before his arrival. After a barrage of introductions, he found himself confronted with his wildest dream: a thick, meaty bowlful of mutton stew.

He approached it like a stalking lion: cautious, respectful, determined. When finally he lifted the bowl to his lips, something like an explosion took place inside him. He drank slowly, letting the soft shreds of meat caress his tongue and the wonder of their energy suffuse him. At last he returned the bowl to the table and let out a hearty sigh. 'The gods are great,' he pronounced and everybody cheered.

They feasted and talked until the sun had disappeared and the light of oil lamps shone in their eyes. Rab stole glances at Atia across the table. She was so lovely in the low light. Her auburn locks tickled her cheeks, making feathery shadows, and her soft, sensuous lips seemed to glow with a new shade of red.

He wanted to kiss those lips. He wanted to spend the rest of the night kissing them.

And yet it seemed fated that he was to spend the rest of the night among a troupe of friendly strangers.

'A story!' shouted Gamilath.

'Ah, yes, let us have a story,' repeated Shudat.

'A story! A story!' sang Hageru's boy and girl. Their hosts were gazing at them expectantly and Atia and Livius looked piteously lost.

'It is Nabataean custom for a guest to entertain his host with a story,' explained Rab.

'I fear that the only stories I know are of war and of the gods,' said Livius.

'And I know none at all,' said Atia. She sent Rab a pleading look.

Rab sighed. He was not going to get any time alone with Atia—but perhaps there was another way to speak to her.

Rab levelled a playful smile at the two children and stretched his arms theatrically. 'Then I believe it is up to me to ensure that our wonderful hosts learn the story of the enchanted horse.'

'The enchanted horse!' shouted the children in unison. They clapped and cheered gleefully as Rab cleared his voice and began.

'If you were to step outside this tent right now

and start walking south-east, you would pass over rows and rows of golden hills that would stretch out into a great sand sea, and beyond that sea you would encounter a rich, verdant land between two rivers. In this land there are great herds of horses.'

'I love horses!' shouted the girl.

'That is well,' said Rab, 'because in this fair green land there was once a girl much like you who also loved horses. One day, a trader came to her village and sold her father the tallest, smartest, most beautiful horse her father had ever seen.

'But when the girl's mother saw the new horse she became worried. "She is ugly," said her mother. "And just look at that bump on her back. She will never be able to carry a hunter or a warrior. You must sell her back."

'Now, the little girl had a brother much like you,' said Rab, pointing at Hageru's son. 'And together the brother and sister begged their father not to sell the new horse and vowed to take care of it themselves.

'They decided to call the horse Thirsty because whenever she stopped to drink from a stream it was as if she was trying to swallow up all the water in it.

'"Where do you think all that water goes?" the girl asked her brother one day.

'"I think it goes into the bump on her back," said the boy.

'"Maybe you are right," the girl replied.

'One day, the boy became very sick, and the medicine to save him lay beyond the sand sea. The father prepared several of his best horses to make the dangerous crossing.

'"Take Thirsty," said the girl. "She will survive the journey. She keeps water in her bump."

'So the father agreed and he set off across the sandy desert. The sun beat down each day. So much sun—and no water to be found. All the horses perished—except one. Which one do you think that was?'

'Thirsty!' shouted the children.

'You are right!' shouted Rab. 'With Thirsty to carry him, the father was able to return with the medicine and the little boy was saved. The mother was amazed. "I am sorry that I called your horse ugly," she said. "She is the most beautiful creature in all the world." And every day from then on they celebrated the beautiful, tall horse with the strange long legs and beautiful, perfect bump. The end.'

'But it wasn't a horse at all!' shouted Hageru's daughter.

'It wasn't?' said Rab, feigning ignorance.

'It was a camel!' shouted the boy.

'Really?' said Rab in mock surprise. 'Are you certain?'

Scandalised, the children shouted and howled,

followed by a quiet laughter that told him that he had succeeded with at least two members of his audience. He braved a glance at Atia. She was studying the floor.

She did not look at him for the rest of the night, and he feared his scheme to affirm her beauty had failed miserably.

He half-wished his fever would return, for now it was no longer proper for her to sleep beside him and she had rightly moved her bed mat to the place where the women slept.

He gazed across the darkness, trying to make out her shape. He thought about the softness of her body against his and grew warm. Perhaps his fever had not passed, after all. Perhaps the only thing that could remedy him was her.

The next morning, he opened his eyes to discover Atia's mat unoccupied. 'Where is Atia?' he asked Hageru.

'She and Livius have gone with my sisters and brother to tend the flock.'

'Your brother?'

'He arrived early this morning.'

Rab discovered the group standing at the top of a hill overlooking part of the canyon. A tall, muscular-looking Nabataean man who appeared to be roughly Rab's age was speaking animatedly while the others peered down the slope. Spotting Rab, the man smiled and gestured to him. 'Greetings, Brother!'

Brother? Rab was not this man's brother and he did not like how closely he was standing to Atia.

'Rab, this is Yamlik,' said Atia as Rab joined the group. 'He is a sailor and a trader. He just returned from Barygaza in the land of India. Is that not wondrous?'

'Well met, Brother,' said Yamlik, grasping Rab's arm with heavily ringed fingers.

Rab forced a grin. 'Well met.'

'I was just showing your companions our magic carpet,' he said. Yamlik gestured down the canyon at an unexpected swathe of green.

'Is it not amazing, Rab?' asked Atia. She was shaking her head in wonder at the sight of the grassy field. 'I have no idea how they do it.'

Rab stiffened. It was just an irrigated pasture, by the gods. 'They simply employ an Archimedes screw to reach the groundwater,' Rab said shortly. He turned to Yamlik. 'Purchased in old Amman, I presume?' he asked.

'Indeed it was—with the proceeds from my last sea journey.' Yamlik petted at his own short beard in a way that Rab found maddening.

Yamlik gestured to a bump in the ground running up the slope. 'The screw lies inside a pipe hidden beneath the earth just there. Whenever we need to water the field, we hook a donkey to a wheel that turns the screw. Water is lifted from a spring through the twisting spirals inside the pipe.'

Was Rab mistaken, or was Yamlik looking at Atia more than he was Livius? And did Atia's smile appear just a little brighter as she listened? 'It is truly remarkable,' she said.

'Just amazing,' Livius parroted, though he was gazing at Gamilath, not the pipe.

'Utterly magnificent,' Rab said with sarcasm and felt Atia's elbow in his side.

'We have several others installed at other springs nearby,' explained Yamlik, 'and we rotate the sheep between the fields they serve.'

'But how do you defend the fields?' asked Rab.

'I am sorry, I do not understand,' said Yamlik.

'From Romans, I mean. How do you prevent them from taking your pastures?'

Yamlik was shaking his head. 'We have never had any need to defend our pastures from Romans. Besides, Hageru's husband will soon become a Roman himself. He has already completed ten years of military—'

'That matters not at all,' Rab interrupted. If he heard about another Nabataean joining the Roman ranks he would lose his wits. 'You must take precautions now. The Romans will come eventually and demand unreasonable taxes. If you cannot pay them, you could lose everything. You must be prepared to fight.'

Rab sensed Atia watching him closely. Gamilath was shaking her head. 'I am afraid that we have spent all our money on obtaining the screws,' she said.

'Then you must sell more sheep,' urged Rab, feeling his nerves grow short. 'You must arm yourselves well.'

Atia moved to touch his arm. 'Rab—' she said, but he yanked his arm away. He knew what she was going to say. She was going to tell him to be reasonable. But he did not need a Roman telling him to be reasonable.

Yamlik flashed a righteous frown. 'If you spend your days preparing for a fight, how can you ever be at peace?'

Rab's breath seeped through his teeth. 'I think I need to go change my bandage,' he said, then he turned and walked away.

That evening after dinner, Yamlik retrieved a scroll from the shelf and carefully unfurled it. He gave Rab a glance and began to read.

'You have heard it said that you should love your neighbour and hate your enemy. But I say to you, love your enemies, bless them that curse you, do good to them that hate you so that you may be the children of your father in heaven, for he makes his sun to rise on the evil and on the good and sends rain on the just and on the unjust alike.'

Atia was shaking her head in admiration. 'Words of wisdom,' she exclaimed. 'May I ask which philosopher penned them?'

'A man called Jesus of Nazareth,' said Yamlik. 'He met my grandfather many years ago when he journeyed through these hills.'

Atia's mouth fell open. 'Your grandfather knew the prophet of the Christians?'

'Yes. Do you know of him?'

'He is quite infamous in Rome,' said Atia, 'though I find his message fascinating.'

'You, too?' said Yamlik, his eyes sparkling.

Rab found himself loathing the excessively handsome man with the colourful rings and closely trimmed beard. Yamlik was the worst kind of Nabataean. He spouted his high-minded philosophies while less fortunate people suffered all around him. Did Yamlik think he could just erase the need for vengeance against Rome? And did he really believe that he could just swoop in and steal the woman Rab loved?

Rab cleared his voice. 'I believe it is time for another story,' he pronounced.

Yamlik shot Rab a look of alarm, while Hageru's children erupted in cheers.

'Are you really going to gift us yet again, Rab?' asked Shudat.

'It is the traveller's obligation, is it not, Sister?' Rab said magnanimously. 'And also his greatest joy.'

'You are too generous,' Shudat said and everybody gathered around the dinner table as Rab cleared his voice.

Chapter Sixteen

'This is the story of a trader,' Rab began. He shot a look at Yamlik. 'A rich, handsome sea trader.' Rab gazed at the floor for an unusually long time, as if he were contriving the story just then.

'This particular sea trader had a problem, however. He loved himself too much. He loved the sound of his own voice and the brilliant things it said. He loved his bronze skin and muscular limbs and every single hair of his closely trimmed beard. But mostly he loved his face, for it seemed to him to be astoundingly handsome. His favourite thing to do was to stare into his copper mirror and admire himself as he floated across the sea.'

Rab glanced out at his audience, his gaze lingering on Yamlik.

'One day, the sea trader was staring into his mirror and failed to see a large reef lurking in the water beneath his boat. The boat crashed into the reef and the trader was hurled overboard.'

The children gasped, but Rab's eyes flickered with a savage glee. 'Then the poor trader was ripped apart by a troupe of passing sharks. Every inch of him was consumed—including every single hair of his closely trimmed beard.'

The children stared at Rab in wide-eyed horror.

Atia glanced at Yamlik, who was petting his own beard in alarm.

There was a long, confused silence. 'Apologies,' Rab said, glancing at the children. 'I had forgotten how very cruel that particular story was.'

It was Yamlik who salvaged the moment. 'Well, as a sea trader myself I can say with certainty that I will never again gaze into a copper mirror.' Everyone laughed.

Everyone except Rab, of course. He was smiling so tightly now that Atia feared his teeth might begin popping from his mouth one by one.

Livius lifted a honey cake from the tray. 'How do you say *I love honey cakes* in Nabataean?' he asked Gamilath and normal conversation resumed.

Atia watched Rab retreat to his bed mat. He appeared to be busying himself inspecting his water bag.

Meanwhile, Yamlik was saying something to Atia about his travels in India. 'Do you know of the Buddhists?' he asked. He had apparently met a number of them and found them to be fascinating.

Atia wished that she could find Yamlik fascinating. In truth, all she could think of was Rab and how oddly he had been acting since he had recovered from his fever.

First there had been the story about the camel. She had never heard any tale like it in all her life. A creature believed to be an ugly embodiment of one thing, finally found to be a beautiful embodiment of another. Rab had given Atia a significant look after he had finished, as if he had shaped the story to send her a message.

As if she, somehow, was the camel he had described.

The idea of it might have offended her. What woman wished to be compared to a camel? Yet the thought had sent a flutter of joy through her heart. The camel in his story had not only been beautiful, she had been strong and enduring and had ultimately saved the little boy's life. *I am sorry that I called your camel ugly*, said the mother in the story. *She is the most beautiful creature in all the world.*

But perhaps Atia was ascribing a meaning to the story that simply was not there? It would not have been the first time that her own wishful thinking had got in the way of reality. And the reality, she reminded herself, was that Rab had rejected her. He believed her to be ugly on the inside—just like all the other Romans he loathed, though for perhaps different reasons.

She decided to forget about the camel story and was glad she did, because the next day he seemed almost hostile to her. First there had been the strange, confrontational manner in which he had responded to Yamlik and when she had tried to comfort him he had yanked his arm away from her and stormed off.

And now this bizarre tale of the sea trader.

'Ana oheb kaykat aleasl,' Gamilath was saying in Nabatean.

'Ana ahubby al kayak lazy,' repeated Livius.

'A noble effort,' Gamilath said. She slid Atia a look. 'Again.'

The two continued to practise the sentence until it was rolling off Livius's tongue. Then Livius stood and fixed his gaze on Gamilath. He cleared his voice and knelt before her, taking her hand in his. *'Ana oheb Gamilath,'* he said gently. *I love Gamilath.*

Gamilath's eyes quietly filled with tears. She took one of her bracelets and slid it on to his arm. *'Ana oheb Livius,'* she said. The silence was so very sweet that it seemed unholy to break it.

The voice that finally did was full of irritation. 'Excuse me, but why have we not yet departed for Rekem?' Rab asked. 'We have been here for three days now. We are due in Rekem in five.'

Hageru and Gamilath exchanged a look. 'Livius's knee is not yet fit to sustain a march,' said Hageru. 'Nor have you fully recovered from your infection and fever.' She glanced at Rab's bandaged arm.

Rab shook his head. 'Livius can stay here and I am fit enough to travel. We must arrive in Rekem in no more than five days,' he repeated. 'There are consequences if we do not.'

'Rab is right,' Atia said. 'We must leave as soon as we can. Tomorrow, if possible.'

Rab caught Atia's gaze. His expression was full of gratitude.

'But Livius's knee is not yet healed,' Gamilath protested. 'It cannot withstand a long march.'

'We must leave him here to recover,' said Rab. 'Atia and I will go on our own.'

'Nonsense,' said Yamlik suddenly. 'We will simply take the camels.'

'You have camels?' asked Atia.

'Of course we have camels,' said Yamlik with a grin. 'Are we not Nabataean?'

Rab's plan could not have failed more miserably. In the moment, he had thought it brilliant. A revelation, of sorts. It had come to him just after Livius had pronounced his love to Gamilath. *Lovestruck fool!* Rab had thought. *Livius should just stay here.*

It was then that he had recognised the genius of the idea. Why should Livius not just stay? There was no real reason for him to continue on to Rekem other than his own sense of duty—something that had obviously been obliterated by a pretty young woman with jingling bracelets. Why should Livius not just stay with Gamilath and allow his knee to fully heal before returning to duty? And in that case Rab and Atia could simply continue on to Rekem together.

Together and finally alone.

It was the manner in which he had spoken his revelation that he feared had ruined it. He had not left enough time after Livius had made his grand pronouncement. Worse, the tone of Rab's voice had been wrong. It had been full of impatience and disdain. He feared that he had sounded almost jealous of Livius.

He had not been jealous, of course. If anything, he had been exasperated. How on earth could a man presume to fall in love in only three days? And how could the object of his affection somehow do the same? And how, by all the gods in all the heavens, could there be no opposition to the matter? The whole thing was so idyllic as to be ridiculous.

Thank the gods Atia had affirmed their need to

depart. She had saved him once again—this time from being labelled a malcontent. Unfortunately, Atia's urgency caused Yamlik to leap into action, obviously eager to prove his usefulness to her.

And Livius had insisted on accompanying them, not only because he was obligated to fulfil his mission, but also because a Roman military escort would be necessary to get them past any military checkpoints.

Following Yamlik's offer of camels and Livius's declaration of duty, Gamilath had pronounced that she would also join the group, for she could not allow her brother to return unaccompanied from Rekem with three camels in tow.

And thus now, instead of two lone travellers, they were a caravan of five: Yamlik, Atia, Gamilath, Livius, and Rab.

They set off early the next morning and Rab consoled himself that he would find a chance to speak with Atia soon. Five days was a long time and travelling on camels meant they would have plenty of energy for discussion.

But Yamlik insisted that the caravan travel in the traditional formation of a single line, with Yamlik in front, then Atia, then Gamilath, then Livius and finally Rab. The women were to remain in the middle of the caravan, Yamlik insisted. It was Nabataean tradition.

And so Rab decided that he loathed Nabataean tradition, along with Yamlik himself. He also loathed the sun, for its movements marked the passage of time. The hours were ticking by. If he did not speak to Atia soon, he feared he never would.

He imagined himself shouting at her from behind. *Atia, I wish to thank you for saving my life. Also, I have considered your proposition and the answer is yes. I will accept your gold coins. Anything to be close to you one last time. Also, I love you.*

They had travelled across a high plateau those next two days, with no shade in sight. By the time they made their camp each evening they were too exhausted to do anything but fall upon their bed mats.

They started early the third morning, plunging into a small, beautiful *wadi* by the name of Phaeno where an unlikely stand of oaks gave them shade enough to pitch an early camp.

'What are those?' Atia asked as they unloaded the camels. She pointed at the cave-like openings along the cliffs. 'They look as if they have been made by men.'

Rab seized the moment. 'They are copper mines,' he said. 'During my fa—during King

Rabbel's rule, they were used to produce funds for the water system that serves Rekem.'

Atia gazed up at the mines. 'Strange that such a powerful source of revenue is not in use now,' she remarked.

Rab wanted to seat himself beside her and describe the mines' long history—how they had been worked continuously by the people of the *wadi*—a clan that could name their ancestors back for a thousand years. He wanted to tell her how ancient arrowheads had been found in in one of the mines and strange drawings upon its walls. But once again he found himself at the mercy of another man in charge.

'Come now, let us eat,' said Yamlik. 'And then we shall have a story.'

That night they stared up at the stars while Yamlik told the first part of a two-part Nabataean epic. Rab paid no attention at all to Yamlik. He focused instead on the constellation Libra, wondering if Atia saw it, too, and if she was thinking of him at all. By the time Yamlik was done, Rab could barely keep his eyes open.

The next day, the route grew stonier and starker. Small bushes and tufts of dry grass gave way to no vegetation at all.

They crested a high pass, pausing to appreciate one of Nabataea's most remarkable sights: a *wadi* so wide and long that it could barely be perceived save from above. 'That is Wadi Arabah,' said Rab. 'Its sands flow—'

'All the way to the Red Sea,' interrupted Yamlik.

Atia gazed in wonder at the sight. 'Does it ever fill with water?' she asked.

'Once every few years,' said Yamlik. 'Nabataeans believe that when it does, it carries all their troubles away.'

'Let us hope it fills soon, then,' Atia said. She gave Rab a meaningful look, as if she wished the same for their own troubles. But with only one night left, what hope could there be?

'Let us hope it fills this very night,' said Rab.

Chapter Seventeen

She wondered if the camels were the reason she
could not sleep. Miraculous creatures, they ferried her across the punishing landscape like a
princess of the sands. The beasts never seemed
to tire. They walked neither fast nor slow. Their
tempers were neither short nor long. The only
thing they did to an extreme was drink.

Whenever they came to a cistern or a spring,
they would lower their long necks into the water
and partake. The previous afternoon, Atia had
watched a spring completely drained by the five
thirsty camels. Rab had said that they would not
have to drink again for ten days.

The camels were made for the desert, which
meant that there was no reason for Atia to exert
herself at all during the day, which meant she was
not tired when they arrived in camp each evening.

Which meant she could not sleep.

Her restlessness was especially keen tonight—

the last night of their journey. Tomorrow, they would plunge down into the network of hills and *wadis* surrounding Rekem—the great city of stone.

At last she would gaze up at rock-carved buildings that many said rivalled the Egyptian pyramids. 'Herodotus died before Rekem was built,' Atia's own tutor had told her once. 'Or else he would not have given us seven wonders, but eight!'

Still, Atia would have gladly bypassed the great city if it meant spending just a few more days with Rab—or even just a few more hours. All she needed was enough time alone with him to tell him what she had been unable to say that day by the stream: that she had meant no offence by offering him the coin, that she had only wanted to compensate him for any distaste he might experience with a woman such as she, that she had not meant to cheapen their connection, but to ensure its equality.

If they could just have some time alone, she would tell him all that and more. She would fill his ears with her apologies and, once they were full to brimming, she would ask him for one small favour: would he be willing to kiss her lips one last time? It was all she needed—just a small reminder of his lips, of how good they tasted, of how they seemed to melt with hers, of the things they said to her without speaking a word. She wanted something to remind herself what it felt like to be alive.

Atia rolled over on her mat. Beside her, Gamilath lay atop her own mat, deep in slumber. Atia envied Gamilath's sound sleep, but did not begrudge it. She had delighted in seeing her and Livius's love bloom.

Propriety demanded that the two sleep apart in the presence of Gamilath's older brother, but Atia knew that it would not be long before they were huddled together inside some secret cave, their limbs intertwined.

The thought made Atia smile. Livius deserved happiness. He had only five years left of his army contract. Soon he would have the freedom to start building a new life. And tomorrow he would march into Rekem with the assurance that his duty had been fulfilled.

Atia's own duty, in contrast, was just beginning.

She rolled over again and stared into the darkness. She knew Rab was lying there somewhere just out of view.

Since they had set out on this last leg of their journey, he had been more distant than ever. He had said only a handful of words to her over the past several days and, whenever she looked at him, he always seemed to be gazing off into the distance, as if he were already riding away from her into the desert.

Atia rose from her mat and slipped into her sandals.

She felt better the instant she began to move her legs. The sky was cloudy with stars and against their milky backdrop she was able to make out the snaking path of the small *wadi* in which they had camped. She stepped forward in that stream of sand and began to follow its wide bed.

It felt so good to move. Her feet pressed into the sand as she walked, making a soft, whispering noise against the desert's perfect silence.

She glanced at the western horizon and caught sight of a small speck of light. It was growing rapidly, swelling into a large yellowish sphere that began to climb into the sky.

How long had it been since she had watched a full moon rise? As it made its way higher it grew whiter, as if shedding its own skin. Eerie shadows appeared. Soon she perceived the profile of a distant cluster of palms. Palms!

Now she had a goal, for she knew that palms signalled the presence of water, and she was already becoming quite thirsty. She was certain if she could just reach that small cluster of palms, she would be rewarded with a much-needed drink.

She walked and walked, but it did not seem as if she was getting any closer to the palms. Rab had warned her once about the phenomenon of mirage. 'The sun can play with your mind,' he had explained. 'It can make you see things that are not there.'

Atia wondered if the same was not true of the moon. Had it somehow altered her perception, causing her to conjure those spiky palms?

I should just go back, she thought, though now the very existence of the palms had become a puzzle she wished to solve. She continued to walk.

By the time she reached the palms, she was breathless, exhausted and very thirsty. She stalked around the cluster, searching for a man-made spring. *Where there are plants, there is water*, she reassured herself.

No spring appeared, so she wiped her brow and quietly began to dig. She scooped up armfuls of sand, but the tiny grains were like water. For every handful she lifted from the hole, another handful seemed to spill back in.

She dug for what must have been an hour. Now she was very, very thirsty. She needed to make a decision—take the long walk back to camp or throw her energy into finding the water she knew lay just below her feet.

She continued to dig. She had to find the water—if only to prove to herself that she could. She heaved up armfuls of sand, certain she would find it soon. But when she stopped to assess her progress she saw that she had made very little.

If only she were a camel. Then she would not be thirsty at all. Earlier that day, Rab had noted that if they had ridden camels directly from Bostra, their journey would have lasted twenty days instead of the thirty-nine it had taken so far.

Thirty-nine days. It was hard to believe they had departed Bostra just thirty-nine days ago. It felt like a lifetime.

It was then she realised: today was the day she was supposed to die.

On the twentieth day of the ninth month of your thirtieth year, the old woman had said. Atia had tucked the information away in the deepest part of her mind—never to be forgotten.

And yet, she *had* forgotten. Somewhere between Bostra and Rekem, that ominous date had slipped her mind. She had been so consumed with trying to forget—forget the tears, forget the battle, forget the camel trainer with the eyes flecked with gold—that it seemed she had also forgotten the date of her own demise.

A creeping panic was overtaking her. Were these her last moments on earth?

She had never expected to cheat her own death. In the past she had sometimes even yearned for it. But now that her time had come, she felt her breaths quickening in rebellion and her heart beating out its protest.

She did not wish to die. Not any more. Not when she had just learned what it meant to live.

She looked all around the oasis, searching for possible sources of her demise. She closed her eyes and listened for the sound of her doom. What would it be? A chorus of hyenas' laughter? The soft crunching of pebbles beneath a lion's paws?

'Ha, ha, ha!' she laughed, daring them to come. She felt herself on the verge of tears.

A voice called from the shadows. 'Atia?'

Chapter Eighteen

Her heart skipped. 'Rab?'

'Atia, are you well?' He stood in the moon shadow cast by the palms, his body barely distinguishable from the rest of the night.

'I am perfectly well,' she replied. She felt a wave of relief, followed by a rippling of dread. Was it to be Rab, then? Was he to be her assassin?

'What are you doing, Atia?'

'Is it not obvious that I am digging for water?' The moonlight poured over her shoulders, illuminating the small hole she had managed to excavate.

He appeared to shake his head. 'What is obvious is that your head is tilted backwards, your mouth is pointed at the sky and you were just laughing in the way of a hyena.'

She could imagine the smirk on his face. 'I was not laughing at the sky,' she insisted. 'I was laughing at…my imminent success.'

'You were celebrating a success you have not yet enjoyed?'

'I am in no mood for your teasing,' Atia grumbled, though in truth there was something extremely comforting in it. 'I know there is water here and I am quite certain that I am on the verge of finding it,' she pronounced.

'It must be a heady feeling to be that close to success,' he observed, clearly enjoying himself.

'It is quite gratifying,' she said. 'At least we can agree on *that*.'

Her statement seemed to give him pause. 'Would you like some help?'

'No, I do not need your—' she began saying. In truth, she *did* need his help—most desperately. Why was it so hard to accept? 'Yes,' she finally admitted.

He extended his hand. 'Come,' he said.

He lead her to a dark area beneath one of the palms. *The perfect location for a strangling,* she thought morbidly. Yet she knew instinctively that if she was meant to die tonight, it would not be at his hand.

Perhaps they were meant to die together.

'Here is your water,' he pronounced. He bent to clear away a pile of leaves and she watched the milky moonlight spread its light across a sprawling black pool. She gasped. Water. Pure, clean, lovely water. It had been there all along—through all her desperate digging. She had been so convinced of the difficulty of the problem that she had not seen its solution right before her eyes. 'You have my gratitude, Rab.'

How nice it was to say his name aloud. Perhaps it was to be her last word. She imagined a crocodile springing up out of the inky water and removing her head from her body. Or perhaps the pool itself would be her demise. Death by drowning. An ironic ending in this dry place.

Rab bent to the spring and cupped the water in his palms. 'Did you not say you were thirsty?' he asked.

The water inside his hands was like the sand had been inside hers: she could see it slowly slipping through his fingers. She peered at the ground. Why could she not bring herself to drink?

He did not push her. He only sat down at the edge of the pool and gazed up at her. 'It is strange,' he started saying. 'We have travelled all these days across the desert and not once have I told you a travelling story.'

Atia cocked her head. 'You told stories at the home of Yamlik's family.'

'They do not count.'

'Why not?'

'They were told beneath the shelter of a tent for the benefit of our hosts. To qualify as a true travelling story, it must be told beneath the stars for the benefit of the travellers.'

'Like Yamlik's epic?' Atia said.

'Like Yamlik's epic, except exciting and interesting and finished well before sunrise,' said Rab.

Atia laughed and Rab patted the ground. 'Will you let me tell you a travelling story, Atia?'

Atia sat down before him, sensing a deeper agenda at work.

'There was once a beautiful, wealthy kingdom that lay beyond the Middle Sea,' he began. 'Its rulers were peaceful and good, and they built a city full of sculptures and gardens and wonders to behold. The King and Queen lived in a splendid palace with their son and three daughters, all of whom they loved dearly. But the King had a special place in his heart for his son, for the two shared a passion for the world beyond.'

Atia recalled that Rab had three sisters. Her curiosity stirred.

'Whenever the King journeyed to a faraway land he always brought back something for his Queen and something for his son. Horns from Britannia. Carpets from Persia. Masks from the land of Punt. Once the King travelled to a place called India and upon his return he gifted his wife and son each a beautiful wood-carved elephant, for they were the most noble, wondrous creatures the King had ever seen.

'Soon after his trip to India, the King's dear Queen died. He placed her mummy inside a grand tomb along with jewels and riches and bags of golden coins. To this great horde of wealth he added all the gifts he had given her throughout his life—the horns from Britannia, the carpets from Persia, the masks from the land of Punt. He put them all inside the magnificent tomb with the exception of one—the wooden elephant, which he gave to his son to remember his mother by.

'One day an evil general marched into the kingdom and declared its citizens heathens. The King and his family retreated to the rooftop of the palace and watched from above as the soldiers invaded the city, burning and raping and looting. They watched in despair as the soldiers unsealed the door to the Queen's tomb and poured inside, taking everything of value.

'"Father, we must fight!" urged his son. "Call the army!"

'But the King only sobbed. "The soldiers greatly outnumber our own," he said. "We cannot win."

'"Let us fight and die, then," said his son, "with honour."

'But the King would not listen. He pulled a small vial from his pocket and tipped it to his lips.'

Rab paused. He gazed at Atia across the darkness.

'By all the unruly gods, Rab, continue! What happened next?'

'The King tipped the bottle of poison to his lips,' Rab repeated, 'and began to drink. The son moved to stop his father, but he did not reach him in time. The King took a final swallow, then smashed the emptied vial upon the ground.

'"Remember what this kingdom was once, dear boy," the King said. "And never forget the elephants." By the time the enemy soldiers arrived on the roof the King was dead.'

'No!' exclaimed Atia.

'The son escaped,' Rab continued, 'and he vowed to avenge his father. Over the next dozen years the Prince built up a secret army comprised of every able member of that fine kingdom.'

'Even the women?'

'Of course the women—or are women not equal to men?'

Atia did not know what to say. She had never heard of such a thing in her entire life. Women were not equal to men in Rome. Was it different in Nabataea? She supposed that in fantastical stories like this one, they could be anything they liked. 'What happened then?' she asked.

'The great army of citizens marched on the occupied capital and freed it. In honour of his victory, the Prince adorned the top of each column of the palace with a stone elephant.'

Atia sighed. 'A happy ending.'

'But the story is not yet finished. The son,

who was the new King, placed the two wooden elephants in his bedchamber before a large mirror. And every evening he would stare at his twin elephants and remember his mother and father, who taught him to love the world beyond. And then he would turn to the mirror and look at himself, who had decided not to be defeated by it.'

When she spoke, her voice was trembling. 'I have often felt...defeated by the world,' Atia said. She gazed at the dirt, then began to trace her finger in it.

'I know,' whispered Rab.

'For many years, I sought to escape from it.'

'I know.'

'You *know*?'

'About the tears?' he asked. 'Yes.'

'But how?'

'You are not the only one with a talent for observation.'

He gazed into her eyes and tried to convey what words could not: that he had been observing her since the day they met.

'Do you find me weak, then?' she asked.

'You have battled a demon stronger than all the world's armies and emerged triumphant. You are the opposite of weak,' he said. 'You are heroic.'

A shy smile traversed her face and she resumed her strange sketching in the dirt.

'The hero of your story was very brave.'

'I agree. The King's son never gave up.'

'I am not speaking of the King's son. I am speaking of the King.'

'But the King took his own life,' Rab protested. 'How could that ever be brave?'

'He chose death over humiliation. That is brave.' She paused, still sketching the ground. 'My mother took her own life,' she whispered.

Rab sighed. He had suspected as much. When she had spoken of her mother that evening beneath the stars, the pain in her voice had stung his own ears.

His father and her mother—both killed by their own hands. She continued to move her finger through the dirt.

'I am very sorry,' Rab said.

'It was a long time ago. My father wanted a son,' she said, 'and my mother could only produce daughters.'

She was hard at work now. He could see her bent over her design, tracing long, swooping lines, scratching deep into the earth: two elephants. 'After my mother delivered her fourth daughter, my father beat her very badly. He destroyed her beautiful face, do you understand?'

'By the gods,' gasped Rab.

'Then he sent the baby to the dump.'

'An orphan's home, you mean?'

'I mean where the people dump their trash. He did not wish to support another girl.'

Rab squeezed her hand.

She smiled tightly, blinking back her tears, failing in the effort. 'But my mother got her revenge. That is all that matters.'

And left you all alone. He stayed silent.

'She did get it,' Atia repeated, as if having to convince herself.

'Sometimes the easy thing to do is to die,' Rab said.

She was shaking her head. 'You say that, yet you support the Nabataean rebels. Are they not simply going to their deaths?'

'The rebels seek justice,' said Rab. He felt his jaw tense.

'I understand that. So did my mother, yet you think her death a shame.'

Rab paused. He pictured the dead bodies on the beach.

'How many rebels do you guess there are?' asked Atia.

'At least a thousand, maybe more.'

'But there are five thousand soldiers in a Roman legion,' said Atia. She appeared to do some calculation in her head. 'And there are two legions stationed in Arabia Petraea alone, plus several more in the Judean and Syrian provinces. It is an unwinnable fight.'

'You speak like a politician.'

'I am a politician's daughter.'

'The rebel numbers are increasing by the day,' said Rab. But that was a lie. The rebel numbers were not increasing, because many Nabataeans who should have been rebels were already in business with Romans. Or marrying them. Or worse—joining their cursed ranks.

'Rab, what is it that you fear?' Atia asked suddenly. She had ceased her sketching. She was gazing at him across the darkness.

'I fear that the Nabataean people will be made into beggars in their own land. I fear that—' He stopped himself. 'What is the point of this?' he asked. It only made his jaw ache and his heart beat too quickly. It only made him dig his fingernails into his palms so hard they left bruises. Why had his father let the Romans in? That was what he really wished to know. His biggest fear was that he would never find out.

She was waiting for his answer. He had the feeling that she would have waited a thousand years. 'I fear that the Nabataean people are being lost,' he said at last. 'I fear that our splendid culture is being erased and that one day our greatness will be forgotten.'

He exhaled, though it was not simple breath that emerged from his chest. It was a great chaotic storm and it swirled all around them and blanketed them in angry dust.

He stared up at the sky. The stars had disappeared, swallowed up by the light of the moon. *The moon is like Rome*, he thought, *fat, yet hungry.*

He imagined himself falling towards it, as if to slay it. He unsheathed his sword and slashed it through the air, but found that there was nothing to slay. Only light. White and insubstantial. Meaningless and diffuse. The more he fought, the more exhausted he became. Nabataea was being erased, and he could do nothing to stop it. His heart filled with despair.

He felt her hand reach for his.

Chapter Nineteen

She wove her fingers with his and squeezed. He squeezed back. He pulled her gently towards him and she scooted next to him until she could feel the cloth of his sleeve pressing against her arm. Her heart was beating.

'What about you, Atia?' he whispered at last. 'What is your greatest fear?'

Her greatest fear? *That these are our last moments together*, she thought. *That after tomorrow I will never see you again.*

But how could she tell him that, after what he had just said? He feared the demise of his very culture and she only feared the loss of him. His thoughts were nobler than hers. His troubles greater.

Still, he had spoken from his heart, and she was obliged to speak from hers. 'I am afraid that I will die without ever having lived.'

And there it was. A selfish thing to say—especially after his virtuous admission. But it was the truth. 'Rab, I have wasted so many of my days…'

Rab squeezed her hand again and gazed up at the moon. 'I wonder if I have not wasted many of mine as well,' he said.

What did he mean? Was he simply reassuring her, or was it possible that he regretted their estrangement? Or could he have been referring to something larger still?

'You are neither a camel trainer nor a trader, are you, Rab?' she asked. She hardly knew what had compelled her to speak. Rab sucked the air, saying nothing. 'You are the rebel leader.'

Now he ceased to breathe at all, or so it seemed. The air was deathly still. He turned to her, the moonlight illuminating the confession in his eyes. *Yes, I am. And you have just placed yourself in danger.*

She tried to stop herself, but it was as if the Fates themselves were speaking through her. 'And your father…was no pomegranate farmer.'

His brows made a sharp angle, but his eyes waited.

'Your father was King Rabbel the Second.'

He released her hand and appeared to reach for his blade. Suddenly, it all made sense. It was now—now was to be the moment of her death. She had exposed his secret and put the rebel army at risk. She would need to be eliminated.

She considered attempting to run. She could leap up suddenly and dash off into the desert. Ha! As if she could outrun Rab. As if she could escape Morta's shears.

Besides, running would make her a coward and she was not a coward. She was her mother's daughter, by the gods, and she would face her death without fear.

She pulled her hair aside and bared her neck. She held her breath. A soft wind rustled through the leaves of the palms, then quieted. A frog began to croak. *I do not fear you*, she thought. *I love you. Go ahead, deliver me my death.*

When Rab finally spoke, his voice was full of curiosity. 'So when did you know?'

She gulped the air. 'When did I *know*?'

She glanced at the object in his hand. It was her fallen scarf.

'I presume this is yours,' he said. He smiled sweetly as he handed her the ripped garment. It was the same scarf she had been wearing the day they met.

She gazed at the scarf in puzzlement, running her finger along the ripped seam.

'When did you know I was the rebel leader?' he asked again. 'Or when did you begin to guess it?'

She spoke carefully. 'I guessed it when I learned that it was you who saved me from Plotius. No mere trader could possibly defeat a giant like Plotius.'

'Very observant,' said Rab.

'But it was not just that. It was also the way you led us on the trail. You were too comfortable in the role. You commanded our group better than Plotius ever could.'

'You flatter me,' he said.

'I merely observe. Also that day at the baths—' She felt the heat of a blush.

'Yes?' he said. 'Go on.'

'Your exposed flesh bespoke a good deal of physical training.'

He grinned, then closed his eyes, as if imagining the moment.

If he was going to kill her, he certainly would not be smiling like that. Her cautious optimism was slowly transforming into a deep, bodily relief. 'But I knew for certain only just now after you told your story.'

Wonder flooded his expression. 'Indeed? And how did I give myself away?'

'When you spoke the King's last words you faltered and your voice changed. I sensed you were on the edge of tears.'

'They were my father's last words—*the elephants*.'

He released her hand. Why was he releasing

her hand? 'What do you think he meant by them?' she asked, hoping to keep him talking.

'I have asked myself that question for thirteen years now,' he said, rising to his feet. 'I have yet to discover a satisfactory answer.'

He was smoothing his robe when she realised that he was not going to kill her at all. He was going to leave her.

No, no, no, she thought. Her heart squeezed. But of course he was going to leave. She had exposed his true identity. She would be obliged to tell her father and he knew it. He would likely be gone before the dawn.

'Please do not go,' she blurted. 'I do not plan to tell my father about you—or anyone else. Just stay here a bit longer. We can speak together more, or just be still. I am not your enemy and I promise to keep your secrets.' She realised that she was babbling, but she hardly cared. He was leaving her. 'Please just stay. I do not wish to expose you, or bore you, or vex you, or engage in some ridiculous debate. I only—'

'Atia?' he interrupted. He was standing inside the shadow of the palms, his expression unreadable.

'What, Rab? What is it?'

'I would not leave you if the Emperor himself appeared before us with a hundred legions at his back.'

He was smiling at her—she could tell by the tone of his voice. One of those sweet, genuine smiles that was rarer than rain.

And he had not been lying. His figure remained fixed in place beneath the shade of the palm. He seemed to be busying himself with some quiet task. A sandal was tossed aside, then another. She began to hear the soft sounds of moving cloth. There was only one thing he could be doing.

Or undoing, rather. She saw the shadow of his robe fall to the ground, followed by the thin strip of his loincloth, then watched his dark silhouette slip quietly into the pool.

She was overcome by the vision of him. The moonlight poured down on to his naked torso in a play of light and shadow. The contours of his body—his sculpted arms, the twin bulges of his chest, the rippling plane of his stomach—seemed both more magnificent and less real, as if she were not viewing a male body, but some idealised version of a male body that she had fashioned inside her own mind. *A mirage.* The water reached his hips, concealing the rest of him beneath its shimmering surface.

Thank the gods.

She did not know what she would have done if he had been as exposed as he had been that afternoon in the stream or that morning at the baths. Probably she would have simply run away in terror—not of the man himself, but of her own desire for him.

In one fluid motion, he lowered himself beneath the surface of the water and re-emerged in a splashy burst. He shook out his long hair and water splattered across Atia's skin. She cried out, then laughed.

He caressed the water's surface with his arms, beckoning. By the gods, it was as if he were caressing her own skin.

'I will disappoint you,' she told him.

'You will only disappoint me if you do not come in.'

What was that expression on his face? Surely it was a trick of the moonlight making him appear so very sincere. His hair hung in ropes around his cheeks and his bare skin dripped with water. It was as if he wished for her to see him exactly as he was. A warrior without his armour. A statue of Achilles stripped of his paint.

Curse the moonlight. She did not trust it.

And why should she? It seemed to be in league with the desert itself. Together they conspired to trick her—to conjure this man from the very dust. Of course he was not real, for he appeared to be offering her everything her heart desired.

Not just offering it to her: begging her to take it.

He stretched out his hand.

Yes, curse the moonlight, for he was so very handsome in it. So very difficult to resist.

And there were so many good reasons to resist him, though she could not think of a single one just now. He had hurt her once, yes? In some distant time and place he had wounded her pride. He had also frustrated her. She vaguely remembered something about that. She cast about her mind for the details, but her thoughts had become so very crowded with him.

She stood and stepped into the shadow that he had only recently occupied. She removed her tunic and let it fall to the ground. Curses, why had she tied her breast band so tightly? She battled with its large knot and willed it free. Her loincloth was mercifully easier to remove. It fell from her limbs like the skin of a snake.

'Take my hand,' he said.

She paused. *This is simply a mirage*, she told herself. *A beautiful dream.* Besides, if she lived beyond this night, she would likely never see Rab again.

'It sounds as if we must both find our courage to live,' he said.

He might have said something more, but Atia did not hear it. She could only hear those words— so loud and weighty, like a dare handed down from a god.

Go ahead, then, Atia, she told herself. *What are you afraid of? Live.*

She placed her hand in his and stepped into the pool. The water was not cool, nor was it warm. It seemed to be precisely the temperature of her own skin.

She plunged into its depths, submerging herself, then burst to the surface. He was smiling down at her, but the expression in his eyes had changed. Their guileless sweetness was gone—replaced by something urgent and serious and... hungry.

'I want to make love to you, Atia,' he said.

He was several paces away from her in the pool, yet she felt as if he had whispered in her ear. She feared him and desired him all at once. The last time they had met like this, he had changed all the rules—at least all the rules that she had ever been taught. What would he demand of her this time?

She did not even dare to imagine. She felt paralysed with longing for him. She held his gaze, but knew not how to proceed. She had imagined their moments together in the stream a thousand times, not daring to dream beyond them. Now she had no idea of what to do or how to be. In this small desert spring, she was very much at sea.

'I want to make love to you, too,' she said.

He smiled, then scooped up a large helping of

water. 'Come, you must be very thirsty,' he said. His voice was husky and low.

'I am,' she said, though she had quite forgotten her thirst.

'Will you not drink from my hands?'

Suddenly her thirst came roaring back. She stepped towards him, bent to his hands and began to drink. The water tasted sweet and she felt an almost holy relief as she sipped it.

She let her hands sink slowly into the water.

His column of taut flesh was not difficult to find and when she wrapped her hand around it, she felt a strange thrill. His pleasure was hers to give, she realised. And he trusted her with it.

She was humble in her power. Tentative and careful. She began to stroke him beneath the surface of the water. He was watching her closely, as if it pleased him to see her face.

But of course that could not be. Impossible.

In an effort to move her nose out of his view, she stepped closer to him, not knowing that in so doing she would trap the air between them until it became almost unbearably hot. To alleviate the burning heat, she pressed her cool, wet breasts against his chest.

But that seemed only to transfer the heat— from the surrounding air to a place deep inside herself, a place that she hardly knew how to keep cool. She could feel his heart pounding against hers—like a soft fist knocking at a door.

And between them, something larger than a fist. It was growing within her grasp. Larger. Harder.

'By the gods, Atia, what are you doing to me?'

She hardly knew. She only continued to stroke, as if her small, rhythmic movements might somehow bring him the kind of pleasure he had given her that day in the stream. If she concentrated hard enough, could she make him begin to moan? If she kissed him just here, at the bottom of his neck, and then let that gentle kiss deepen into a suck like…this, could she make him begin to shake and quiver like he had done to her?

'Yes,' he murmured.

Yes. She was doing well. Yes. He was feeling pleasure. Yes. He was beginning to moan. Yes…

'No,' he spouted suddenly. His chest appeared to empty itself of air. He cringed as if in pain, then slowly, gently removed her hand from its important work. He hugged her tightly against him. 'You are going to send me to the moon, my dear,' he whispered in her ear. 'But I will not travel there without you.'

Chapter Twenty

He raked his fingers through her wet hair and breathed in the scent of her. Then he wrapped his arms around her chest and pulled her close. *This is all we are going to get*, he thought. One night. One single night in a lifetime of thousands. He squeezed her tightly against him, as if his arms were strong enough to stop the forces that would soon break them apart for ever.

He stepped back to look at her. If they were never to see each other again, then he wanted to remember her as she was right now, with the moonlight pouring over her skin and her eyes smiling up at him.

He loved her eyes—bright luminous orbs. So intelligent and kind. So radiant with mischief. Of all the changes in her appearance that had taken place during their journey—the leaning of her limbs, the bronzing of her skin, the darkening of her lips—it was her eyes that had changed the most. Their hooded sadness had slowly disappeared, replaced with a lusty, wide-eyed glow.

Her whole being seemed to glow, in truth. It was as if somewhere along the trail she had switched her diet—as if now, instead of poppy tears, she drank the moonlight itself. Had grown luminous on it.

He settled a strand of hair behind her ear. Even in the moonlight, he could still discern its auburn hue. It was his new favourite colour.

He tried to burn her expression into his mind. His own excitement and yearning seemed reflected in it, as if she were a mirror in which he could see his own true wants. Not anger, but humour. Not resentment, but yearning. Not revenge, but love. She moved her hand to cover her nose.

'Do not even dare it,' he admonished. He gently returned her hand to her side. 'I beg you not to do that ever again. Your nose is strong and unique. It blesses your face with a regal intelligence. Do you not see how very beautiful you are?'

Though beautiful was not the word for her. Beautiful described women who powdered their faces and kohled their eyes and painted their lips with the dregs of wine. It was the word applied to ladies who walked graciously through the corridors in diaphanous robes, who lounged in *tricliniums* growing round on grapes.

Atia was not beautiful, for she had long ago transcended that particular word.

She was sublime. Magnificent. She was a woman who had crossed the sweltering wilds of the Arabian highlands in the middle of August. A survivor who had successfully fought off heat and hunger and wicked men. She was a warrior who had done battle with the desert inside herself and somehow emerged victorious.

Beautiful woman? No, she was a goddess to be worshipped for the rest of her days.

And yet they had just this one single night.

Beautiful? Atia? The two words had never belonged together. They were like two truths so different that placed together they became a lie. And yet coming from his lips she finally dared to believe them. *All right, then, I am beautiful*, she told herself, testing the statement inside her mind. *I am beautiful enough for this strong, noble, magnificent man to want me.*

And he did want her. She had felt the proof of it inside her very hand. And now he was bending to kiss her. She could feel his hot breath, see his large, soft lips descending to meet hers.

And then their lips locked and all the desire that she had kept bottled up inside her came pouring forth, and she feared she might topple him with it. 'Mmm,' he said instead and met her yearning with his own as their lips tumbled over each other and their mouths fell into a hungry rhythm.

It was as if they were dancing—a fast, swirling dance fuelled by longing. His tongue swept inside her mouth, possessing it, caressing it. His lips were telling her things they could not take back. There was an urgency to his movements, as if he were making up for lost time. His hot breaths were like tiny confessions of yearning.

His hands. They ranged across her body like thieves, plundering every exposed surface. *Take what you like,* she told them, leaning into their gentle pressure. He kneaded her hips, then caressed slowly downwards. When he finally reached the twin mounds of her buttocks, he moaned.

His kiss grew deeper, lustier. His tongue dipped and plunged, as if he were in the act of consuming her. She gripped the twin flanks of muscle that ran down from his arms, trying to keep up, though her effort was futile. It was all she could do simply to hold on.

'I want you so badly, Atia,' he said. This time, she would not even begin to doubt it. Not with his kisses as urgent as they were, his hands as greedy, his hot column of flesh as relentless as it seemed tapping against her stomach beneath the water.

This was real desire and, incredibly, it was for her.

She knew where this was going. Soon his body would demand release. Then he would turn her around and bend her over and spill his seed inside her. What she could not account for was that she craved this moment. Her desire for it seemed to be growing in direct proportion to the passion of his kisses.

She pressed her body against his and began to move. She wanted him, she realised. She wanted to feel him inside of her, getting his pleasure. Not only that, she wanted to see him doing it. It was the first time she had ever wanted such a thing in her life. The notion filled her with wonder.

She cast her eyes around the pool. She had a strategic mind, or so she had been told once. She figured she might as well use it.

'Just one moment,' she said and floated to the edge of the pool where she had spied a perfectly sized boulder. She gently tipped the large flat rock into the pool, then nudged it with her foot to where she had stood. She stepped up on to its flat surface.

Suddenly, everything had changed. She had made herself almost as tall as he was. Her delicious, succulent lips presented themselves at a much more convenient angle and as he began to kiss them he was able to appreciate more fully their lush abundance.

Her buttocks—bless them—were also much more conveniently placed. He slid his arms around her waist and was able to easily caress their entirety.

'Atia, you are a genius,' he said, marvelling at her successful experiment.

But the experiment had apparently only just begun. She moved closer, stood on her toes, then gently pressed her womanhood against the tip of his desire.

Did she understand the consequences of such an action? Clearly not, because she continued to kiss him as if nothing had changed. His mind split with the awareness of how close he was to joining with her.

Just one night, he told himself. *Make it last.* But his body was no longer obeying his commands. It was doing only what it wanted. He moved himself beneath her folds and pressed against her soft, warm skin. He found her entrance with the tip of himself. Sensation sparked through him, disintegrating quickly into arrow-sharp angst. He felt wild and unfulfilled. He wanted her so badly.

'Does that feel good?' she asked in innocence.

She was like Artemis landing her first arrow

and asking if it hurt. Clearly she had no notion of the power she wielded.

'It feels too good, my love.' Too cursedly good. It was not just the storm of sensation she conjured, not merely the mind-bending combination of lips and hips and skin. It was the way she was moving against him. The slow, subtle purpose. It was the confidence she seemed to be acquiring with each passing moment. She took his lower lip into her mouth and sucked it.

By all the gods in all the heavens, he wanted her. He could not wait any longer. He pushed himself into her and heard her gasp.

Bliss. Sweet, otherworldly bliss. Sensations that she had only ever dreamed of rollicked through her body.

He gripped her back and pushed into her again. Another onslaught of feeling. An invasion of ecstasy that she made no effort to fight. She had never surrendered herself in this way to a man and in doing it the whole weight of her existence seemed to lift.

'You are mine,' he whispered, thrusting into her again. She felt his breath along the curve over her neck. His nose traced a slow path upwards and she sensed him breathing her in.

Her skin seemed to catch fire and her bones felt as if they were melting beneath his grip. She felt his lips behind her ear. Kissing. Sucking. Biting. Pain that was also pleasure. What a wonder it was. Her head fell backwards and she moaned as he moved his mouth over her ear and took her earlobe in his teeth.

He pushed into her as he did this, conjuring a perfect storm of pleasure inside her. She was caught in its howling winds, its pounding sands, its exquisite chaos of desire. 'Yes, Rab,' she gasped.

This was unlike any joining she had ever known. In place of numbness, she felt sensation. In place of dread, she felt yearning. In place of a desire for it to end, she wanted it to last for ever.

She dug her fingers into his back. 'Yes!' she called and heard him groan in response. They had reached the storm's eye. They were falling through it together, weightless, their bodies joined, their eyes staring up at the starry sky.

The pure, mind-bending pleasure. Their bodies pulsed together with a closeness that seemed to transcend the flesh. He collapsed on to her shoulder and emitted a long sigh.

She closed her eyes and basked in his closeness. When he lifted himself off her she did what she had never allowed herself to do: she laid her head on his chest.

It was as if she had been drugged—as if instead of poppy tears she had drunk a dozen drops of him. But in place of numbness, she felt its opposite. Awareness. Ecstasy. Love. She had never felt more alive in all her life.

She supposed that she could die now. If this was to be her last night in the world, then it had been worth it, after all. 'Rab, I love you,' she said.

How could he ever have guessed that in his disgrace he would find glory, in all the wrong he had witnessed and caused, that he would somehow learn what was right? That in his enemy he would discover the love of his life?

'Atia, I love you, too,' he said. He squeezed her tightly in his arms. 'And I will love you for the rest of my days.'

It did not matter that that these were their last moments together, that after tomorrow, he would likely live out the rest of his life with only the memory of her. There would never be a woman whom he admired more, who had inspired him more, whom he loved more. There would never be anyone but Atia.

'Rab, you are crying,' she said.

'Am I?' he said, smiling. 'It must be the moonlight.'

'It hurts your eyes?'

'No, it illuminates your beauty. It moves me to tears.'

She smiled and shook her head. 'Flatterer.'

'Wrap your legs around my waist.'

She flashed a mischievous grin and did his bidding. For a moment he felt as if he was rising inside her again already. 'You are an enchantress,' he said, carrying her to the bank. He laid her down atop his own robe and gazed at her naked form.

'You are like Venus lying there,' he said.

She grinned playfully. 'You mean the Nabataean Venus, I hope. What is her name?'

'Uzza. But I am afraid you will have to remain Venus, for Nabataean gods do not have a physical form.'

'Is that true?'

'I speak only the truth to the woman I love.'

'Then tell me the truth. How can we see each other again?' she asked.

He felt a wave of despair. 'If you are to be married, then I cannot stand in the way.'

Could he? Would he really just sit back and do nothing as she was sent to her next loveless marriage? Would he really be content never to see her again?

He watched her gaze at the stars, though she did not seem to be seeing them. There was pain in the lines around her mouth and the glow had drained from her cheeks. It seemed as though he was already losing her—the woman who had conquered his mind and annexed his soul. The goddess who had swept into his life and showed him the real meaning of it: not glory or revenge, but love.

He pulled his *ghutrah* from the shore and retrieved her scarf from beneath her tunic. 'Atia, can I ask you a question?'

Chapter Twenty-One

❧

When she awoke the next morning, she was lying on her bed mat, staring up at the clear blue sky, a mysterious question echoing in her mind.

She laboured to gather her wits, wondering if she had expired, after all. Sandstone cliffs surrounded her and she could feel a layer of fine dust settled on her cheeks. If this was the realm of departed souls, then it was remarkably similar to the wilds of Arabia.

She breathed in the air with suspicion. It smelled sweeter than usual and the sky's blue was more vivid somehow, as if the gods themselves had added another coat of paint. She perceived a soft buzzing of a bee somewhere close. It seemed as if she could feel the very wind created by its wings.

She adjusted her position on the bed mat, heedless of the hard ground. Most mornings she woke up groaning, her hips bruised, her limbs crushed.

Now it was as if she were floating above the mat entirely. Her body did not ache—it purred—and a strange happiness wrapped around her heart.

Beads of hot sweat tickled her skin. She reached to wipe her brow, only to discover a cloth wrapped around her hand.

Beneath it, she felt the dull throb of a wound. She closed her eyes and visions of the night before flooded back in. His words—so thoughtful and tender. A question uttered with heart-melting sincerity. His love offered to her on a silver tray.

'Yes,' she had answered.

Then—a dagger. He had yanked it from its sheath. 'A Nabataean tradition,' he had explained and sliced a single stroke across her hand. He had scored his own hand quickly after and they had pressed the wounds together in a silent bond.

'Atia, I am yours,' he had said. 'Forever.'

She could still hear the soft ripping noise of his *ghutrah* as he split it in two, could still imagine his gentle movements as he bandaged her wound with the resulting strip.

She had reached for her shawl and had done the same to his wound, splitting the garment in two and tying one of the resulting strips around his hand.

She gazed at her bandaged hand now. No, she was not dead. She was married.

A leather slipper stepped into her view. Her heart leapt. 'Rab?'

'Good morning, my love.' He squatted low. 'You can call me Husband if you like.' She sat up and gazed into his eyes and felt a rush of love so powerful it nearly sent her back on to her bed mat.

'Good morning, Husband,' she said, trying out the word. It felt something like singing a song. 'Is this a dream?'

'It is my dream,' he said, offering her his hand.

Then it is mine, too, she thought, and took it, letting him pull her to her feet.

Nearby, Gamilath and Livius were preparing breakfast. Just beyond them, Yamlik was adjusting the saddle of his camel.

'But how did we get back to camp?' she asked.

'I carried you, of course,' he said. 'You were fast asleep.'

'But it was so far, Rab!' She pictured him walking for what must have been hours, her heavy body limp in his arms. 'Rab, yesterday... I was supposed to die. It was written in the stars.'

'No wonder you looked so alarmed when I pulled out my dagger!'

She smiled scoldingly. 'It is no jest. I felt certain that yesterday was to be the last day of my life.'

Perhaps it had been, in a sense. Of her old life.

He placed a strand of her hair behind her ear. 'You have no idea how happy I am that it was not.'

She gazed at him with new eyes. This strong, brave, wondrous man was now her husband? How could it be? She had never expected this, had never even dared to dream it. It seemed that she had not died, but instead had somehow been re-born.

'What now, Rab?' she asked. 'If I am betrothed to the Legate—'

'We will find a way,' said Rab. He cradled her hand in his. 'I can be patient.'

'The Legate will jail you if he discovers it.' She did not even want to voice the other possibility.

'Then we will find a way out of jail.'

'And in the meantime I will bring you tea and honey cakes?'

'Precisely—you can hand them through the bars. Only you must promise not to drug me without my consent.'

'I promise,' said Atia. She tried to laugh, but instead unexpected tears pooled in her eyes. 'And now that I am alive, you must promise to stay that way also.'

Gamilath called everyone to breakfast and was handing Atia a round of bread when she caught sight of Atia's hand wrap. She froze, then glanced at Rab's hand in turn. Atia could see her expression change as she recognised the signs of the Nabataean marriage ritual.

'You are married?' Gamilath asked. Atia gave a shy grin. 'Congratulations!' Gamilath exclaimed, embracing Atia.

Livius nodded knowingly. 'Did I not say I have a nose for such matters?' He embraced Atia in turn and then the three were joined by Yamlik, who bowed to Atia, then Rab. 'Fortuna favours you, Brother.'

'I know, Brother,' said Rab. 'I know.'

Atia's grin lasted all morning. Neither the burning sun, nor the treacherous hills, nor her growing anxiety could vanquish it. It was not until they descended into the Wadi of Moses that the grin became a grimace. 'What is that horrible smell?' she asked Gamilath.

But she only needed to look more closely for the answer. It was camels. Thousands of them. They languished within a massive courtyard surrounded by rooms. 'It is the *caravanserai* outside Rekem,' said Gamilath. 'The sixtieth caravan lodge on the route. There are five more between Rekem and the sea.'

Atia could not stop staring. So many camels! Some stood naked and unburdened, their tall humps mimicking the nearby hills. But many still bore the heavy squarish loads that they had ferried across the Arabian desert.

'Frankincense,' Atia uttered. Bags and bags of it. More frankincense than could have been burned in all the sacred temples from Thebes to Londinium. Not surprisingly, armed men patrolled the area. They walked softly among the camels, their bronze sheaths swinging.

Atia considered the value of this dusty camp. If the profit on a single camel load of frankincense was worth six hundred *denarii*—the equivalent of two Roman soldiers' salaries for a year—then the camels carried what amounted to the price of legions on their backs.

Though the camels themselves did not know it. They were snorting and groaning beneath clouds of flies, their hooves stirring up dust. Atia had never seen such a confluence of beasts and burdens in all her life.

'Why do they not enter the city?' she asked.

'Rekem is holy ground,' explained Rab. 'Before the Romans came, the only camels allowed in the city were those bearing offerings for the Great Temple. Now the only camels allowed are those bearing the Roman tax payments.'

Rab gestured to a group of Roman soldiers making their way through the crowded space. 'Those are the tax assessors,' growled Rab. 'They calculate the value of each load and send twenty per cent to the Legate's offices inside the city.' Rab spat angrily upon the ground. 'Before the Romans came, there were double this number of camels.'

Their group took a sharp turn and Atia craned behind herself for one last glance at the sprawling caravanserai. And it was as if instead of walking away from the camels, the camels themselves were receding, as if time itself were leaving them behind, until all she could see was a blur of colours behind a layer of hot, wavering air. And then even that disappeared and their mighty groans faded.

The air was still as they made their way steadily down the *wadi* leading to Rekem's entrance. Massive geometrical rock formations began to appear alongside their route—towering house-sized squares that looked like the building blocks of giants.

'These are Dushara blocks,' Gamilath explained. 'Tombs carved in homage to our faceless god.'

Atia could hardly take her eyes off the eerie house-sized monuments. Their angles were perfectly square, as if fashioned by a divine hand.

They rounded a bend and Atia's breath caught in her throat. 'Can we stop the camels?' she choked. Yamlik stopped their small caravan and Atia gazed up at a towering edifice unlike any she had ever seen. Instead of resting on a base of rock, this splendid temple had been carved into the rock itself.

The bottom portion of the structure looked much like a Greek temple, while the top looked entirely Egyptian—complete with towering obelisks.

Obelisks! The sacred spiked pillars seemed perfectly at home above the Grecian columns, as if the two cultures often merged in such ways.

Atia had heard about such stone-carved monuments all her life, yet she still could hardly believe her eyes. It was one of the most wondrous things she had ever seen. An architectural chimera. Beautiful and strange.

Rab wore a delighted smirk. 'My father was just a boy when that monument was carved. But come, we have not yet even entered the city,' he said.

They continued down the *wadi* until they arrived at a natural cleft between two massive rock formations—like a gateway to another world. Donkey carts and pedestrians were moving in and out of the massive slot as if it were the most natural thing in the world.

'This is Bab al Siq, the gateway to Rekem,' said Yamlik. 'The camels are allowed no further.'

The travellers dismounted and said their goodbyes. As Gamilath and Livius embraced, Livius whispered something into Gamilath's ear. Gamilath was shaking her head as she tied Livius's camel behind her own. 'I did not hear that,' she said and gave him one last, long look before turning away.

Livius was wiping his eyes. 'So much dust in this damned desert,' he said.

'We will find a way to get you back to her,' Atia said.

Livius pasted on a grin. 'I am afraid I have five more years left of soldiering to do before I can even think of such a thing,' he said. 'I told her not to wait for me.'

'We will find a way,' vowed Atia, though she could hear the resignation in her voice. To leave the Roman army before the end of twenty years was like disobeying the Governor of Arabia: one simply did not do it.

Atia gazed at her wrapped palm. 'We must remove these now, Husband,' she told Rab, 'lest we tie our own nooses.'

They had just removed the wraps and tucked them away when she heard a familiar voice. 'Friends!'

Her breath caught in her throat. She turned and there he was, marching towards them in full armour: the demon himself.

'Plotius,' she said. Behind him marched six

soldiers. *Only six?* Atia wondered. Had there not been ten when they parted?

'We have been waiting for you for days,' Plotius said. 'I was beginning to think you had perished in the desert.' He removed his crested helmet and flashed a wicked grin. 'Imagine my relief when you came lumbering into camp on those ridiculous camels.'

'Well met, Plotius,' said Atia as she attempted to conceal her shock. Against the odds, Plotius had made it to Rekem. But how had he done it? She glanced at his hip belt and saw the answer to her question, for attached to it was the box that had likely contained her dowry. It appeared that he had bought his way to Rekem, just as he had vowed he would. *Let him explain that to the Legate*, she thought.

'I did not expect to see you here, Plotius,' she said.

'You did not expect it or you did not wish it?' Plotius gave Rab a glance.

'Where are the other soldiers? I count only six here.'

'They died with honour,' said Plotius.

Atia's heart squeezed. 'How?' She closed her eyes, not wanting to hear the answer.

'We found the rebel camp and attacked them at night. Killed at least fifty of the dirty Arabs.' Plotius clapped one of his soldiers on the back and laughed. 'We got our revenge, did we not, Soldier?'

'Yes, Commander,' the young man said.

Atia felt ill. For the first time in weeks, she craved the tears. She closed her eyes and let the craving transform into anger. 'You killed fifty rebels and lost four of your own men and you are *laughing*?'

'I am laughing in triumph, stupid woman. There is nothing more honourable than to die for Rome.'

'You are a savage,' she said and spat upon the ground.

Now he was laughing even harder. 'You are going to regret that, Atia,' he said. He took her roughly by the arm. 'Now come. I promised your father that I would deliver you to the Legate and that is what I intend to do.'

'Unhand me,' said Atia, yanking herself free. Rab stepped between them.

'If you dare touch her again, Plotius, I will rip off your arm,' he said. The two men stood eye to eye. Atia saw Plotius reach for his sword.

'Stop!' Atia shouted, pushing between them. 'There will be no more violence! We will enter the sacred city and fulfil our mission, then go our separate ways.'

'I would not count on parting ways so soon,' said Plotius. He gave Atia a significant look, then stepped backwards and bowed. 'After you, my Queen.'

Atia's vision grew blurry with anger. 'I am not your Queen,' she said and set off down the Siq at a near run.

It wasn't until she was well down the limestone road that she noticed her surroundings. She peered up at the massive stone blocks on either side of her and felt a rush of awe.

Where on earth was she?

This was more than just a slot canyon, she realised. It was a towering temple, a miraculous confluence of time and stone.

And it was cool. She slowed her pace and marvelled at the perennial shade created by the towering monoliths on either side of her. Birds danced between them, their black wings evanescent shadows against the ancient browns and pinks.

'Praise Dushara,' said a man in Nabataean. A small group was huddling around an unfinished rectangular carving in the rock. She peered over the men's shoulders and caught sight of a recently sacrificed goat.

The men were dipping their fingers into the animal's blood and splattering it on to the blank façade. The stone was not unfinished, Atia realised. It was perfectly complete. While the Nabataeans personified the gods of other cultures, they rarely depicted their own. The men were simply praying to their faceless god.

'Praise Dushara,' she echoed. She perceived the soft trickle of water somewhere near. The sound was so subtle and peaceful—as if the water was flowing through the rock itself.

And so it was, for two small channels appeared to have been carved into either side of the cliffs. The miniature canals flowed along at eye level and when Atia peered down into one she beheld a miracle: pure, clear water. She crossed the road and peered into the other channel and beheld a clay pipe. *Drinking water*, she thought—just like the pipes that served the finest *domas* in Rome.

Atia had scoffed when Rab had told her that the Nabataeans 'cultivated' water, but now she was beginning to understand what he meant. She imagined a giant cistern high in the hills where the water 'farmers' collected their crop of rain.

They rounded a corner and came to the end of the Siq and several of the soldiers gasped. Atia stopped in her tracks. Rising before them was a monument so magnificent that Atia could hardly believe it to be real. Glowing in bright yellows, reds, and blues, the plastered, painted, columned façade seemed to decorate the desert with glory.

Statues posed at each of its two levels: visions of fearsome Amazons, winged Victories, Greek gods and a cornucopia-bearing goddess that defied definition. They all presided over the towering columned hall, which seemed to Atia to be the most beautiful monument in all the world: Queen Chuldu's Tomb.

Rab came up beside her and she had to fight the powerful desire to take his hand.

'That is the tomb my grandfather built for my grandmother,' he said under his breath. 'He loved her very much.'

Plotius pushed past Rab, bumping him out of the way and taking a position beside Atia. 'There will be plenty of time to gaze upon the tombs later,' he said and she wondered what he could possibly mean.

She could not dwell on the question, for as they continued deeper into the city there was simply too much to see. There were tombs everywhere, each with a more elaborate façade than the last. There were hundreds of them. Big ones and little ones. Plain and colourful, spare and ornate. There seemed to be no stone surface left untouched by the holy monuments.

Atia gazed and gawked. The city itself seemed to be a kind of temple, a grand celebration of those who once were. Atia stared up at a terrace area where a cluster of especially elaborate façades loomed. She caught Rab's stare. *Behold the wonder and the glory of Rekem*, he seemed to say. *Do you understand now why I cannot let it go?*

They followed the sacred way ever downwards past a massive Roman-style theatre with benches carved directly into the rock.

Just beyond the theatre a host of bare-chested workers were standing on a high wooden platform supported by poles that had been burrowed into the rock. They were chiselling away at a half-completed façade.

'So that is how they do it,' remarked Atia.

'From the top to bottom,' said Rab. 'They move their scaffolding downwards until a pile of rubble forms beneath them, then they stand on the pile.'

'Where are the slaves?' asked Plotius.

'Nabataeans do not keep slaves,' stated Rab.

'But there are many tribes that inhabit the Nabataean backcountry, are there not? The Thamuds, the Safaites, the Lhyanites. One would think—'

'The Nabataeans are not invaders, nor are we enslavers,' interrupted Rab. 'Not like you Romans. We are traders. We labour beneath the same sky as everyone else and we are all equal before the gods.'

Plotius scowled, but Atia felt her spirit swell. Was this what it felt like to be proud of one's husband?

'You seem happy, Atia,' said Plotius. 'Does the city of stone please you?'

'More than I ever could have imagined,' she said, catching the glint of Rab's eye in the sunlight.

Slowly the high cliffs subsided and the tombs gave way to a sloping area full of houses, shops, and—incredibly—trees. Date palms and figs and verdant acacias lined a canal running parallel with the street, their roots suckling at the remarkable, unbelievable gift: water in the desert.

They crossed beneath an arch and Atia had to blink as she beheld another miracle: a park. A lush, green park with mature shade trees and stretches of grass. There were meandering pathways, lovely pergolas and benches that seemed meant for lovers.

At the centre of the expanse was a large blue pool with an elegant pavilion at its centre. The artificial island was connected to the shore by several flat footbridges that appeared to float atop the placid waters. Atia spied a group of giggling children running across one of the bridges.

The Nabataeans are geniuses, she thought.

She glanced at Rab, but his attention was consumed by the building adjacent to the park. The massive marble columns and wide entryway of the giant structure told Atia that it could be none other than the Nabataean royal palace.

Or the old royal palace, as it seemed. Now men

in Roman togas were ascending its high stairs and Roman soldiers stood sentinel at its entrance.

Plotious led their group up the stairs and into a sprawling open-air reception hall flanked by a massive triple colonnade—the largest Atia had ever seen. Atia stopped to admire the sheer grandeur of the space, which rivalled anything she had seen in Rome.

'In my father's time, this part of the palace was an *agora*,' whispered Rab as Atia passed by him and Atia caught the wistfulness in his voice. 'During the day, merchants sold their wares in the cool of the shade here and at night it would be transformed for royal banquets.'

Atia tried to imagine the space filled with torches and revellers instead of Roman soldiers. It was a difficult vision to conjure, for it seemed that the legion had made the old palace the centre of its activities. There were soldiers everywhere. They buzzed about like flies, some cleaning their armour, others jousting with swords and others absorbed in more quotidian tasks: cutting hair and mending tunics and even playing dice.

But as their group journeyed across the great hall, Atia paid no mind to the throngs of soldiers, for her attention was riveted by the columns sustaining the colonnade. It was neither the columns' size nor their elegance that captured her eye, but the massive stone heads adorning their capitals, their wrinkled trunks bending gracefully into themselves. Elephants.

A realisation struck her.

Chapter Twenty-Two

The elephant heads mocked him from above—proud and strange. He had not been inside the palace since that terrible night thirteen years before and had almost forgotten about his father's stone elephants, constructed early in his reign.

Rab paused beneath one of the columns, fighting his emotion.

'Rab, I must tell you something about the elephants,' said Atia. 'I have had a revelation. I—'

Plotius stepped between them. 'What must you tell him about the elephants?' he asked.

Atia tensed. Rab could see her mind working. 'That they are…they are Indian elephants and not African,' said Atia.

'And how do you know this?' asked Plotius.

'Their skin is wrinkled,' replied Atia. 'And just look at the size of their ears.'

Plotius was distracted long enough for Rab to toss his quick-witted wife a wink.

'Why does it matter what kind of elephants they are?' asked Plotius. 'You are trying to delay. Come.'

Plotius motioned to the soldiers and they climbed another set of stairs and set out across the threshold that had once been Rab's father's throne room. On the dais where his father's throne used to be, a giant bust of the Emperor Hadrian loomed.

They passed the small Greek theatre where his father used to meet with the popular assembly and stepped past the temple where his father used to make offerings to Dushara. Rab spied a statue of Jupiter where the stone block for Dushara used to be and felt a pang in his heart.

Behind the temple lay a series of rooms in which his family used to dwell. Now they were occupied by Romans and Nabataeans sitting in client chairs fanning the hot air.

'Wait here,' said their escort and he entered Rab's old bedroom. When he re-emerged, he motioned to Plotius. 'Legate Julianus will see you now.'

Their entourage filed into the room as their escort announced them. 'Honourable Commander, these travellers have been sent by Governor Severus himself. They bear an urgent message for you.'

A stocky, sharp-eyed man a little older than

Rab stood up from behind a large desk and bowed to the visitors. Seeing Plotius's face, he quirked a brow. 'Well met, Plotius,' he said. 'It has been a while.'

'Indeed it has,' said Plotius, moving around to grip the Legate's arm. The two men exchanged a meaningful look, though Rab could not discern if they were friends or foes.

'Please, sit,' said the Legate, gesturing to a group of client chairs in front of his desk. As Plotius, Atia and Rab took their seats, Rab noticed a beautiful sober-faced Nabataean woman standing behind the Legate. She slid Rab a glance.

'This is my translator, Shaquilath,' said the Legate, motioning to the woman. 'And behind you are my guards, Rufus and Gaius.' Rab glanced at two large scowling guards standing against the adjacent wall. They hovered just behind Plotius's own guards, who had formed a kind of phalanx behind the chairs. The Legate sat back, apparently at his ease. 'Now tell me, with whom do I have the pleasure of speaking?'

As Plotius opened his mouth to speak, Atia was already introducing herself. 'I am Atia Severus, daughter of Governor Severus, and this is Rabbel, son of Junon, our guide. We come to you with a letter from my father.' Wasting no time, she reached into her rucksack and passed the sealed letter across the desk.

The Legate unsealed the letter and scanned it. Rab looked down to find Atia gripping the arms of her chair. The Legate gave Rab a long, scrutinising look and drew a breath. 'I believe I shall read this aloud, since it relates to all three of you.'

In the days that followed, whenever Rab thought back on that moment, he cursed himself for not having seen the sign. It was in the Legate's eyes when he looked at Rab: an unusual pity, as if he were looking at a dead man.

'"Dear Commander Julianus",' Julianus began. '"If you are reading this scroll then my daughter stands before you, along with two escorts: a Nabataean man who calls himself Rab Junon and my own tribune, Plotius Gnaeus Longinus."'

The Legate glanced at Rab, cleared his throat, then continued.

'"The Nabataean man is not who he says he is. His true name is Tainu Obodas Rabbel the Third. He is the oldest living heir to the Nabataean throne and also the leader of the Nabataean resistance. I command you to execute him swiftly and discreetly at your earliest convenience."'

Rab choked, then coughed. The world began to spin and his vision blurred.

Beside him, he heard Atia shout, 'No!' She moved to stand, but two soldiers stepped forward and held her down.

Then all Rab could see was Atia. She was

no longer seated beside him, however. She was standing beside a blue pool, reaching out to him. She was getting smaller and smaller, fading away into a blur of dust. 'No!' she shouted, over and over again, but her voice was growing weak, replaced in Rab's mind with Plotius's mocking laughter.

When Rab's wits finally returned, Plotius was laughing still and Atia was convulsing with sobs.

The Legate had resumed his reading. '"My daughter's second companion is Plotius, my finest tribune. I have sent him to you so that you will make him your second in command. You will find no better ally in defeating the rebels than Plotius. His loyalty lies with Rome and Rome alone."'

The Legate looked up again from the scroll. He turned to his translator, who closed her eyes for what seemed an unusual amount of time.

The Legate nodded, then returned his eyes to the papyrus. '"In addition, I command you to preside over the marriage of my daughter to Plotius."'

'What?' said Atia. Plotius's face split with a grin. Atia was shaking her head so vigorously that her hair fanned the air.

But Rab did not feel the wind, because he was sinking. Deep down into his chair, which opened into a fissure in the floor into which he travelled until he found himself in the realm of lost souls.

Atia. His wife. The only woman he had ever truly loved was to be given over to a man who would use and discard her as he would a stolen sheep. And Rab, in all his physical strength and skill, could do nothing to stop him.

For Rab himself had just been condemned to die.

He felt the squeeze of hands on his shoulders. They held him down, pinned him to his seat. He was breathing too hard. He feared his heart might explode. *Swiftly and discreetly at your earliest convenience.*

The Legate was speaking again. "'Plotius carries my daughter's dowry with him and will provide you with the sum of five thousand *denarii*, representing his first year's salary, along with a small gift to you as a token of my gratitude. A wedding feast is not necessary. My daughter, as you can see, would only be embarrassed by such a display.'"

Rab saw Atia's eyes touch the floor, and in that instant he understood why it had been so difficult for her to believe in her beauty.

"'One last command as relates to Atia,'" continued the Legate, his eyes nearly at the bottom of the scroll. "'I am assuming you have received this scroll with its seal unbroken. If it was broken, however, I order you to flog my daughter for disloyalty. Ten lashes will suffice.'"

Atia's expression was unflinching, as if she was threatened with such punishments all the time.

The Legate took a long breath. '"In sum, you will kill the Nabataean rebel leader, marry my daughter to Plotius and place Plotius beneath your command. Do all these things quietly and with haste. Consider them a test of loyalty. I will pay a visit to Rekem as soon as I am able." Signed Legatus Augusti Pro Praetore Magnus Atius Severus.'

The Legate did not even look up as he issued his command. 'Take the Nabataean to the holding cells.'

The arms that held Rab down yanked him up and dragged him towards the door. Rab heard a shriek, but it had not come from Atia. He turned to see Livius's enraged figure lunging towards the guards. 'Unhand him!' Livius shouted. He was waving his dagger like a madman. 'He is my friend!'

'Take him, too!' commanded the Legate. A guard kicked the dagger from Livius's hand and seized him.

Now both Rab and Livius were being dragged out the door.

Rab strained to look behind him. *Just let me*

see her one last time, he thought. A single kick to his backside told him he would not even be granted that one small wish.

In the past, Atia might have carefully swallowed her tears. She might have stared at her own toes and wondered why they were so crooked. She might have smiled and said she felt a little ill and could she please be excused so she might attend to her delicate constitution?

Not any more.

'Legate, you are making a mistake,' she told Julianus.

The Legate raised a brow. 'Is that man not the rebel leader?'

'He…he was the rebel leader. He has vowed to cease his activities.'

'Cease his activities?' said Plotius with a scoff. 'He led four dozen rebels to our camp at the Bitumen Lake.'

'Rab knew nothing about the rebels,' protested Atia. 'We all would have died that day had he not called them off us!'

Julianus frowned. 'How many lost?' he asked Plotius.

'Of the Romans, eighteen men, Commander,' said Plotius. 'But we got our revenge. We tracked the little Arab bastards to their encampment. Slaughtered fifty of them in their sleep.'

The Legate glanced briefly at the Nabataean woman whom he had introduced as his translator. It was unusual for a Roman man to employ a woman in any official capacity and the woman's disapproving expression gave Atia a reason to hope.

'My father is mistaken in ordering Rab's death,' Atia said. 'Rab saved our lives. He has also vowed to disband the rebel army.' *Once I convince him to do so, that is.*

Plotius scowled at Atia. 'Rab is a murderer and a traitor to Rome. As my future wife I command you not to speak of him again.' Plotius turned to Julianus and the tone of his voice changed. 'When I serve beneath you, Commander, you can be assured that I will work tirelessly to eliminate all of the remaining rebels. I will hunt them down and slaughter them in their sleep.'

The Nabataean woman sucked in a breath. The Legate was shaking his head.

'I fear I cannot make you my second in command, Plotius,' he said.

'Excuse me?'

'I do not feel that you are qualified at this time to take on the position. As for the rebel leader, he will remain in my custody until I am able to discuss the matter with the Governor himself.'

Atia nearly burst into tears. 'Bless you, Legate,' she breathed. She buried her head in her

hands and tried to calm herself. *He will remain...*
She heard the phrase over and over again in
her mind. She had just been granted the gift of
time—time enough, she prayed, to get Rab and
Livius free.

The fires of rage burned in Plotius's eyes. 'The
Governor himself has ordered my promotion,' he
hissed. 'You read it yourself!'

'And yet as the Legate it is my right to choose
whom I place in my confidence. I will take the
matter up with the Governor when he arrives.
In the meantime you may stay with the legion
here in Rekem, or you may return to Bostra. It
is your choice.'

'You are making a mistake, Commander,' Plotius growled.

'Perhaps I am, but that is between me, the Governor and the Emperor.'

Plotius's face had taken on the exact colour of
the inside of a fig. 'And my marriage to the Governor's daughter?'

'Because that appears to be contingent upon
your position in the legion, I am afraid I cannot
allow it. We must wait until I can confer with
the Governor.'

Plotius stood. Something in his eyes had
changed. They were no longer burning. On the
contrary, they appeared frozen and black. Dead,
almost. 'But the dowry,' he was saying. 'The

coin.' He unclipped the box from his hip belt. 'Do you not wish to receive the Governor's gift?'

Plotius was rounding the corner of the Legate's desk. He was unhinging the box. 'No!' shouted Atia. He was pulling something from the box. A dagger. Atia lunged across the desk.

Chapter Twenty-Three

'Go to Hades,' said Rab. He stared at the disgusting wad of spit that had just landed in his cell. He did not need to look up to know who had hurled it.

'I am afraid I have already arrived in Hades, my friend,' said an unmistakable voice. Rab peered through the bared opening in the door of his cell and saw guards pushing Plotius into the cell next door.

'Then may you drown in the River of Woe,' said Rab.

'I would welcome any river at all,' Plotius said. 'It is too damned hot in here.'

'When we are dead we will not know it,' called Livius from the cell next to Plotius.

Rab returned to his small cot and lay back, trying to make sense of it all. Had Plotius's execution been ordered, too? And how could Rab ever repay Livius for trying to help him as he had done?

'I had my suspicions about your link to the rebels,' called Plotius from next door. 'But heir to the Nabataean throne? That was unexpected.'

'You claim ignorance of the Governor's order to execute me?' asked Rab.

'I admit that I did not know, though I suppose he kept it from me to prevent me from killing you directly.'

'You are a monster,' said Rab.

'No more than you,' said Plotius.

'I am better than you.'

'If you are so much better, then why do you command your rebels to attack Romans?'

'The rebels do not attack, we defend,' said Rab. 'This is our land. It does not belong to Rome.'

'You should have told that to your father,' said Plotius. Rab stayed silent. He *had* told that to his father. His father simply had not listened.

Plotius yawned. 'You know that if the Nabataeans had fought the invading Romans, they would have lost,' he said.

'That is not necessarily true,' said Rab.

'Go ahead and live out the rest of your days in a dream world,' said Plotius. 'You are the one who is doomed.'

'And you are not?'

'Of course not. When the Governor comes, he will set things right. Then it will be Atia inside this cell and not me.'

'Atia?'

'She will have to face the consequences of what she did.'

'And what was that?'

'She saved the Legate from the sting of my blade,' said Plotius.

'She *what*?' called Livius from down the hall.

'She jumped in front of the stupid man before I could put the dagger in its proper place.'

'And where was that?' asked Livius.

'In his gut, Livius,' growled Plotius. 'Where the Governor ordered it to be thrust if the Legate did not do as he was told. I am a soldier just like you—only I follow my cursed orders.'

Rab imagined Atia jumping to the Legate's aid while Plotius approached with his dagger drawn. By the gods, she was brave. 'Is she injured?' asked Rab.

'How should I know?'

Please, Great Dushara, let her be uninjured.

'When the Governor comes, everything will be put right,' Plotius was repeating. 'I followed his orders exactly and he will reward me for it.'

Rab closed his eyes. *When the Governor comes*, he thought. By that time, Rab would already be dead.

* * *

Atia opened her eyes and wondered if she was alive. The morbid puzzlement felt familiar, as if she had experienced it several times before. As if it was becoming something of a habit.

She did not dare attempt a breath, though her wits were returning rapidly. She had recovered enough of them to wonder if she had not misunderstood the day of her own death. Perhaps it was not yesterday, but today. Though she really had no way of knowing what day it was at all.

She spied a woman floating above her. Thank the gods—she was not alone. The woman's long, curly tresses cascaded down her stately shoulders like vines, and an elegant white robe flowed all around her. Perhaps she was not a woman, but the goddess herself: 'Juno?'

'Not Juno,' said the woman. 'Shaquilath.'

'Shaquilath,' Atia said. Such a grand name, as if it could contain the hope of the world. 'The Legate's translator?'

'The very same,' Shaquilath said. 'I have been caring for you for the past two days.'

'Two days? Where is Rab?'

Shaquilath frowned and placed her hand on Atia's head. 'No fever so far. It is a good sign.'

'Where is he?' A lightning bolt of pain shot through Atia's arm. 'Where?'

'He lives.'

At last Atia took a breath, then slumped on the mattress. Everything came back to her at once. How Rab had been condemned to die and been seized by the guards along with brave, foolish Livius. How Atia had lunged forward just as Plotius had thrust his knife towards the Legate's belly. How the blade had sliced cleanly through the flesh of her upper arm, then penetrated into her very chest.

'May I see him?' Atia asked softly. She convulsed with a cough, then cringed.

'You are in no shape to go anywhere, I am afraid,' said Shaquilath. 'My husband has forbidden it.'

'Your husband?'

Shaquilath held up her hand and opened her fist, and Atia beheld a small diagonal cut in the middle of Shaquilath's palm. It took Atia several moments to apprehend its meaning: Shaquilath was married to the Legate.

Shaquilath put her finger to her lips. 'Shhh,' she said.

'I will not tell a soul.'

'I know you will not,' she said, 'for I see you have had a similar injury.' Atia gazed into her own palm. The gash had almost completely healed. She traced her fingers along the small scab that remained and wondered if somewhere Rab was doing the same.

'The heart knows no borders,' Atia mused.

Shaquilath smiled. 'It gives me cause to hope. How long can Romans tax and rob and plunder the Nabataeans if they are also joining souls with them?' She poured Atia a cup of water. 'And yet it is that very joining that will ultimately destroy the memory of us.'

'As long as your great tombs stand, you will be remembered,' said Atia. She drained the glass.

'It seems that is our only hope,' said Shaquilath. She began to unwrap the cloth that had been tied around Atia's arm. 'Our beautiful memorials of death will be our eternal life.'

'Tell me, is Rab is safe?'

'Yes. He is safe and provided for in a large holding cell not far from here. As you know, my husband has vowed to take no action until your father arrives. After that I cannot say.'

'Gratitude,' said Atia, feeling bleak. She imagined the Legate trying to explain to her father why he had not followed orders. He would be fortunate to escape with his life. 'I will pray for your husband, then,' Atia said.

'Gratitude,' said Shaquilath. 'I will pray for him, too. He has good intentions for this province…and *all* of its residents.'

Atia thought of her father and felt bleaker still. Emperor Hadrian demanded money from the provinces and her father was committed to send-

ing that money at all costs. How could the Nabataeans generate the taxes Rome required without
continuing to impoverish regular Nabataeans?

If only they could strike gold somewhere in
the desert. Shaquilath lifted Atia's wrap and
slowly removed the bandage around her chest.
Atia gazed down at the wound. It was like a great
hole in the earth.

An idea came to her. 'Have you not heard of
the copper mines in Wadi Phaeno?' she asked
Shaquilath.

'I am sorry?'

'Rab told me that they generated great wealth
once.'

'I have heard of them…' said Shaquilath.

Atia could see Shaquilath's mind turning. She
applied an oily salve to Atia's wound and gently
pressed a dry cloth against it.

'I see what you are thinking,' Shaquilah said
at last. 'To reopen the copper mines and use the
profits to pay our taxes to Rome.'

'The traders would love you for it,' said Atia.
'And Rome would be none the wiser.'

'It is a brilliant idea,' said Shaquilath. She
wrapped a second cloth around Atia's arm and
tied it off. 'I will tell my husband. We owe you
a debt.'

'Not one that you have not already paid many

times over,' said Atia. 'But if you wish to help me, I ask for only one thing.'

'Anything that is in my power.'

Atia lowered her voice to a whisper. 'The key. He cannot do any good from a cell. And I promise you that he will do good.'

Shaquilath drew a breath, then nodded. 'It will take time.'

Atia glanced at her newly bandaged wound. 'Time, I have,' she said.

Shaquilath refilled Atia's cup of water and then retrieved a small bottle from a shelf. 'What is that?' Atia asked.

'Tears of poppy. They will help with the pain.'

'No, thank you,' Atia said. 'I would prefer to feel the pain.'

'Are you certain? Your recovery is only just beginning. I can just leave it here if you like—'

'No,' said Atia. 'No thank you, that is. Please take it with you. I am certain.' Shaquilath nodded gravely, seeming to understand. Atia closed her eyes and thought of a key hanging on a hook somewhere—a key that would soon be in her hand. And then she thought of Rab. Alive. There was no better medicine.

Rab awoke to the smell of rain. *Impossible*, he thought. Rains did not begin to fall on Rekem until October. Was it October already? Of course it was, for he had arrived in Rekem at the end of September and many days had passed since then. He had been loathe to count them, however, for each day he woke wondering whether it would be his last.

Rab lay on his cot listening to Plotius's soft whimpers, followed by his terrifying scream. Plotius was having another nightmare. He had them so often that Rab had begun to expect them, though it was Rab who should have been having them. Plotius would surely be set free soon, whereas Rab was a dead man.

After many moments, Rab heard the sounds of Plotius rising from his cot and making water in his bedpan. The commander gave a loud, anguished yawn. 'What news, Livius of Gaul?' he called from his cell.

'I have a new pimple on my backside,' called Livius, drawing Plotius's laughter.

'And what news from your side of prison, Rab, son of Junon?' Plotius asked.

'The air smells like rain,' Rab stated.

'Are you sure that is not my piss you are smelling?' Over the past twenty days, Plotius had softened, and the three had become uneasy neighbours.

'I smell it, too,' said Livius. 'Moisture in the air.'

'Rain in Rekem?' replied Plotius. 'Does that happen often?'

'Not often, but when it rains, it pours,' said Rab. He looked around his cell and felt a growing alarm. The stone walls had been cemented together in a haphazard fashion and Rab could pick out at least a dozen holes large enough for daylight to enter. Or water.

But that was not what really worried him. The problem with their cells was that they were located entirely under the ground. The three men had been imprisoned in what was essentially a cistern—a place where water would naturally collect. Rab studied the sandstone floor, which had been sealed over the years by the footsteps of its residents. He felt a chill.

'In the dream I had last night it was pouring rain,' remarked Plotius.

'And did that dream take place in Rekem?'

'No, it was in Hispania, in my childhood home.'

'I did not know you were from Hispania,' said Livius from his cell.

'The Baetica region. My father was a centurion for the legion based there. He was in the dream also—though in truth it was more like a memory. So was my mother and my older brother.'

'What were they doing?' asked Rab.

'Just the usual. My father was beating my older brother and my mother was trying to protect him. In the dream I was standing in the doorway, try-

ing to get their attention. Our donkey cart was in
danger of being washed away by the rain.'

Rab paused. 'Why was he beating your older
brother?'

'The same reason he always beat my older
brother—because he was not a real man. He refused to join the legion and do his duty to Rome.'

'I see,' said Rab.

'Anyway, in the dream the donkey cart got
swept away and I was running after it, screaming.'

'I was aware of the screaming part,' said Rab.
'So did your brother eventually join the legion?'

'No, unfortunately. My father beat him a little too hard one day and he failed to wake from
it. But he was not a real man. Real men fight,'
said Plotius.

Rab listened closely and thought he could hear
a small quiver at the edges of Plotius's voice. 'Of
course, I do not need to tell *you* that,' Plotius said.
'Rebel leader.'

Plotius had meant it as a kind of compliment,
but Rab could not take it as such—not while entertaining visions of a father beating his son to
death for refusing to be a killer. And yet in a
sense that was what Rab was doing with his rebel
army: raising up a generation of killers.

Rab heard the soft patter of rain upon the stone
ceiling. Just as he looked up, a drop landed on
his check. He moved to wipe it, as if it were a

tear, but another quickly took its place, and then another. And even though they were just small drops, he felt as if he were already drowning.

Chapter Twenty-Four

Twenty days. That was what Atia was thinking when the drops began to fall. She was sitting in the park's small rose garden, wondering at the sky. It had been twenty days since Rab had been locked away somewhere in Rekem and still Shaquilath had been unable to grant Atia's wish.

'Soon,' Shaquilath had reassured her. 'Be patient.' But how could Atia be patient when her beloved sat awaiting his own death? How could she explore the wondrous city when any moment her father could arrive and order that death delivered?

Twenty days. Enough time for the rainy season to arrive—or so it seemed. The drops fell on the roses' small leaves, making them tremble. Shaquilath had predicted the rain that morning, but it still seemed like a miracle to Atia's sun-dried mind. How many times had she dreamed of this moment—of feeling the caress of rain upon her cheeks?

'A hundred drops will fall or maybe even a thousand,' Shaquilath had said, 'but the gods will lose their will. The real rains do not arrive until January. I have never seen a street become a river in October.'

Atia had nearly choked on her honey cake. 'The streets turn to rivers here?'

'Rivers like great, terrifying dragons that can swallow you up. When the winter rains come to Rekem, the entire city moves to higher ground. But do not worry. The clouds gathering now do not make dragons. They make kittens.'

Atia looked up at the thunderclouds roiling in the sky above her. She was not so sure about the kittens. As if to confirm her suspicion, a fat, watery drop landed on her cheek. She lifted her arm to wipe it away and cringed with pain. She had passed twenty days in Shaqulath's tender care, yet it still hurt to move her injured arm.

Nor was her endurance even close to normal. She walked each day in the park, trying to build up her strength. But after only an hour of walking the injury in her side always began to throb and she had to stop to rest in this small rose garden.

She broke off a rose. Twenty days—and each day she moved a little closer to danger. When her father found out she had defended Rab and thwarted Plotius's mission, there was no telling what he would do.

She was just stepping out on to the main road when she saw one of the legion's guards bounding up the stairs of the old palace. 'Halt!' Atia shouted, hailing him from the street. 'What news?'

'It is the Governor of Arabia Petraea,' said the guard. 'He has arrived in Rekem. He is entering the Siq as we speak.'

Atiab braced herself against a nearby column. It was as if just by thinking about him she had conjured him into existence.

She thought about trying to run, though she could barely even walk. She considered trying to hide inside one of the tombs. There were hundreds of them to choose from, after all, and most were family tombs with empty burial slots.

Atia pictured herself curling up inside one of those small spaces in the rock and simply disappearing from the world. She could bring food and water and stay there for days. Months even.

But what about Rab?

How could she cower and hide while her own husband faced death? No. She could not sit still while a good man died. She had to be brave. She had to face her father.

Slowly, she began to walk towards the Siq. The rain was falling harder now. The canal alongside the street had begun to overflow and Atia felt her *stola* growing heavy with wetness.

Finally, she saw him. He was seated atop a horse in his travelling armour and short military tunic, and as he approached, she saw how his left leg bulged. 'Greetings, Father,' she called, waving. 'Welcome to Rekem.'

He stopped his horse and squinted down at her. Was it the rain, or did his face look very pale?

'Atia, hello,' he said. 'I did not expect such an enthusiastic greeting.'

She forced a smile. 'It is good to see you, Father. It appears you have brought the rain,' she said. She glanced behind him at what must have been a hundred soldiers. 'Along with a good chunk of the legion.'

'The business of Empire waits for no man,' he said, repeating his favourite phrase. He glanced at his leg, which appeared to have been padded with many layers of fabric. And in that moment she knew that her father's days were numbered.

She swallowed her emotion and turned to walk alongside his horse.

'I see that your arm has been injured,' her father said, almost as if he were happy about it.

'A minor wound,' she lied. 'It is almost healed.' She said nothing about his leg, but she noticed that every time the horse took an awkward step, he cringed.

'How was your journey?' Atia asked politely.

'Rather hot,' he said, 'though I expect not as hot as yours was.'

'I expect not.'

They walked along in silence. The rain poured down. As they passed the residential area, Atia noticed many people bearing rucksacks full of what appeared to be household goods. They were walking uphill, heading for higher ground.

Meanwhile Atia and her father continued downhill until they reached the steps of the palace. Several guards clustered around her father's horse and helped him down from it. He put his arms around the men's shoulders and leaned on them heavily as they helped him up the stairs.

Atia tried to act as though everything was normal—that the rain was not coming down at an alarming rate, that her pale-faced father did not appear to be on the verge of death. They paused at the top of the stairs and shook themselves dry beneath the wide colonnade.

'So tell me, Atia, are you pleased with your marriage to Plotius?'

Her father would learn the whole truth from the Legate soon enough—there was no reason to lie. But lie was just what Atia did. 'Of course, Father,' she said. 'But I would have been happy with whatever husband you chose for me.'

And I have certainly not already chosen and married one of my own.

'And the camel man—you watched him die?'

'I did, Father.' An easier lie. Much less specific.

'Did it not become clear to you on the journey who he was?'

'I am afraid not, Father.' Now the lies were piling up as if she were building a great tower of them. 'But you must remember that I am just a woman. I often do not see such signs clearly.'

'Quite true.'

But it was not true. Atia was a great observer and had been all her life. As a test, she tried out another lie. 'I have also come to understand how very weak I am.'

'Weak and lacking in fortitude,' her father agreed. 'You are like your mother in that way.'

But Atia's mother had been strong and Atia herself had plenty of fortitude. She had endured three terrible husbands, after all. She had survived the Arabian desert and helped others do the same. She had even saved the Legate's life.

The next lie she conjured she could have recited in her sleep: 'If only I had inherited Mother's beauty.'

'Your lack of it has been a source of many of my troubles,' her father said. 'Such an unfortunate nose.'

But her nose was not unfortunate. It was strong

and unique. It blessed her face with a kind of regal intelligence, or so Rab had told her.

For the first time in her life, Atia realised that she was not the only liar in her family. Her father had been feeding her lies about herself for her entire life.

He glanced at the rose in Atia's hand. 'And what of the roses, my dear?'

'I'm sorry, Father?'

'Do Arabian roses smell different than the roses of Rome?' Atia remembered him asking her a similar question once.

'Yes, Father.'

'And do you find them superior or inferior?'

'Superior,' she said. A truth amid the lies—like a rose amid thorns.

He peered at her closely. 'There is something different about you,' he said.

'The journey did me good, Father,' said Atia. Another truth. 'I found happiness.'

Instead of congratulating Atia on that happiness, or on her supposed marriage, or on anything at all, her father gave a mighty *harumph*. He gazed out across the open-air reception hall. 'It is just like Julianus not to send an escort,' her father grumbled. 'Where in Hades are his offices?'

'At the back of the palace,' said Atia, pointing across the hall.

Her father started out across the large open

space, his soldiers making a tight formation behind him. He paused in the middle of it, breathless, and motioned the soldiers on. Then he turned to Atia. 'Are you stupid, Atia?' he called. 'You stand there like some dull-witted child. Accompany me at once!'

Never again, Atia thought. *In anything.*

'No, Father,' she called back. She hardly knew her own voice.

'What did you say?' The rain was coming heavily now. It was pounding down upon the courtyard's fine marble floor and had soaked through her father's crimson cape.

'I lied to you, Father,' Atia shouted above the din. 'I am not married to Plotius. I am married to Rab, the rebel leader!' Her father gripped his stomach as if she had delivered him an actual blow. 'Rab is a good man,' she said, 'and I love him!'

Her father's eyes blazed. 'You dirty, disloyal, contemptuous little harlot!' he shouted. He began to limp back towards her. 'Come here this instant!'

Atia shook her head and stood her ground. 'All my life I have lied, Father,' she continued. 'I have lied to you about my feelings. I have lied to others about your malicious acts. I have lied to myself, telling myself that you are a good man. But you are not a good man and killing is no way to get power or to keep it.'

He was closing the distance between them, his expression murderous. 'You will suffer greatly for your disloyalty, Atia. You and the damned Legate.'

'The Legate Julianus is a good man,' she shouted. 'He seeks peace and justice for all the people of this province. He is what a real Governor should be.'

'Julianus is a traitor,' shouted Atia's father. 'I will kill him myself!'

Suddenly, Julianus's voice resounded across the hall. 'Whom will you kill, Governor Severus?'

Julianus was not alone. What seemed like half of his legion had appeared beneath the colonnade. The soldiers were fanning out into the hall and greatly outnumbered her father's own military escort, which had been quietly surrounded.

'Traitor!' shouted her father. Abandoning his pursuit of Atia, her father turned and began limping towards Julianus. But in his haste, her father slipped on the slick marble and fell on to his injured leg. 'Ow!' he shouted.

The last thing Atia saw before she turned down the palace steps was Julianus arriving before her father's writhing figure and offering his hand.

'Goodbye, Father,' she whispered.

She took the long way around the palace to her

living quarters and, by some miracle of the gods, Shaquilath was there when she arrived.

'My father has arrived in Rekem.'

'I know,' said Shaquilath with a strange grin. 'It seems he brought the rain.'

'You knew that he was coming?'

'The desert has ears.'

'He is not long for this world, Shaquilath.' The two women shared a look. It meant that there was hope for the Nabataeans yet.

Atia heard the loud drum of thunder. 'Please, tell me where Rab is now?' she begged. 'I must find a way to free him.'

'And you will free him,' said Shaquilath. She held up a small key.

Atia nearly swooned. 'How?'

'I told my husband that the prisoners needed to be moved to safety.' Shaquilath gazed out of the window at the rain, which now seemed to be coming down in sheets. 'That part was certainly true.'

Shaquilath handed the key to Atia. 'I have spoken to my husband about reopening the copper mines. He thinks it is a genius idea.'

Atia smiled. Hope, indeed. 'I have a feeling that you have had great influence in that particular opinion and many others.'

'Perhaps,' said Shaquilath with a wink.

'Now tell me, where is Rab?'

'In the swathe of rock just to the west of the Great Temple. Look closely and you will see a set of stairs carved into the rock's base.'

'I owe you the debt of my own life,' said Atia.

Shaquilath was shaking her long, curly locks. 'There is no debt, for we are sisters.' Atia gave a deep bow, then turned to leave.

'Atia?'

'Yes?'

'Be careful. I was wrong about this storm. It is no kitten.'

Rab stood atop his cot, which had now become submerged. What had begun as a few drops, and then a few puddles, had grown into something of a pond inside his cell—a pond that was rapidly becoming a lake.

If the rain did not stop soon, he realised, they would all be drowned.

He laughed aloud. For countless days he had waited in terror for the appearance of his executioner. He never could have dreamed that his killer would trickle in on liquid legs.

'Rab, why do you laugh?' shouted Livius.

'He laughs so that he does not cry,' replied Plotius.

'Why does the water rise so quickly?' asked Livius.

The ignorance of the question struck Rab as

funnier still and he laughed louder. When he finally regained his wits, he said simply, 'Water is the desert's greatest blessing, and also its greatest curse.'

'Are we going to drown, then?' said Livius, his voice trembling.

'It appears that way,' said Plotius.

'I am afraid we are,' laughed Rab.

'You have both gone mad,' said Livius.

'I would rather die mad than sane,' roared Plotius.

'I would rather not die at all!' shouted Livius.

Meanwhile, the water had risen to the level of Rab's knees. There was nothing he could do to stop it. He took a deep breath and thought of Atia.

And it was as if he conjured her from the very mist.

'Rab, I am here,' she said in her silken voice. 'I have come to save you.'

Rab's heart ceased to beat. Could it be? In seconds, a face appeared at the small opening in his cell door. 'This will only take a moment,' she said.

A key moved inside the lock and Rab pushed hard against the door, thrusting it open. She tumbled into his arms in a rush of water. 'Atia!' he shouted.

And it was as if the flood was no longer flowing around him, but flowing within him—a flood of love.

'Hello, Husband,' she said. Her body was convulsing with sobs. Or was that his own body?

'It seems that you have once again saved my life, Wife,' said Rab.

'You know I would never let a good man die.'

And in that moment Rab vowed to do anything in his power to be that good man until the end of his days.

They waded through the rising water and thrust Livius's door open. 'Thank all the gods in all the heavens!' Livius shouted, his tears mixing with the water, which had risen to the level of their chests. 'We must leave this place now!'

'There is one more prisoner, is there not?' asked Atia. She pointed at the last closed door. 'Who lies within?'

'Not a good man,' said Rab, expecting Plotius to voice his protest. But the former commander stayed silent. Rab gazed into Atia's eyes. 'It is Plotius. And it is your choice.'

Atia shook her head, then thrust the key into the lock.

Chapter Twenty-Five

They had been walking for three days when they finally saw the camel. Though walking was not quite accurate in Atia's case. To escape Rekem, they had found the highest ground they could and made their way south, scaling cliffs and scrambling over boulders until the torrential rains ceased.

But Atia could not sustain their pace as they made their way into the night and so the men had taken turns carrying her upon their backs. They hiked relentlessly through the darkness, desperate to put distance between themselves and the search parties who would surely be pursuing them.

Of the three men, it had been Plotius who had carried Atia the longest. 'Are you sure you are not tired, Plotius?' she had asked as the sun rose on the third morning.

'I would carry you to the end of the earth, *domina*,' he had said.

Now a barren plain stretched out before them. In the distance, unusual rock formations made strange shapes against the morning sky. 'In that case you can put me down now, Plotius,' said Atia, 'for I believe that we have arrived at earth's end.'

Plotius gently set her on the ground, and she breathed in the rain-crisp air. She bent to the ground and scooped up a sample of earth. It was as orange as the dawn.

'You are becoming Nabataean,' said Rab, watching the sand slip through Atia's fingers.

'I should hope so, since we are presently marching into the very heart of Nabataean rebel territory.'

Rab cringed. 'That was a very Roman thing to say.'

'Ah, no!' she said. 'May Venus—I mean Uzza—forgive me!'

'Much better,' he said, then tossed her a kiss through the air.

She had missed this—their light-hearted banter. She had longed for it almost as much as she had longed to feel his arms around her. And yet she worried that they might soon part ways for ever.

The night before, Rab had announced his plan

to lead them to the largest of the rebel camps, which lay in a particularly desolate area by the name of Wadi Iram. 'There is really no other choice if we wish to survive,' Rab had explained. 'The camp is well provisioned, though I need not tell you that its existence must remain a secret.'

After almost two days without food, the thought of any provisions at all was welcome, and Atia and her Roman companions vowed on their lives never to reveal its location.

'Will we not be killed on sight?' asked Plotius.

'Not if I say otherwise,' said Rab with easy authority. 'Besides, it is a violation of Nabataean honour to deny a person sanctuary in the desert— no matter who they are.'

Atia sensed that Rab was looking for more than sanctuary, however. The deeper they travelled into Wadi Iram, the lighter his mood, as if he was looking forward to rejoining his brothers in arms.

As if he could not wait to resume their bloody work.

It was her greatest fear. If Rab meant to continue to lead the Nabataean rebellion, then Atia would have to let him go. She could never again be a part of the pursuit that had resulted in the slaughter that day on the beach.

'Just a day and a half more of walking and we will be there,' Rab was saying. He was pointing at an outcropping of stone so far in the distance that it seemed to blur in a layer of liquid heat.

But there was movement inside the heat. Atia squinted her eyes. Yes, just there. A tall, loping figure was emerging from it, as if conjured from the desert itself. Atia blinked.

'Rab?'

'Yes, my love?'

'Can a mirage move? I mean, on four legs?'

'What?'

Saying nothing, Atia pointed at the figure, which was growing larger by the minute.

Rab squinted at the rider emerging into view. 'No, it couldn't be,' he muttered.

By the time Atia recognised the boy, Rab was running towards him with his arms spread open.

'Rab?' said the youth, swinging down from his tall camel with catlike agility.

'Zaidu!' Rab shouted.

The reunion was as exuberant as it was tearful, and soon Rab had mounted the camel behind Zaidu and vowed to return.

After only a few hours, Rab and Zaidu came loping back across the desert with a small herd of camels. 'One for each of you,' cried Zaidu. He grinned playfully. 'So we can race.'

And race they did—across a flat, lifeless plain dotted with haunting, massive stone formations that seemed to float like giant ships in a barren sea. They rounded one of the stony ships and made their way up a small canyon.

They turned, then turned again, as if inside a maze. Finally, they emerged into a large flat area surrounded on all sides by cliffs. A natural fortress.

At least a thousand men and an equal number of camels were camped within its protective rock walls, and Atia wondered how they could survive in such a stark place. The answer to her question lay just beyond the men at the base of the rocks. There, clusters of luxurious date palms basked around the unlikeliest of sights—a lake.

There was water flowing into the lake from above. It was being conducted in vertical channels down the cliff face in one of the strangest, most beautiful sights Atia had ever seen.

'You asked to see the secret water,' said Rab. 'Here is one such place.'

Atia, Plotius and Livius laid out their bed mats at the outer edge of camp. 'You will not be bothered,' said Rab. 'I have ordered my men to treat you as guests.'

Atia marvelled as Rab walked among the rebel soldiers, shaking hands and slapping backs. The men treated him with the respect afforded an honoured leader, but the expressions on their faces as they greeted him betrayed something more: love.

Atia's spirit swelled, then collapsed. Her husband was a great leader, or so it seemed. The men appeared as though they might do anything for him. Including killing.

'We must sleep apart tonight,' said Rab as they sat together around their small campfire that night.

'Of course,' said Atia.

It was the perfect opportunity for a jest. She could have said that she expected it, but she did not have to like it. She could have gazed across the fire at her fellow Romans and said, 'One of them will do just as well.' She might have jested that she would try not to call out Rab's name in her sleep.

There were many ways she could have kept the conversation alive, but instead she let it die. Her humours were all out of balance. Dread was slowly eclipsing the love inside her heart.

He was going to go back to his war against Rome.

He was the heir to the Nabataean throne, by the gods. Why wouldn't he? Did she think he would simply renounce his mission and travel off with her into the desert? She understood better than most the obligations that came with such high levels of leadership. And the sacrifices.

The tiny flames sputtered and she dared to

lean against him—one of the few expressions of love she had allowed herself since their reunion. Now she feared it might be one of the last.

'Rab!' she said suddenly. She lifted her head, sucked the air. How had she forgotten? 'I never told you about the revelation I had.'

'Revelation?'

'About your father's last words. About the elephants!'

The next morning, Atia awoke to the sound of men's footsteps shuffling in the sand. She sat up and rubbed her eyes. The rebels were gathering below a cliffy sandstone ledge above the camp. A tall, muscular man was stepping on to a naturally flat part of the rock above them. He wore a flowing white robe and matching *ghutrah*, and as he lifted his arms, he appeared as venerable and strong as a Roman Emperor.

'Greetings, Brothers!' he pronounced to a spate of cheers. 'I stand before you today as a proud man, for I see the Nabataean spirit alive and well among you.'

It was Rab—or Prince Rabbel, as he was known. Atia's husband. The love of her life.

The Prince of the Nabataeans.

Atia marvelled at his poise as he stood before his men, who seemed to grow taller themselves as their leader praised them. 'Together we are more than what we are alone,' he was telling them, 'and I am fortified by the certainty that we will accomplish much in the coming months.'

The men erupted in another round of cheers and Atia moved quietly across the camp to join them.

'But it is the nature of our endeavour I wish to speak to you about now,' continued Rab, 'for I have recently understood it in a different way.' Rab paused and gazed at the cloudless sky, as if gathering his thoughts. 'As you know, I have long burned with anger towards my father, the late King Rabbel. I have never been able to understand why he gave up our precious kingdom without a fight.'

Grunts of anger and assent rippled through the crowd.

'I am speaking to you now because I believe I have my answer.'

Rab paused significantly and the men quieted. 'In order to convey this answer, I shall relate a story that I only very recently learned.' Rab scanned the crowd and somehow found Atia. He gave her a slow, reverent nod. 'It is the true story of a Greek seaman named Hippalus. Now, this seaman was restless and also very curious. He traded successfully along the shores of Arabia, but always wondered if it would be possible to cross to India.

'Hippalus noticed that in summer the wind blew east across the Indian Sea, while in winter it blew west. So one summer day, he risked his life and set out across the open sea, faithful that the east wind would carry him. A month later he found himself very much alive and arriving in the port of Barygaza, India. He returned to Arabia the following winter with a caravan's worth of Indian frankincense and spices, which he ferried all the way to Pelusium for half the cost of the overland caravan route.'

Rab paused while his men absorbed the statement. They were exchanging quiet looks of horror.

'I do not need to tell you what those convenient winds stand to do to our lucrative frankincense trade. It is just a matter of time, Brothers.'

There was a long silence. Several of the men glanced wistfully at their camels.

'When I learned of Hippalus's discovery,' Rab continued, 'I finally understood my father's last words. As he lay dying, he told me not to forget the elephants. For many years I believed him to be mad, but now I understand what he was trying to say. You see, my father visited India several times during his reign, and what he loved most were its elephants. To my father, elephants were not just from the land of India, they represented the land of India itself.

'Brothers, what my father was trying to tell me was that the golden age of Nabataea is over. The overland trade routes to southern Arabia that once sustained us are being overtaken by routes to India from the sea. My father did not wish to give up Nabataean lives to protect a kingdom that was already doomed.'

The men whispered among themselves and shifted on their feet. 'This cannot be,' someone said.

'But it is,' said another. 'My cousin works on one of the ships that Prince Rabbel describes. They are not subject to Roman taxes. They are making a fortune.'

'It does not change the past,' said someone. 'The Romans stole our kingdom. We must take it back.'

'But we can never take it back. For every one of us there are thirty of them.'

'We must make trouble for the Romans, then!' shouted another. 'Endless, debilitating trouble!'

The loudest voices in the crowd seemed to be growing angrier with Rab. But Atia heard several men whispering together about the late King Rabbel. 'Perhaps he was not such a coward after all.'

Rab was rubbing the inside of his palm. Atia could see him tracing the length of his wedding scar. He took a breath and continued.

'So far I have told you what our great King

wished to be known,' said Rab. 'Now I will tell you what *I* wish to be known. Over the past months, I have come to know Roman soldiers.' He glanced at the figure of Plotius, still slumbering at the edge of camp. 'I can say that there is an emptiness in their hearts that we can scarcely understand. Killing is their profession, you see. It is like trading for us. They are raised to do it. It is all they know.'

Rab scanned the crowd. 'If we fight the Romans, our souls will grow as empty as theirs.' Rab paused, letting the men consider his words.

'I know this because in my thirteen years of hating Romans, my soul grew empty and I did not even know it. I was fortunate, though, for the gods sent me someone who filled it back up again.' Rab caught Atia's gaze once again. And it was not desire or lust she saw burning inside his eyes this time. It was love.

'Brothers,' he continued, 'we must not let the injustices of the past fuel our anger. We must continue to work for change, but we must do it from the inside out. If we continue to kill, we are no better than killers. We must be better than our oppressors. We are all equal beneath this vast sky are we not? Well?'

About half of the men shouted in unison, 'Yes!'

'I stand before you today to propose that we disband,' said Rab. 'Let us distribute the wealth we have accumulated among ourselves and let it fund works that will improve Nabataean lives. Let us cease our work of violence and approach the challenge before us in the true spirit of Nabataea—that of peace and equality. It is only by passing on the values we cherish that our greatness will live on.' Rab bowed his head and raised his hands. 'I leave the matter with you,' he said.

Rab stepped backwards on his ledge and bowed his head while the men clustered into groups and began to talk. Atia listened closely as the men exchanged views and tried to persuade one another of their positions. Each man was given plenty of time to speak and she recognised many of the rhetorical techniques used by Roman Senators. *Pure democracy*, thought Atia. *In the wilds of Arabia.*

The groups appeared to take votes, then gradually grew quiet. A man from one of the groups dropped to his knees. 'We elect to follow your will, Prince Rabbel,' he said and bowed his head. Another man followed, then another. Soon all the men were on their knees bowing in agreement to Rab. Only Atia was left standing.

Then, slowly, Rab, too, bent to his knees and bowed. To Atia.

The camp had been abuzz for the rest of the day as the riches of the war chest were distributed and the men packed their provisions and made their plans. Many had set off that very afternoon. The rest waited for the light of the following morning to ride off on their camels, though there were some who lingered well into mid-morning.

'Let me guess where you are going, Livius,' said Atia. She closed her eyes and pretended to think. 'Perhaps to a certain tent in the hills east of the Bitumen Lake?'

'How on earth did you guess?'

'I have a nose for these things,' Atia said with a wink.

'I suppose that we did find me a way back to her,' mused Livius, 'though I never guessed it would involve becoming a renegade.' She could see Livius's sense of duty at war with his pulsing heart.

'It is quite possible that Rab will be pardoned,' said Atia, 'and in that case you will be, too.'

'And what on earth would make you think that?' Livius asked.

'I have a feeling that this province will be getting a new governor soon,' said Atia.

Livius's expression changed. 'I will await that happy day. And in the meantime I will count myself fortunate that I will not be the only renegade in my party.'

'Or even the highest-ranking renegade,' said Plotius. He was tightening the straps of his camel.

Livius gave Plotius a mock salute. 'The Commander speaks truth.'

Atia grinned. 'I see that the Commander has also learned to appreciate the merits of a camel,' she said.

'I have learned to appreciate more than just that,' Plotius said. He gave Atia a low bow. 'I only hope that one day you will be able to forgive me,' he said.

'You are forgiven,' said Atia. 'It is what you do now that truly matters.'

'I am going to attempt to be the good man whom you would not allow to die.'

'You honour me, then,' said Atia and bowed back.

She caught sight of Rab saying goodbye to his nephew. She could tell just by Rab's expression what he was saying. *Go back to your lessons and study hard. Take care of your mother and aunts. And no more camel racing, do you understand?*

She saw them embrace. Zaidu swung up on to his camel and joined up with the final group, which was slowly filing out of camp. Livius and Plotius were soon atop their own camels at the back of the party and it was not long before Rab and Atia were watching them disappear around a bend.

'It is not too late, you know,' said Atia. 'We can still join them.'

Rab was shaking his head. 'And journey for forty more days and nights before I can lie with my wife in peace? I refuse. Besides, you have not yet heard my proposal.'

'Proposal?'

'I have a proposal for you Wife, but I can only express it to you in a high place, such as the top of that rock there.' Rab pointed over Atia's shoulder and grinned.

Atia did not turn to look, for she knew exactly where he was pointing. 'You mean the rock that overlooks the lake, yes? The terrifying, precipitous diving rock?' Atia had seen a few of the younger men jumping from the tall boulder the day before. She had not envied them their fun.

'I seem to remember the last time you forced me up a steep cliff I lost my breakfast on your robe,' Atia said.

'Such a fond memory that is,' Rab said. He stood before her and slowly began to walk forward. 'It was our first embrace.'

'Embrace?' asked Atia. She took one step backwards and he stepped forward again, closing the distance. 'You were carrying my lifeless body up a sheer cliff with my vomit running down your back.'

'Your body felt so good against mine,' he said. 'I remember thinking that I had met my match.'

'You did not think that!'

'I certainly did. And since we are speaking honestly, I will admit now that while you rested against me I made bold to touch your backside.' He stepped forward again and she stepped back.

'What? While I was beyond my very wits?'

'It may have been more of a caress than a touch,' he said. Somehow, he was still pushing her backwards.

'I feel as if I am being herded,' she said.

'I have always fancied the shepherding profession,' he said. Before she knew it, they had arrived at the base of the diving rock. He scrambled on to its steep face and extended his hand. 'I will not let you fall, my love. Come.'

She took his hand and they slowly made their way up the long, steep swath of rock. 'This is a first for us,' he remarked cheerfully, trying to keep her from thinking about the ground, which was becoming more and more distant.

'What do you mean, *a first*? You do not expect me to jump, do you?'

'No, not at all,' he lied. 'I was talking about walking together. You know, side by side. Alone.'

She thought for a moment. 'You know, you are

right. We have walked for hundreds of miles, yet never really walked together.'

'And never been able to have a conversation without the whole world hearing.'

They arrived at the top. 'And never been able to do this.' He bent his lips to hers and before she could protest he was kissing her—the longest, slowest, most delicious kiss he had ever given in all his life.

He squeezed her against him and could feel her nerves disappearing. 'Do you know how many hours I have spent dreaming of this?' He let his hands wander to her breasts. 'Atia, I want you so much.' The morning sun beat down upon them, and he started to think about the water just below. How wonderful it would be to touch her in its cool depths.

'My proposal is this,' he began. 'I wish to travel to the land of India with you. We can find a ship and sail with the wind, just as Hippalus did. We can stay as long as we like—one month, three months, a year.'

'We can see the elephants?' she said.

'Yes!' he said. 'And we can sail back with a load of incense and spices and make our fortune. What do you think?'

'You know that I would follow you anywhere, but I have always longed to know India. And by going there we can learn the sea route and help other Nabataeans do the same. It is a brilliant plan and you are a magnificent man.'

'I am glad you think so, because you are stuck with me,' he said.

He stood behind her and wrapped his arms around her and they gazed out at the blue pool for a long while. 'How does the water stay there?' she asked. 'I mean, how does it not just seep down into the sand?'

'Bitumen,' he replied. 'From the Bitumen Lake. The pool is lined with it. So are all our cisterns and pools. It is the secret of our success.' He was kissing her again. He could not help it. 'You are my bitumen,' he said.

'Is the pond very deep?'

'It is very deep,' he said between kisses.

'How do you know?'

'Because I have made the jump many times and never touched bottom.'

'It is growing quite hot,' she said. She was arching her head back in that way that drove him mad. 'It would be nice to take a dip in the pool.'

'It is a long walk down to the shore,' he said, 'and I am rather tired of walking.'

'I am rather tired of walking myself,' she said, taking his hand.

And suddenly they were not walking at all. They were flying.

* * * * *

MILLS & BOON

Coming next month

THE EARL'S COUNTESS OF CONVENIENCE
Marguerite Kaye

'We're alone now.'

It was absurd, the way Eloise's stomach lurched when he said that, as if he'd told her something she didn't know. Something exciting, that made her pulses flutter and her mouth go dry. 'There are probably at least two footmen guarding the ballroom doors. And gardeners— there are bound to be gardeners out there, looking up, catching a glimpse of the newly married Earl and his Countess surveying their domain.'

'The newly married Earl and his Countess enjoying a rare moment of privacy together,' Alexander said. 'Relishing the opportunity too, because once they launch themselves into the preparations for their wedding ball, they are not likely to have many more such moments.'

One of his hands was resting lightly on her waist. The other was at the nape of her neck. Heat was radiating from the point where his fingers made contact with her skin. If they were being watched, it would seem odd if she simply stood there like a wooden mannequin. Eloise put her hand on Alexander's shoulder. Her legs brushed his. She reached up, feeling the smoothness of his freshly shaved jaw under her palm, curling her fingers into his hair. It was as silky as it looked. Her heart was hammering, but she was acting, that was all, she was playing her part as the recently married Countess of Fearnoch, deeply in love with her husband.

She stepped closer. Her breasts brushed his chest. His hand tightened on her waist. If she really was alone with her husband for the first time that morning, she would…

His lips touched hers before she had finished the thought, and her heart began to beat wildly. There was a pause, an aching pause, and she realised hazily that Alexander was giving her time to draw back, but a newly married countess would not draw back from kissing the husband she loved, so she did not. And he kissed her.

Continue reading
THE EARL'S COUNTESS OF CONVENIENCE
Marguerite Kaye

Available next month
www.millsandboon.co.uk